NO REGRETS

Published by Acorn Digital Press Ltd, 2013.

ISBN 978-1-909122-42-0

www.acorndigitalpress.com

NO REGRETS

BERNARD O'KEEFFE

AN INVITATION YOU CAN'T REFUSE

For Jo, Caitlin and Rory

1

"Maybe she left you because you'd become – I don't know – boring."

If it had been anyone other than Jerry who came out with the words, I might have reacted differently. But this was the most boring person I had ever known, the man nicknamed Captain Sensible at college, and it hurt.

It hurt because it may well have been true.

And whenever I run through the possible reasons for taking on the bet (I was drinking more than I was used to on that particular evening, I was saying goodbye to one of the most miserable years of my life etc.) I always come back to that particular comment, the cruelty of that final word ironically sharpened not only by the nature of the man delivering it but also by the mock uncertainty, the savage hesitation, of the "I don't know" that preceded it.

It was New Year's Eve, a night when you would normally find me at home, looking forward to seeing out the year with an evening in front of the telly or an early night with a good book. But that year had not been an ordinary one, and when Jerry rang up and asked me out for a New Year's Eve drink, the idea of seeing the year off in some kind of public way, or at least in some place other than the house which, in recent months, had become so empty and so unhappy, seemed attractive, or at least more attractive than it had seemed in previous years.

What's more, I could, for the first time in as long as I could remember, find fewer reasons for staying in than I could for going out.

"Here's to a better one," said Jerry.

"Yeah. A better one," I said.

"And to Alex."

"Yeah, of course. To Alex."

We sipped our beers, licked our lips, and looked at each other with uncertain half-smiles.

"This time last year…" said Jerry.

"Yeah. I know."

This time last year Alex would have been throwing his annual fancy dress party.

"Makes you think, doesn't it?" said Jerry. I nodded. "But I'm sure Alex wouldn't have wanted us to be – you know – maudlin or anything."

"Of course he wouldn't."

"He would have wanted us to get on with things. To have a drink and get on with things."

"Of course he would."

We raised our glasses.

Alex had always been the one who got on with things, the wild one, the one who had been there, done that and worn out the t-shirt while we were still consulting the map. And now he had gone, knocked down by a car in the fast lane, meeting his end in the place where he had metaphorically lived for so long.

"You know what Alex would have said, don't you?" said Jerry.

"Go on. Tell me."

"He'd have said you've got to—"

"Got to what? Look forward? Be positive?"

"Make the best of things. Make the best of it because you don't know how long you've got. Ironic, eh?"

Jerry sighed and moved his glass around the table in slow circles as if he was about to try to contact our dead friend.

"But we're not here just to talk about Alex, are we?" he said.

He sipped his beer, licked his lips and looked around the pub. Then we looked at each other. Now that we couldn't talk about Alex, the conversational options seemed dramatically reduced, and when Jerry gave me a must-be-tough smile and cleared his throat I sensed what was coming. I just knew what he was about to ask.

"Look, Rick," he said, "We go back a long way, don't we?"

"We do," I nodded.

"So I hope you don't mind me asking you a personal question."

"Go ahead."

"And I think we've had enough to drink for me to ask you this."

"Just ask it."

"And it's something I've been thinking about for quite some time—"

"For God's sake, Jerry, just ask it!"

"OK." He took a breath. "Why do you think Sarah left you?"

I sighed and looked towards the bar. Another drink suddenly seemed a very good idea.

"Maybe," I sighed, "things just weren't working out."

"And what does that mean?"

I shrugged. It was a question I had asked myself with depressing and baffling frequency over the last couple of months.

"Look," I said, "I came out for a drink not an inquisition."

"That's fine." Jerry held up a pair of back-off hands. "If you don't want to talk about it, that's fine. I quite understand. These things can be… difficult."

"It's not that I don't want to talk about it—"

"No, honestly, I understand, I really do. I can see you're sensitive about it—"

"I'm not sensitive about it, it's just that I don't really know the answer, and it's easier to say things weren't working out than it is to try to find the real reason."

"And what do you think that real reason might be? What, deep down, do you tell yourself in your darkest moments? When you ask yourself why? Why, after over twenty years of marriage did she walk out on me for another man?"

I had forgotten Jerry's habit of asking questions. Once he got hold of one he didn't like to let it go. It may have made him a good lawyer, but it didn't make him good company.

"Do you know what, Jerry?"

"What?"

"I don't really know."

"And I don't really believe you,"

I paused and looked round the pub – the large groups at smiling tables, the intimate couples in corners, the crowds at the bar, all laughing, all talking, all getting on with each other.

"Maybe we just didn't get on with each other any more."

"And what does that mean – not getting on with each other? It doesn't just happen, does it? There has to be a reason."

Jerry liked finding reasons for things.

"Perhaps," he said, "you'd become a little predictable?"

"Predictable? What do you mean?"

"It can happen, you know. It's easy to get stuck in a routine. Easy to do the same old thing."

I looked at Jerry. If anyone knew about being stuck in a routine it was him.

"For example," he said, "When did you last surprise her?"

"What do you mean? Creep up behind her and go 'boo'?"

"No. Surprise her by doing something different, something unexpected?"

We paused, while I trawled my memory for moments of surprise.

Jerry leaned forward, started to say something and stopped. He sat back, took a breath and then leaned forward again.

And then he said it.

"Maybe she left you because you'd become – I don't know – boring."

"Boring?"

"Yes, boring. Perhaps you'd become a little boring."

I had only had three pints but suddenly the pub, the world, the universe, swayed out of control. From the mouth of the man whose mind wore a cardigan, whose life carried a kite mark, who had more than one pair of slippers, had come a word which began to scroll across my mind, getting larger and larger: Boring. Boring. Boring. Boring

"What?" I spluttered.

"Only an idea," said Jerry, holding his hands up defensively.

But the word had taken hold and was now anchored in a sentence: Sarah walked out on me because I was boring.

"Did she ever say anything?"

"What do you mean – say anything?"

"Anything about you becoming, you being – you know..."

Boring. "No. Never. Well, not in so many words."

"What did she say, then?"

"Just the old clichés. We'd drifted apart, become different people, the spark had gone, it wasn't my fault."

"And you think that's the real reason?"

"Why not?"

"No one 'drifts' apart. There has to be a reason. Maybe you didn't go out enough."

"I never go out if I can help it."

"Exactly."

"Are you trying to tell me that if I had gone out more my wife wouldn't have left me?"

"It's not that simple, obviously, but it's symptomatic."

"Oh it's symptomatic, is it? Symptomatic of what?"

"Of a state of mind."

"Oh for fuck's sake! No wonder I don't go out if it means listening to this sort of bollocks!"

"But you admit that you didn't go out much?"

I nodded.

"And Sarah did."

I nodded again.

"With this Colin bloke?"

"I suppose so. I didn't ask."

"And what's he like?"

"Colin?"

"Yeah, this bloke Colin. What's he like?"

"Look, Jerry, I'm not sure I really want to talk about Colin."

Colin was a teacher at Sarah's school. More than that, he was a PE teacher at Sarah's school, one of those angular-jawed, Neanderthal types who sing *Swing Low* at Twickenham. It had never occurred to me that this was the man who Sarah had been with when she had said she was going out with people from work. People always sounded plural to me – I never imagined it was just one person, let alone one person called Colin.

"Sorry," said Jerry, "I'm only trying to—"

"I know. And I appreciate it. I really do."

"It must be difficult"

It was difficult all right. I had always expected to find more gaps in my life as I grew older, but I hadn't expected to find quite so many quite so quickly. Suddenly there were so many gaps you couldn't see any life at all.

"You've got to do something about it," said Jerry.

"About what?"

"About—" He paused. "About your state. About what's happened."

"And what do you suggest?"

Jerry looked thoughtfully into his beer as if the answer might be floating round in it somewhere. He shook his head sympathetically. "I don't know," he said, "but there must be something."

We drained our glasses. Jerry picked them up and headed for the bar while I, yet again, looked at the crowd of New Year's revellers, wondering how my own family, or what used to be my family, would be marking the occasion. What would Sarah be doing? In a pub with Colin? At some party? Or maybe at home, curled up in his arms on a sofa? Or maybe curled up in his arms in bed? And where would Ellie and Danny be? At New Year's Eve parties no doubt, doing God knows what – drinking too much, taking drugs, maybe even, like Sarah, in the middle of some sexual act?

Jerry came back with the drinks, and sat down opposite me with a sigh.

"I've got it," he said.

"Got what?"

"The answer to what you should do."

"Go on then, tell me. As long as it's not to be positive, or to get on with it, or to make the best of it."

"You should get out more."

"Get out more? What do you mean? Get out more as in 'get a life'?"

"Yeah. Why not?"

"Because I don't want to. Because I don't need to."

"Want and need aren't quite the same thing, are they?"

"Look, Jerry, let's quit the philosophy lessons shall we? I don't want to go out more, thank you very much. You might think I need to, but I don't. The simple fact is I prefer to stay in most of the time."

"You can't have that attitude."

"Yes you can. I've had it for years."

"But why?"

"Why not? I spent years and years going out. I met people, I made friends, I did all those things you're supposed to do. But there came a time when I just didn't fancy it any more. There's no rule you know. There's nothing that says you have to go out if you want to stay in."

"OK," said Jerry, leaning towards me across the table, as if about to deliver some intimacy, "but can I ask you another question?"

The Young's Special had weakened my resistance. I waved my hands as if inviting him to deliver a punch.

"Ask away."

"Sex with Sarah."

"For me or for you? Either way, a little unlikely tonight, I'd have thought."

Jerry smiled. It was almost a laugh.

"What was it like?"

"What do you mean?"

"In those last few months – what was it like?"

I shrugged and paused, thinking back to the once-a-week couplings (two if we were feeling particularly rampant). Nothing unusual came to mind. No strange requests, no surprising practices, no sudden production of uniforms, creams, toys or handcuffs.

"I only ask," said Jerry, "because that's what they say is the tell-tale sign of things not being right."

"You don't need to know about my sex life to work that out, do you? She left me. So things can't have been right, can they?"

"It's OK. If you don't want to talk about it that's fine. I understand. I can see you're sensitive."

"I'm not sensitive!"

"No need to shout."

I looked around. Heads had turned in our direction.

"Look," I said, lowering my voice and leaning across the table towards Jerry. "I don't mind talking about it. It was fine."

"Fine? Not great? Not fantastic?"

"Well, no. I don't suppose it was. But then at our age, and after so long, what do you expect? Is your sex life fantastic?"

"This isn't about me, it's about you."

"So what if my sex life wasn't fantastic? What do you expect?"

"My point exactly. What do you expect? Maybe that was the problem all along – low expectations. Still, all that can change now, can't it?"

"What do you mean?"

"Your wife has walked out on you after twenty-four years of marriage. You either see it as a huge problem and wallow in your misery or you see it as an opportunity."

"I'm not interested in all that kind of stuff. Not at my age. I'm not interested in opportunities."

"What do you mean at your age? Haven't you heard? Forty's nothing. Fifty's nothing. Sixty's nothing. Old is the new young."

"Look, forget it OK?"

"We all need it."

"No we don't."

"You're lying."

"Look at priests. Look at nuns. They get by without it easily enough."

"But look at them. They're miserable. Look at you. You're miserable too."

"I'm fine."

"How long have you been without it then?"

"Without what?"

"Sex."

I shrugged. "I don't know. I haven't been counting."

"If there's one thing you most definitely have been doing it's counting. You know exactly how long it's been."

"I'm managing. OK?"

I must have said this with some force because Jerry stopped suddenly and shot me an apologetic glance.

"I'm sorry," he said, "I didn't mean to push. I know it must be hard – or not as the case may be."

It was Jerry's own joke, so he laughed loudly.

"I'm sorry," he said, "It's just that – well it's just that Sarah was the one who cheated on you. She's the one who walked out. It means that—"

"It means that I could have gone out and had a retaliatory shag at the first opportunity? Is that what you mean? It gave me loads of opportunities?"

"Well, I don't mean to put it that crudely."

"It's your fantasy, isn't it Jerry? You ask about it because it's what you would really like to be able to do yourself."

"That's ridiculous!"

"I don't think it is. Because do you know what? Before it actually happened to me I thought the same way as you. I had this occasional fantasy. What if? What if my wife walked out and left me for someone else and I was free again, free to play the field? What would that be like? The funny thing is though, that when it actually happens, it's the last thing you think of. There's a whole load of voices in your head, but not one of them is saying, 'She's cheated on you. It's your turn now. You get a free shot.'"

I looked away from the table, tired of this relentless probing.

"Look, Jerry, I didn't come out for this kind of thing. If I wanted analysis I'd go somewhere else for it. And anyway, I thought you were here to cheer me up, not to make me feel worse."

Jerry shook his head, as if I had somehow missed the whole point.

"You don't get it," he said. "Sometimes you need to face up to a few things before you can move forward."

"Like sex with my wife for the last twenty-four years possibly not being very good. Like she had more fun with Colin than she did with me?"

Jerry gave a half-nod. "Who knows?"

"Like my wife left me because—"

Suddenly Jerry's face lost focus. He loomed in front of me, changing shape like some freaky light show or a brightly coloured kids cartoon. And then he became invisible. All I could see in front of my eyes were bright neon letters spelling out the truth I couldn't bring myself to utter: My wife left me because I am boring!

I shook my head to clear it, but all this did was increase the size of the letters:

My wife left me because I am boring!

I shook my head again.

My wife left me because I am boring!

"Rick! Rick! Are you OK?" Jerry's face came back. "You were saying your wife left you because..."

I have become more boring than Jerry!

"Rick?"

"Sorry?"

"You were saying your wife left you because..."

"Was I?"

"What were you going to say? Because you didn't go out?"

"No, not that."

"Because she thought you were boring?"

"No. Not that. I'm not boring!"

"I didn't say that. I said because she *thought* you were boring. Because you didn't go out."

"Just because I don't go out much doesn't mean I'm boring, does it?"

Jerry pursed his lips and looked away, like a frustrated teacher unable to get his point across.

"Look, Rick, it's New Year's Eve. What do you normally do on New Year's Eve?"

"Normally I stay in."

"I know *you* do, but I meant what do people do – other people."

"What's the point of all this?"

"Just tell me. What do other people do on New Year's Eve?"

"They go to their friend's fancy dress party – if their friend is still alive, that is."

Jerry shook his head sadly.

"To Alex," he said, lifting his beer in another toast.

"To Alex," I said.

"That's what I mean," said Jerry. "Just think of Alex. You can't take anything for granted can you? You just don't know what's round the corner. It could be a speeding car. You need to make the most of what you've got while you've got it. But to get back to my question – what else do people do on New Year's Eve?"

"They get drunk and they—"

"Yes?"

"You want me to say they make New Year's resolutions, don't you?"

Jerry smiled triumphantly.

"And once I've said it, you're going to suggest *I* make one, aren't you?"

Jerry smiled again.

"Well, forget it," I said, finishing off another beer and suddenly unsure whether it was my fifth or sixth. I couldn't remember the last time I couldn't remember how many I'd had. I couldn't remember the last time I spoke in so many italics.

"New Year. New You."

"What?"

"It's time to change."

"I knew it – a New Year's fucking resolution."

"Why not?"

"Because they're stupid, that's why not. And because no one keeps them."

"I keep mine."

"Oh yeah? Such as?"

I knew I shouldn't have asked him. Whereas throughout my life I had broken every one of my half-hearted New Year's resolutions, it seemed that Jerry had kept every one of his. Giving up smoking. Losing weight. Working for charity. Reading an improving book each month. If there were medals for keeping New Year's resolutions Jerry's would be gold.

"Are you telling me you've never kept a New Year's resolution?"

"Well, no. Not properly."

"Well, do you know what you should do?"

"There's no point. I won't do it."

"You haven't heard it yet."

"OK then tell me."

"Your resolution should be to get out more."

"Why? Do you think I'm boring? Do you think that's why my wife walked out on me? Because I'm boring? That's it, isn't it? You think I'm fucking boring!"

"I didn't say that."

"Just because I don't live a life like Alex—"

"To Alex!" Jerry lifted his glass in a toast.

I did the same. "Yeah – to Alex!" I said, "But just because I don't live like Alex, it doesn't mean I'm fucking boring, does it?"

Jerry looked over his shoulder and gave a don't-worry smile to those at the bar who had yet again turned their heads in our direction.

"Calm down," he said, "you're shouting. Look, I'm not saying you're boring at all. I'm just asking you a few questions. Like – have you ever wondered what might have happened if you had gone to Alex's New Year's Eve party each year instead of staying at home?"

"Of course I have. That's why I ended up staying at home."

"All those people you could have met. All that fun you could have had."

"I'd run out of costumes. I couldn't go as Boy George every year."

"That's not the point. The point is you stayed at home."

"Look. It was my choice, OK? I wasn't rude or anything. I always sent my regrets. I didn't have to go. It was my choice, my free choice, my existential choice."

"I'm sure it was. But what would the world be like if everyone refused invitations? There would be no parties for a start."

"Heaven!"

"And you say you're not boring?"

"I'm not."

"Prove it."

"I don't need to, thank you very much."

"Not because you can't do it?"

"Of course not."

"Do you know what, Rick? I think you're so stuck in your ways, that even after your wife has walked out on you, you can't change them."

I couldn't believe what was happening. Captain Sensible, the master of middle-class routine and predictability, was accusing me of being stuck in my ways. Was it really happening or was I experiencing a Young's Special hallucination?

"Jerry, you're wrong."

"Like I say, prove it."

"OK. How?"

"You should make a New Year's resolution. And what you should do for your New Year's resolution is accept every invitation that comes your way."

"Don't be silly."

"I'm not."

"Every invitation?"

"Every invitation. Whenever you get an invitation, an invitation of any kind, you accept it. You don't even pause to think. You just accept it."

"But I can't do that."

"Why not?"

"It's silly, that's why."

"What's silly about it?"

It was so silly I didn't know where to start. "Well, if you accept every invitation, you have no choice, do you?" I said.

"That's right."

"But you need choice, don't you?"

"Maybe that's exactly what you don't need."

"That's ridiculous!"

"It's no more ridiculous than other things I can think of."

"Like what?"

"Like doing nothing when your wife walks out on you."

"I won't do it."

"Why not? Chicken or something?"

"It just won't work."

"Of course it will. Take tonight, for example. If you'd received an invitation to a New Year's party tonight you would have had to go. If someone, like me for example, had asked you out for a drink you would have had to accept."

"I did. I'm here."

"Exactly. But if you hadn't felt like it you wouldn't have been able to say no – you wouldn't have had a choice."

"And what do you mean by every invitation?"

"Just what I said. If you're invited to go somewhere, or to do something, you accept."

"OK, smart arse, so what happens if on this New Year's Eve I had received two invitations – one from you for a drink and the other to a party. Which one would I accept then?"

Jerry paused, pondering the dilemma.

"You see?" I said triumphantly, "it's not quite so straightforward is it? In fact, it's a crap idea. An unworkable, crap idea."

"No. It's simple. You have to go to the one you accept first."

"And what if they arrive simultaneously? What if they both drop on your mat at the same time or they both pop up in your inbox at exactly the same moment?"

Jerry had the look of a man who hadn't thought things through. It was good to see a lawyer caught out. Then he smiled triumphantly. "Whichever you open first," he said. "You can't open them both simultaneously, can you?"

"It's still a shit idea," I said. "It just won't work. I mean, how do you enforce it? How would anyone else know that you'd kept your resolution?"

"Ah," he said. "That's straightforward. It's no different from any other resolution. No one can police it apart from yourself. If you don't mean to keep it then there's no use making it."

"Well I don't mean to keep it, so let's forget it, shall we?"

"You're frightened, aren't you? You don't think you could do it? And do you know why that is? It's because you're bor—"

"I'M NOT BORING. OK?"

"OK, do it then."

"I just want to know what an invitation is, that's all. Not an unreasonable request, is it? Try this. Do that. Come here. They're all invitations aren't they?"

"OK," said Jerry "for the sake of this, an invitation is one that is directly addressed to you."

"Has to be written, does it?"

"No it can be face to face. But it has to be specifically addressed to you. So something like 'Come along and try our new Indian restaurant' isn't a personal invitation is it? But if it said 'Dear Rick

Matthews, come along and try our new Indian restaurant', then that would be different. As it would if the owner was looking you in the face and asking you."

"What if he emailed me?"

"Again, it depends whether he addresses you by name."

I looked long and hard at Jerry and he looked long and hard at me, as if we were locked in some mental arm wrestle.

"I don't think you're up to it, Rick."

"Bollocks."

"You're not up to it for two reasons. First you're scared. Second you can't. You're so set in your stay-at-home, don't-go-out ways that you just can't change it. You won't admit that it led to the collapse of your marriage and you haven't got it in you to make a change. That's the truth, isn't it?"

"Of course I can do it."

"Go on then. Do it."

"OK. You're on. I'll do it."

"For a whole year?"

"One whole year."

"I'll do it. What do you want? A handshake?"

I reached out and shook his hand.

"Every invitation?"

"Every invitation."

And that was it. The beginning of my year of No Regrets.

2

January

I crawled out of bed on New Year's Day, went downstairs and, recognising the vaguely familiar pains and throbbings in my head as the symptoms of a hangover, put on the kettle and went in search of Anadin. Failing to find anything that might help in the medicine box previously stocked by Sarah, I crawled back to bed and slept fitfully for a couple of hours. Something felt generally wrong. There was no doubt that I was suffering the effects of too much drink, but there was another less identifiable unease, and it was only when I stumbled downstairs, flicked on the computer and opened my inbox that I realized what it was. The words flashed in time to the pounding throbs in my head as details of the previous night's ludicrous resolution shone, with frightening clarity, through the dark hangover fog.

> From: Jerry Palmer
> To: Rick Matthews
> Subject: Last Night
>
> Morning! (or more likely afternoon…) And Happy New Year! And don't forget… Every Invitation. For one whole year.
>
> Jerry

I hit the reply button and typed:

I was drunk. Ridiculous idea. Forget it.

Rick

Surely Jerry would understand. He must know, as I did, that it was simply a stupid idea that I had no intention of seeing through. It's what you do when you're drunk. You shake hands on all kinds of things.

My head throbbed. A light sweat seeped through my pores and every time I swallowed it felt as if I was scraping my throat with something sharp. It was a long time since I had experienced anything like it, and the idea of embarking on a scheme that meant I ran the risk of feeling like this more often filled me with horror. I went through the medicine box once more, but the best it could come up with were travel sickness pills (which I considered taking on the off-chance), and then I went back upstairs. Maybe going back to bed might be the best way to tackle the day, and even the year, ahead.

When I reached the landing I gently opened Danny's door. The smell of alcohol and last night's aftershave was enough to tell me he was home, but I put my head round the door just to check and to hear the reassuring breaths of a deep sleep – a habit I started when he was newly born and just out of hospital and which, for the following nineteen years, I had been unable to kick. There he was, sprawled across his duvet, a young man in what was still a young boy's room, the books and posters on the walls and shelves telling the story of his nineteen years.

I closed the door and walked across the landing. Turning the handle quietly and peering through the crack, I heard no breathing, so I pushed the door wider and looked in. This bed was empty, but it was, by now, a familiar enough scene. Gone were the times when we wouldn't sleep until we heard the door shut behind her at whatever hour and the reassuring turn of the double-lock. Gone were the times when we would bring our mobiles to bed so that we were ready for late-night texts about whether she would be back and where she might be staying. Gone were the times of 'we'.

The chances were she had slept at a friend's house, or crashed at wherever the party had been. But then another thought came to me.

Maybe she wasn't here because she had decided to go to Sarah's. Maybe she had rung Sarah rather than me. Maybe she would wake up in Colin's house rather than mine.

I sent her a text, wishing her a Happy New Year, and decided that, tempting though it was to crawl back into bed yet again, a walk might be less defeatist.

Before going out I checked my emails.

From: Jerry Palmer
To: Rick Matthews
Subject: Our bet

Rick,

Just as I said, then? You won't do it because

1. You can't
2. You're chicken
3. You're boring.

I pressed reply

I AM NOT BORING!

Stepping out into the cul-de-sac of neat Edwardian terraced houses, I turned to see Harry waving in my direction as he carried out a recycling bag.

"Happy New Year!" he called.

"Happy New Year!" I called back.

"Remember – if you're free at lunchtime," said Harry, "we're having our usual drinks party. Drop in if you can."

Every year Harry and Jill invited the road in for drinks on New Year's Day. And every year I avoided it. Sarah always said that we should go out of politeness, and had, on a couple of occasions, turned up by herself just to show we weren't rude, but I had never seen its appeal.

"No problem if you can't," said Harry. "We'll quite understand."

My instinct was to do what I had always done – to smile politely with a 'We'll see', knowing that Harry knew full well that I was not going to show.

But this was a New Year. This was a New Me. And this was An Invitation.

"I'd love to come, Harry," I said. "What time?"

Harry almost dropped his blue bag. Then he smiled broadly.

"Really?"

"Yes really. I'd love to."

"Great. See you later, then. Six-thirty-ish?"

It all felt wrong somehow. The way those words "yes", "really" and "love to" had tumbled out in that order – it was as though my brain-to-voice computer program had just crashed. Accepting like that had gone against all my well-established instincts and I began to feel faintly nauseous. I liked my neighbours. Whenever we spoke in the road they were friendly and polite, but I always enjoyed the sense of distance we managed to maintain, and it never occurred to me that it would be a good idea to get to know them any better, never crossed my mind that I would ever say yes to Harry's New Year drinks.

I walked down the road towards town. My head still hurt and I wondered whether, after all, going back to bed would be a better way of dealing with my hangover than going to a drinks party. Surely I needed sleep and recovery more than I needed to keep up this ridiculous resolution?

I walked for ten minutes more then turned back.

When I got home I was surprised to see Danny sitting at the kitchen table, munching cereal.

"A bit early for you isn't it?" I said, looking at my watch.

"And a Happy New Year to you too."

I flicked on the kettle and spooned some coffee into the cafetiere, trying to be natural and relaxed in a situation that I still found strange. Danny kept his head down over the newspaper. It seemed only yesterday that he would happily chirp away, reading out parts from the football pages that particularly amused him, happy to share whatever he was thinking with whoever happened to be in the kitchen at the time.

Now all that was gone.

"Good time last night?" I said, trying to make it sound effortless and casual.

"All right."

"Where were you?"

"What's it to you?"

"Just asking."

Danny turned the pages of the paper. "I was at a party at Phil's. Where were you?"

"I was out for a drink. With Jerry."

"I thought you didn't normally go out on New Year's Eve?"

I walked over to the table and sat down opposite him. He still kept his head down.

"Well this year," I said, "I went out. Perhaps it's time for a change."

"Perhaps there's been enough change as it is."

"Look, Danny, I'm finding it all very difficult—"

"And I'm not?"

"I didn't say that."

Danny turned another page. "This isn't a good time to try to have a 'chat'". He mimed the quotation marks.

"So we won't have one."

In other words I wouldn't ask him how his first term at Oxford had gone, I wouldn't ask him about his comedy act and, most importantly, I wouldn't ask him when he was going to his mother's.

"And to save you asking, I'm going to Mum's later today. OK?"

"OK," I said, "That's fine."

There was so much I wanted him to tell me, like what he felt about it all, like what he spoke to Sarah about, like whether she had given him any more explanation of why, on that early November day, four weeks into Danny's first term at Oxford, she had decided to leave.

3

"I think we need to talk."

That was how she started the conversation. It was a familiar enough beginning. We had, over the last twenty-four years, had many just like it. They mainly came at the end of protracted sulks, of days, and sometimes weeks, when one of us had harboured unarticulated resentments, had bottled up our anger. And they usually began in this recognisably calm manner. This wasn't going to be one of those rare explosive moments, when, impulsively and heatedly, we would shout things like "I've had enough", "I can't take much more of this" or "You make me sick", increasing the ferocity of the insults until one of us would ask the question "So what should we do about it then?" and we would both back off, knowing that we didn't want to chase this particular row to where logic threatened to take it.

So when Sarah said, "We need to talk" it seemed the prelude to just another statement of her discontent with something specific that I had done or failed to do in the recent past. It could have been anything – not filling the dishwasher, making a joke at her expense that she didn't find funny, insisting on watching Sky Sports when she wanted to watch a costume drama on BBC, correcting or contradicting her on a small detail, not noticing that she had had her hair done or was wearing a new top/trousers/shirt/shoes. I usually realised quite quickly what I'd done wrong, and had few problems, as she launched into the early stages of her attack, in gauging the seriousness of the assault, or in working out the best way to construct my defence.

When Sarah started this conversation on that grey, dark November afternoon, I was expecting something similar, and I was completely unprepared for what followed.

"I have something I need to tell you," she said.

This didn't sound like a question or a nag – more like a revelation or a confession. Maybe she had been stealing my hidden supply of expensive bath oil or sneaking a look at my emails.

"I think," said Sarah, "that we have come to a critical point in our relationship."

"What do you mean?" I said. This was clearly more than leaving the top off the ketchup bottle.

"I mean it's not going anywhere."

I laughed. "Not going anywhere? Of course it's not. Where do you expect us to go?"

"I'm being serious."

"And so am I. What do you mean – not going anywhere? There's nowhere for us to go. We're here."

"That's my point."

"What is?"

"We're here. There's nothing else."

"Nothing else! What else do you want?"

"It's not easy for me to say this, Rick, and, believe me, I've thought long and hard about it and I've agonized over it, turning it over and over in my mind. But I just think things aren't right."

"What are you talking about?"

"And they haven't been right for some time."

"I don't know what you mean."

"That's my point exactly. The fact that you don't know what I mean shows the state we've reached."

"Let's go back a bit, shall we?" I said, realising now that something momentous was unfolding in front of me. "What do you mean by not going anywhere?"

She turned away, composing herself.

"I just think we've grown apart. I could have said nothing and just carried on with the sham, but I've reached the point where I don't think I can."

"Hang on," I said, "What exactly are you saying here? Let's get straight to the point, shall we?"

" I mean that I can't take much more of it."

"You've said that before. You've said that millions of times before, but you always get over it. You're just going through a bad patch. It'll pass."

"This is different, Rick. Really different."

"What are you saying?"

"I'm saying that I think we need some time apart."

"What?"

"I think we should separate."

"What? Separate! Why?"

"Just listen, Rick. Listen to what I have to say."

Then came the clichés. About growing apart. About having changed over the years. About the kids having held us together, but now that they were older, now that they were both away, not being such effective glue. Glue. I'm pretty sure that's what she said, that she described our two children as some kind of glue.

And then there was the stuff about us not having much in common any more. She didn't actually use the word "boring", but looking back on it that was clearly what she was implying. What else could she mean by not sharing interests, not enjoying doing the same things, wanting to go off in directions I wasn't prepared to go?

"I'm not sure," said Sarah, "that we ever did have a lot in common. But it's only recently that I've noticed it."

"You're talking bollocks, Sarah. There's another man, isn't there. Who is it?"

"I am telling you Rick. There's no other man."

I just didn't believe her. Some of what she said made sense. I knew we hadn't done much together over recent years and I had noticed that she was going out much more to music, theatre, and exhibitions, claiming that it was with "people" from school. And I hadn't even probed her, hadn't even felt jealous or possessive. Maybe I should have. Maybe my failure to do anything was just another sign, in her eyes, that we had come to the end of some particular road.

"So let me get this straight," I said. "You want to leave me because you're just fed up with me, fed up with our marriage?"

"It's not that simple. It really isn't."

"It sounds that simple to me."

"This isn't easy for me, you know."

"Well, funnily enough, it's not a breeze for me either."

We paused, and in the brief silence I heard her sniffle. I was half expecting her to break down in tears, but it didn't happen. She managed to keep everything very much under control.

"And let's get this straight," I said. "There's no man."

"No," she said, shaking her head. "There's no man."

She didn't look at me as she said it, and I knew even then that she wasn't telling the truth.

"And what about the kids, our children, our family?"

"Don't think I haven't given this a lot of thought, Rick. It's not sudden and unconsidered, and, yes, of course I've thought of the children. There's no good time to tell them this sort of thing, but I thought I'd wait until Danny was away at university, until they both were."

I laughed in disbelief. "Well, that's very considerate of you, I must say. Wait until the nest is empty and then make it derelict."

"You've got to understand, Rick, this has been very difficult for me."

"What do you want? Sympathy?"

"The kids will understand. It's not as though separation is that uncommon."

"It's uncommon to me," I said. "How many times have you been through it?"

"I mean they both have friends who've experienced it. They'll cope. They're grown up now."

"Are you serious?"

"Absolutely."

"But they're still kids! They haven't even left home. Not properly. They're back every eight or nine weeks. This is still their home, you know, the home that we built for them."

"I know it is."

"OK, then. So you're walking out. How long for?"

Sarah shrugged. "I don't know."

"Is it forever?"

"Again, I don't know."

"So what is it, then? Trial separation? I didn't think those things existed in real life."

"I don't care what you call it. I just know that I need to be apart. I just know it."

"And where will you be staying?"

"With a friend. From school."

"Oh yeah? The same friend from school that you've been going out to all those things with over the last year?"

"Does it matter?"

"Yes. If it's another man it does matter. And I have a right to know."

It mattered so much and I felt I had so much of a right to know that I immediately set out to find out who exactly this schoolfriend was and the exact nature of their relationship. If Sarah had given me her address this would have posed no problem. I had told her I needed it for forwarding her mail but she had insisted, in those first few weeks, on keeping her precise whereabouts a secret and meeting me in town each Saturday morning so that I could hand over anything that had arrived for her.

"Not much this week," I said, passing the modest bundle of mostly junk mail to her across the Starbucks table. "But then not much tends to come through the post any more, does it?"

I thought this might have triggered an amiable conversation, but it was clear that Sarah had no intention of sticking around for a chat.

"I must go," she said, standing up abruptly and leaving her coffee untouched on the table.

"So soon?" I said, standing up as well and trying to catch her eye.

"Yes," she said, and with that she was through the doors and disappearing into the Saturday morning High Street crowds. There was no how-are-you, not even a how-are-the-kids, she just walked away as if we had never spent twenty-four years together, and I was merely her postman.

Hurtful though it was, I gave myself no time for reflection. As soon as Sarah walked through the Starbucks door I rushed after her, almost knocking customers over as I headed for the door and burst onto the street.

There she was, walking purposefully along the High Street towards the station. I started to follow, keeping up with her pace, craning my neck and ducking my head sideways to make sure I still had her in my sights, cursing the crowds of shoppers, but grateful that they formed a helpful protective barrier. Even if she were to turn round it was unlikely that she would see me following her.

If she had taken a bus, or if she had walked towards her car and driven off, I would have had no chance, but luckily the weather was good and she was in a walking mood. Following her in the crowds was easy. It was only when she headed out of town towards Sheen, along sparsely populated pavements, that it became more problematic, but I was determined to find out where she had shacked up and I was determined to do it without being discovered. When she crossed a road and looked both ways at a junction or at traffic lights I had to jump into shop windows or bend down to tie up non-existent shoe laces, and there were a couple of moments when she turned round completely as if uncertain where she had come from, and I had to turn round myself and pretend I was walking in the opposite direction.

But I kept my distance and I tracked her down. I tracked her down to Park Road where she disappeared into one of the neatly terraced houses.

It was then only a matter of waiting until I saw her "friend".

And wait I did. I stayed on the nearest corner for the next couple of hours, ready to rush out of sight should Sarah herself emerge again, and anxious that I didn't lurk too suspiciously outside any one house for too long. I didn't want anyone calling the police.

Then I saw the door open and Colin emerged, Colin the PE teacher.

I could have phoned her or even sent a text, but I decided that the best way to confront her with the truth was to wait until my next Postman Pat role. So I saved it for Starbucks the following Saturday.

"Even less this week," I said, as I handed over the handful of envelopes.

"Oh well," she said, getting up to leave. "Never mind. I must be off."

I stood up as she did and reached out for her arm. I grabbed it firmly and she looked down at my hand as if it was some strange creature.

"Before you go," I said. "There's something I have to tell you."

Sarah raised her eyebrows.

"I know who it is," I said.

"Know who what is?"

"I knew there had to be a man," I said. "These things don't just happen."

"What do you mean?"

"It's Colin," I said. "You're living with Colin. There's no need to deny it, because I know."

Sarah's face contorted with confusion and uncertainty. She made as if to speak but no words came out. She looked more uneasy, more distracted than I had ever seen her before.

She also, I thought, looked profoundly unhappy.

***

I looked across the kitchen table to Danny, his head still bent over the newspaper, and thought of the times when things had been so much simpler. Had I taken it all for granted? Had I taken it all so much for granted that I had become complacent – even, perhaps, boring? Was it unfair to think the fault lay entirely with Sarah? OK, so she had gone off to shag Colin and had probably been doing as much in her concert-going, gallery-visiting, let's-get-out-and-do-things years, and there was only one person to blame for that. But maybe I had in some small way contributed to the whole thing. Maybe I should have done more to make things better.

For the first time I knew what Jerry meant. My wife left me for Colin, Colin the PE teacher, because I had become boring.

But I would show her.

I would show everyone.

4

Harry was a retired judge, balding, affable, and out of touch with the real world in the way that those appointed to pass judgment on it often are. His wife, Jill, was a retired primary school teacher and the two of them constituted Afton Road's senior couple. From number nine, nicely positioned at the end of the cul-de-sac, they had watched the comings and goings over the years: young couples moving in, families growing up, and people moving away. They had seen the fluctuations of the property market and the changing fortunes of their neighbours. A few had moved on quickly, but the majority had stayed for some time, mainly because Afton Road was a very pleasant place to live. Far enough out of Richmond town centre to make it quiet, yet close enough to make you feel you were not far from anything you needed, it was a very desirable location. If it weren't for the inheritance from my parents it would certainly have been well beyond my means, but we had bought at a good time, at the beginning of the eighties, and had watched prices soar around us, not knowing, as the years passed, that our investment would prove to be far more secure than our marriage.

Jill passed round the nibbles while Harry topped up the glasses. The last thing I felt like doing was drinking, but it seemed the only way I was likely to get through my first party in quite some time, so I sank the first two glasses quickly, working on the assumption that a quick top-up of last night's intake would be all I needed to quell my unease. It did the trick, and as I listened to the inconsequential chitchat around me, the kind of stuff I had, until now, been so pleased to avoid, I took in the others at the gathering. Besides Harry and Jill, there was: Phil, a *Mirror* journalist and his wife Henrietta, a solicitor; Felicity, who did something in an ad agency; Sheila, a local GP and her husband John, who worked for some big manufacturing company; Fred, a writer of detective novels and the occasional TV script and his librarian wife Alice; Dave, an accountant, with his latest girlfriend; and another woman who had moved into the road a few months ago, who I had smiled at on the few occasions we had passed, and whose name I hadn't quite caught in the round of introductions.

The group was small enough for it to stand around in the party's early stages in one large circle. Anything you chose to say was said for general consumption – a little like a seminar. This was easy for me. All I had to do was smile and nod and laugh at the right moments; there were enough self-important people there to dominate proceedings, enough loud voices and loud laughs to make it easy to stand there and say nothing while I topped up with Jill's white wine.

But as the party developed the circle broke up, and I found myself caught in a one-to-one conversation with the woman whose name I hadn't quite caught.

"So how did you spend New Year's Eve?" she said.

She was small and dark, with an attractive, confident energy that made her almost bounce as she spoke.

"I went out for a quiet drink. How about you?"

She must have been in her forties, but she looked good for it. Last night's conversation with Jerry about women suddenly came back to me.

"I was at a party, but I didn't stay too long. I knew I had a run this morning."

"A run?"

"I do a bit of running. Nothing serious, but I'm part of this runners' club and the New Year's Day run has become a kind of tradition."

So that explained why she looked so lean and toned. Whereas I had crawled out of bed with a massive hangover, she had been out on a million-mile-long run before breakfast. No wonder she bounced.

I looked at her glass. "And is that why you're not drinking?"

She looked down at her orange juice and laughed. "I may be a runner, but I'm not that kind of runner. No, I just don't fancy it at the moment."

The words 'fancy' and 'it' rolled round my head.

"This is going to sound terribly rude," I said, "but I didn't catch your name..."

"It's Maggie."

Maggie May. Rod Stewart. Or even the Beatles. Oh, dirty Maggie May they have taken her away...I should have stuck to orange juice.

"And you are Rick?" I nodded. "And you're a teacher."

"That's right," I said. "Ravensbourne. The sixth form college down the road. And this is going to sound even more terribly rude, but I can't remember what you do either."

"You can't remember much, can you?"

"A heavy night," I said, trying to make it sound as though such things were the norm.

"But since you ask," said Maggie, "I'm an actress. And before you ask, no I'm not in anything at the moment."

"I wasn't going to ask," I said.

"And I am not what you call 'resting'. I am doing a few commercials and voice-overs."

She was bouncing again.

"Sounds interesting."

"No it's not – it's fucking boring. You don't become an actress to do crappy ads and even crappier voice-overs. You do it to play Lady Macbeth. And when you get to a certain age..."

"You're not of a certain age. You look very... young." She smiled. "And I'm sure all that running must keep you fit."

"It helps."

"How long have you been doing it?"

"About three years. I never thought of it before but when someone asked me along to the group I gave it a go and it kind of stuck."

"So where do you run?"

"Depends, Richmond Park for some of the time, sometimes the river."

"Sounds great."

"How about you? Do you run?"

"Only when I have to," I said, laughing. "You know, catching buses, avoiding the police." Maggie smiled. "But I used to," I said, patting my stomach to indicate the effects of stopping.

"Why did you stop?"

I shrugged. "Just one of those things, I suppose. It comes with age. I used to play five-a-side football too but I don't do that anymore either."

Maggie snorted derisively. "Don't play the age card. There are people twice your age running marathons."

"What? Literally twice my age? That would make them—"

"You know what I mean. So tell me, why did you stop?"

"I wasn't enjoying it, I suppose. And my knees started to hurt a bit. They say it's bad for your joints you know, running."

Maggie shook her head, disappointed at my ignorance. "That's rubbish, you know. Research has shown that running, at whatever age, has beneficial effects. It's good for your joints, good for your circulation, good for controlling weight and research has also shown that running actually enhances your sex life."

"Really?"

"You really should try it again, you know?"

"What? A sex life? I'd been thinking the same thing myself."

Maggie smiled broadly but her smile gave nothing away. Did she think I was flirting with her? *Was* I flirting with her? Is this what you did when you flirted?

"Very funny."

"Actually I was being serious."

My God. I *was* flirting with her.

"I don't believe you. Anyway, I think you should give the running a go again. I don't know what I'd do without it. Sometimes I think it's the only thing that keeps me sane. No matter how crap I feel before I go on a run, I always feel better when I get back."

Her words struck a chord. In my running years that feeling of aloneness, of clearing your head, had helped me forget the stresses of a day's teaching, of dealing with the adolescent Danny and Ellie.

"I'll tell you what you should do," said Maggie. I already feared what was coming. "The Richmond Runners are all ages, all shapes, all sizes." Perhaps I just imagined the look she gave my stomach. "And we're always looking out for fresh blood. Why don't you come and join us?"

An Invitation.

"Really?" I said, playing for time.

"We run on Sunday mornings and Tuesday evenings. Why don't you come along this Sunday?"

An Invitation.

It was definitely An Invitation. By the rules of the contract I had to say yes. I might have been old, fat and out of condition, but I had to say yes. All my instincts were telling me no, all kinds of voices inside my head were mouthing the gentle refusal, all kinds of muscles were readying themselves for the polite smile of regret. But I had no choice.

"Do you know what?" I said. "I'd love to."

"Really? That's great."

"Where do we meet?"

"On the green at nine forty-five. I'll see you there."

"Great."

Fred and Alice came to join us and the conversation moved on. As it did I mulled over the implications of what I had just agreed to do, and kept sneaking glances at Maggie. There were moments when we caught each other's eyes and smiled, and it may have been naïve of me, but I got the sense that she was smiling not just because she had recruited a new member for The Richmond Runners.

***

"Jerry?"

"Rick. How are you?"

"It's ridiculous! I can't go on."

"What are you talking about?"

"This invitation thing. It's crazy."

"I knew you'd bottle it. And last night you seemed so resolute."

"I'm not bottling it. I'm doing it. That's the whole point! I've just been invited to join the Richmond Fucking Runners! That's how ridiculous this is."

"The what?"

"A group of joggers, for fuck's sake!"

"You accepted it, I hope?"

"I can safely say that so far this year I have accepted every invitation that has come my way. I have been to drinks at a neighbour's and I have agreed to join a group of local maniac joggers next Sunday. Two things I would normally run a mile from."

"Very funny."

"What?"

"Run a mile from."

"Look, Jerry, this whole thing could get a little – I don't know – a little out of hand, don't you think?"

"New Year. New You."

"I know all that, but it's still the first of January and I'm knackered."

"Oh, well. It seemed like a good idea at the time, but if you're not up to it..."

"I'm not saying that at all. It's just..."

I paused. It was just what? What was it exactly that I was feeling? If I hadn't accepted Harry's invitation I wouldn't have spoken to Maggie and if I hadn't spoken to Maggie I wouldn't have suddenly needed to find a pair of trainers. Was all this good or bad? Where would it all lead?

"Rick? Are you still there?"

"I'm fine."

I said goodbye to Jerry and crawled upstairs to get some sleep.

I must have slept for several hours. It was seven o'clock when I woke and went downstairs to find Ellie lying on the couch watching an episode of *The Simpsons*.

"I thought I was the one supposed to be sleeping off a New Year's hangover," she said.

"I must have been tired," I said.

"Tired?"

"Yes. I was at Harry's lunchtime drinks."

Ellie was so surprised she turned down the volume. "What? You were out last night and you've been out this lunchtime! What's going on?"

"What do you mean what's going on? I'm allowed to go out, aren't I?"

"Of course you are. It's just that, well, it's just that you don't, do you?"

"There's no rule, is there?"

"No. There's no rule. And I suppose it's, I don't know, a good thing to do…"

"Under the circumstances?"

Ellie turned the volume back up.

"OK," I said, raising my voice to be heard over Homer. "A clumsy attempt to introduce 'circumstances' into the conversation and to instigate a 'chat'. I mimed the quotation marks. "I apologise."

"It's not that I don't want to talk about it, Dad. It's just that I don't know what to say."

"That makes two of us, then," I said.

"If I had something new to say, I'd say it, but all that comes out are huge fucking clichés. Whenever anyone opens their mouth that's all you hear – huge fucking clichés."

I paused, wondering whether or not it was worth pointing out that she shouldn't be swearing.

"I see," I said.

"Nothing personal or anything, but everything's been said."

"Has it?" I said. "It seems sometimes that we've barely talked at all."

Ellie kept her eyes fixed on the TV.

"I know it must be difficult for you," I said. "I know how awful it must be."

"This is 'a chat', isn't it?"

I sat down on an armchair. "Yeah," I said, "I suppose it is. The thing is…"

"Look, Dad, I know it's not your fault."

"Isn't it?"

"Well, no. She's the one who left you, isn't she?"

"Yes, but—" Boring. The word flashed before my eyes. "It's not that simple, though, is it?"

"Seems pretty simple to me. She's left you to shack up with Colin."

Colin the PE teacher.

"You mustn't be too quick to judge."

"Of course not. Just like both of you weren't too quick to judge me and..."

Wiggy. The ridiculous name that she couldn't bring herself to utter had dominated her first two years at Bristol. Trust-fund ski-bum, dreadlocked public schoolboy, body-pierced dopehead – however you chose to describe him, he was exactly the sort of bloke your daughter should avoid as a boyfriend. I knew that no one would ever quite be good enough for her, but surely no one could ever fall as spectacularly short of our expectations as Wiggy. It may have been easy to laugh about it when it was over, when we could refer to the "Wiggy Years" as a thing of the past, but at the time smiling wasn't always easy.

Once, fed up with hearing his preposterous name, let alone having to use it myself, I had decided to confront him.

"Tell me, Wiggy. What's your real name?"

"Rupert," he said.

It stopped me in my tracks. If I was called Rupert I think I might find even Wiggy a better option. I persevered, though.

"So tell me, Wiggy, why have you changed your name?"

He gave me a look as if I was mad, as if calling yourself Wiggy was the most natural thing in the world.

"I just thought it was time to reinvent myself," he said.

I had no idea what he had been like before, but surely it couldn't have been so bad that this incarnation was some kind of improvement. I knew I was playing the protective father, but what else was I expected to do? You name a threat to any man's daughter and Wiggy, without doubt, posed it. Drugs? He had dreadlocks in his hair, didn't get out of bed before one in the afternoon, read philosophy, and had his father's trust fund to subsidise whatever habit he chose to indulge. It would be naive of me to think that he hadn't encouraged Ellie to indulge as well. Sex? You could see it from the way they sat next to each other on the couch, the way they walked down the street, the way they fixed each other with longing, smouldering glances. And this was just the sensational tip of the Wiggy iceberg. As our daughter's university years passed, everything about her seemed to change – her language, her beliefs, her newly acquired enthusiasm for skiing and, in the loafing, Gap year sense of the term, "travel".

Oh, how we leaped and danced for joy when we heard that they had split up. It may well have been the last time that Sarah and I had been united in some act of genuine communal joy.

"Look, Ellie, that's behind you," I said. "All in the past."

"Yeah," said Ellie, "All in the past. I can forget about that now and start worrying about my future. Like what am I going to do when I've scraped my 2.1., *if* I scrape my 2.1 that is."

"There's no pressure, Ellie. One thing at a time."

I looked at her lying on the couch, her eyes glazing over.

"It all goes so quickly Dad, doesn't it?"

She kept her eyes on the screen, and I could see them welling up. I leaned over and touched her arm.

"Everything," she said, "just goes. I just keep thinking about all those times. You, me, Danny, and Mum. All those laughs, all those holidays, all those things we used to do together."

The conversation had taken its usual course, Ellie starting off tough and resilient, reluctant to talk and refusing to open up, only to end up letting it all out and breaking down in tears.

I patted her arm. "Come on," I said. "No point moping around like this. Why don't we go out for a drink or something?"

"What? Another drink? Are you sure you're all right?"

"OK, not a drink then. How about a nice cup of tea?"

Ellie smiled. "Thanks Dad," she said, and I went to the kitchen to put the kettle on.

Later, as we sat at the kitchen table cradling mugs of tea, the phone rang.

"Rick? It's Sarah. Can we talk?"

"What's the problem?"

"I'm just a little worried. About Danny."

"What's happened? Where is he? Is he OK?"

"He's just left me – he's heading home. And he's fine. Or rather he's not. He doesn't, I don't know, seem himself."

"Sarah, can we talk later. I'm just—"

"Why? Where are you?"

"I'm at home. With Ellie."

"I see. Look, Rick, can we meet?"

"Meet?"

We might have spoken frequently, but we had met only a couple of times in the last few months.

"OK," I said. "Let's meet. A drink?"

"I was thinking dinner. Why don't I take you out to dinner?"

An Invitation.

A drink would have been quicker and less complicated. A drink would give me the chance of getting up and leaving early, not an easy option when you're faced with a formal three courses.

But this was An Invitation

"That'd be fine," I said. "Where shall we meet?"

"How about The Raj?"

"Just like old times, eh?"

"Eight o'clock?"

"See you there."

I hung up and put my mobile back in my pocket.

"How is she?" said Ellie.

I shrugged. "OK. Difficult to tell, really."

Ellie took out a tissue and dabbed at her eyes again. "The thing I don't get, Dad, is why Colin? Is it just because he's, I don't know—"

"Handsome?"

"No, I don't mean that. I mean..."

"Younger?"

"I don't know. Different. He's very... different."

"I know what you mean," I said. "It was as much of a surprise to me as it was to anyone."

"And you had no idea?"

"I had no idea about Colin, no. But looking back on it..."

Colin was, apparently, a handsome man, the kind of man you might look at twice if you walked past him in the street. The only time anyone ever looked at me twice was if I bumped into them or if I fell over, but I did like to think I had certain things which

Colin might lack – intelligence and wit, for example. After all, I was the history teacher and he was the one who taught PE (and, if I remembered correctly, it wasn't even PE with Geography; it was the pure, undiluted form).

When I looked at the situation I came to one conclusion. I might have had many enviable intellectual qualities, but I was balanced and impartial enough to concede that Colin had the physical edge. And maybe it was that simple. Maybe, as Jerry had intimated on New Year's Eve, I had become boring not only in general terms but in more specific sexual ones too? What else could it be? The thought that it might be something other than this, that my wife of twenty-four years left me for the intellectual and social stimulation she might find with a PE teacher, was too terrifying to contemplate

"Dad?" Ellie's voice came as if from a distance and I realized I had drifted off.

"Sorry, I was miles away."

"You haven't answered my question."

"What question?"

"About whether you had any idea?

"The truth is…" I picked up my mug of tea and finished it off. "The truth is, Ellie, I really don't know anymore. I really don't know."

5

As Sunday grew closer, I became more and more worried about the prospect of running. Maggie was clearly fit and I assumed that everyone else who was a Richmond Runner would be the same. The chances of other fat, out-of-condition newcomers joining at the same time as me were pretty remote, and whenever I tried to picture the Sunday morning scene all I could see was a group of easy-breathing joggers, most of them Marathon runners of great experience, accelerating away from a struggling, wheezing lard-arse. That lard-arse was me, eyes focused on Maggie's pert, Lycra-clad backside as she pulled away into the distance.

I was so worried by the whole idea that I thought it best to get in some practice. So early on the Friday morning I fished out an old pair of trainers which looked a couple of decades out of date but which still fitted, found an equally old tracksuit, and headed off towards the river.

Taking extra care when I went past Maggie's house, I walked casually down the road, breaking into a jog only when I was safely out of sight. Quite why I wanted it to remain secret I couldn't work out, but as I headed off down the road, keeping what I thought a convincingly steady pace, I figured it was something to do with pride.

My pride stayed intact for about ten minutes. As I started down the hill, I began to sweat profusely. This may have been the result of the fleece tracksuit, but it was a brisk, cold January morning and I sensed that the flooding pores were more a result of my lack of fitness and the excessive New Year booze.

I stopped, bent over, put my head between my knees, and before I could do anything to stop it or to make it less spectacular, I puked up all over the pavement.

Luckily, there wasn't too much traffic about, and even more luckily, there were no passing pedestrians. I wiped the streaks of bile from my chin and headed back up the hill, already working out how I might be able to avoid joining the Richmond Runners on Sunday morning. There was, after all, nothing that said I had to carry on with this stupid invitation lark. I didn't need to go out if I didn't want to. My life. My choice. Why on earth should I feel the need to have my life driven by whatever invitations came my way? So what if I was boring? Maybe I was better off that way. And if the alternative to being boring was puking up on an early morning jog then I knew which one I would choose.

I struggled up the hill and turned into Afton Road. As I did I saw a figure heading towards me. It was Maggie in full running kit, hurtling down the road at a pace that seemed closer to sprinting than jogging. She smiled broadly and waved. I thought for a moment she was about to stop, and was relieved when she carried on without breaking her stride, turning her head to call to me as she passed.

"Fantastic!" she said. "You're into it already. See you Sunday!"

And with that she was gone.

I turned as she went and was quick enough to catch a glimpse of her backside before she disappeared round the corner. It was, as I had suspected, very nice. I smiled, opened the front door and looked in the mirror to find that two streaks of vomit still caked my chin. I hoped Maggie hadn't noticed, and that, if she had, she would make no connection between them and the pile of sick she had probably already passed on the road down to town.

I felt no better after a shower and still worse after a few futile hours trying to do some preparation for the coming term. By way of distraction, I flicked on the computer and checked my emails. At first it all looked like the usual stuff – junk mail from Amazon and iTunes, and offers of investment advice (quite how such things should reach someone with so little to invest always confirmed my sense that digital marketing was deeply flawed). Then I got to one from a name I didn't recognize – Caroline Bingham.

From: Caroline Bingham

To: Rick Matthews

Subject: Balham College Gaudy 1977-80

Dear Rick,

I am writing to let you know that this year's Summer Gaudy is for those who matriculated in 1977-80. It will be held in College Hall on July 7th. We hope as many of you as possible will be able to attend.

A formal invitation will be sent to you through the post but we thought we would email to let you know in advance and to remind you that you can view the list of Old Members from these years by visiting www.balhamom7780.co.uk and that you will be able to see a list of those who have accepted the invitation and who will be attending on June 30th at www.balhamgaudy7780.co.uk.

We hope very much that you will be able to attend. If you would like to confirm your attendance before the official invitation arrives simply fill out the details below and press "Reply"

Name:

Year of Matriculation:

I will be attending on July 7th

I am unable to attend

I read the text several times, knowing that if I were to keep faith with my resolution I had only one option. And yet this was exactly the sort of thing I would, in the past, have taken great pleasure in avoiding. A college reunion was close to my worst nightmare. The prospect of seeing those you barely knew and had long-forgotten was of no significance, but the idea of seeing those you had known but you hoped never to see again, not to mention seeing those you had known and had continued to know throughout your adult life, in the place where you first met them, the place where you had been young together, was truly terrifying.

It was, after all, at Balham that I had met Alex and Jerry. It was at Balham that I had fallen in love with Sarah.

I phoned Jerry.

"Have you checked your emails recently?"

"Why?"

"There's a Balham Gaudy this year. 1977-80."

"Really? Great!"

"What do you mean great?"

"They're good fun. Weren't you at the last one?"

"Of course I wasn't."

"Oh well, you'll be at this one though, won't you?"

"Will I?"

"It's an invitation, isn't it? "

"Yeah. It's an invitation."

"So you have no choice."

"But it'll be awful. What if Sarah's there?"

"You'll deal with it. Come on, it'll be fun"

"Fun? Shit, Jerry. I've suddenly realised – they'll be expecting Alex to turn up, won't they?"

"Not if someone's told them."

I flicked on the old members website. There he was – Alex Barden 1977.

"He's on the list."

"Well, he would be, wouldn't he? You're an old member whether you're dead or alive."

"Someone should have told them."

"It's not the first thing you think of doing, is it?"

"Even so, people should know."

While Jerry suggested that I was perhaps the ideal man to call the college I clicked on the gaudy attendance list and was surprised to find that some names were already there – some had clearly had no hesitation in sending in their acceptance. I scanned down the list of names, recognising a few. Then I filled in my details, pressed "reply" and sent my gaudy acceptance off to Balham College.

I even put the date in my diary.

6

In our very early days a trip to The Raj had been like planning some kind of military exercise. First there was the effort needed to get babysitters. Then there was the angst of getting the kids ready for bed and in a docile enough mood for the babysitter not to be offered danger money. And on top of that there was the stress at the dinner table where you hoped your evening wouldn't be disturbed by a panic phone call, but feared, with every mouthful, that it might.

As the years passed, the visits to The Raj became easier and as the kids developed a taste for Indian food they even started to accompany us on the odd occasion. It seemed entirely fitting, then, that The Raj, which had witnessed most of the significant stages of our relationship, should now be witnessing another.

This first post-split meal had been awkward from the very start, right from the kiss on greeting (on the cheek), through the early conversation about nothing in particular to where we were now – the kids.

Sarah wiped her mouth with a napkin and sighed. "I worry about Danny," she said.

"Funnily enough," I said, "So do I."

"He seems quiet, withdrawn."

"He always has been. I don't think it's surprising. What is surprising is that he hardly says anything, yet he wants to be a stand-up comedian."

"At first he seemed OK," said Sarah, "but over Christmas he seems to have changed in some way."

"Given the kind of Christmas they had I'm not really surprised."

Christmas this year had nearly destroyed me. God knows what it had done to Danny and Ellie who had been ferried, like some human pass-the-parcel, from me to Sarah halfway through the day. They hadn't said much about the bigger picture, ignoring the issue of why they should, at this family time of year, be having to do a split-shift, spending time first with me and then with Sarah (Colin had, strangely, deserted her to be with his family). Instead, they had concerned themselves with the details of exactly when they should move from one house to another and what, exactly, would be available to eat, drink and entertain themselves with at each location. I, at least, had been able to stay in one place, even if the afternoon, when Danny and Ellie had gone off to Sarah's, was one of the loneliest, most miserable experiences of my life.

"He doesn't say much about Oxford," I said. "Has he mentioned it to you?"

"Not much. Just shrugs and says it's all OK."

"Well maybe it is. Maybe that's why he doesn't say much about it. Did you say much to your parents about what you got up to at college?"

Sarah shrugged. "No, but that was different."

"Yeah, we weren't parents. Danny'll be OK. He'll get through it."

"Get through what?"

"Oxford. Us."

I smiled. And then we moved on to Ellie.

"What's she going to do?" asked Sarah.

"A Gap year, perhaps."

"I thought you did those before university, not after."

"Not any more," I said, "and this kind of Gap year has a habit of extending itself into a Gap life."

Sarah almost smiled. "But she seems alright?"

"As far as you can tell about these things."

For about half an hour the conversation went on in similar fashion. But with every mouthful and every sip of beer I found myself hearing less of what Sarah was saying and worrying more about my outing with The Richmond Runners the next morning. Every time I looked at Sarah I started to see athletes. First of all a tracksuited Colin, lithe and supple, jogged into view, and then Maggie trotted past.

"Are you listening?"

"What?"

My mind was in Lycra. Maybe if I took this running thing seriously I too could get myself into a Colin-like state of fitness.

"You were miles away," said Sarah.

"Sorry, I was thinking of… of… Alex," I said, improvising quickly. "You know, it's difficult to think of him gone. He's always been there, hasn't he, ever since college. See? I'm even using the wrong tense – it's almost as if he's still around. Such a bloke – always such fun, always larger than life. Then suddenly he's gone. He steps out into the road and – bang, that's it. No more Alex."

Sarah gazed ahead, as if struck by this truth, or as if suddenly aware of a new one. She looked unhappy.

"I'm not upsetting you, am I, talking like this?"

She took a deep breath. "No, I'm fine."

"It's just that it's funny when your old mate goes just like that. It makes you think. It makes you think that maybe you should make the most of what's left, maybe take a few more chances, a few more opportunities, before you go too."

Sarah looked up. "Opportunities? What do you mean?"

For a brief moment I had to resist the temptation to tell her – to let her know about my New Year's resolution.

"Oh, I don't know," I said. "Do a few more things, perhaps? Because sometimes I think maybe I don't do enough."

Here was her chance to tell me the truth about why she walked out, her chance to hit me with the 'b' word. She said nothing.

"What I mean is there's no point saving things up," I said. "That rainy day might never come. And your leaving – for whatever reason you did – has made me take a long hard look at myself."

Another chance. A chance to say what it was that Colin had that I lacked, what she had left me for. Again she said nothing, just looked down into her lap. I wondered for a moment whether she was crying.

We sat in silence for a while. I turned to my king prawn bhuna, thinking again of my stomach and the next morning's run, while Sarah stayed with her head down, composing herself.

It seemed an age.

Then she slowly raised her head and looked straight at me with moist, tear-filled eyes.

"I have something to say to you, Rick, something I'm not going to find particularly easy."

"Try me."

Here it was. She was going to tell me the truth – the exact reason why she walked out on me. I braced myself.

She leaned back in her chair, took a deep sigh and then eased herself forward again so that she was looking at me close up, her hands waving ineffectually beside her face as if they couldn't find the appropriate gesture.

"I think," she said, "that I've made a terrible mistake."

I looked at her plate. "I don't know. The biryiani looks quite good to me."

"I'm trying to be serious, for God's sake!"

"Sorry. Go on."

"I think I have made a terrible mistake."

She paused.

I waited.

"I think I have made a terrible mistake in leaving you."

My jaw dropped as far as my plate. This was not what I had expected.

"I'm sorry. Could you say that again?"

She kept her voice level and steady, keen to seem in control. "I said that I made a mistake leaving you."

I nodded.

Another long silence. A very long silence.

"OK, so what do you want me to say in response?"

"I don't know. Say what you feel. Say what you think."

"I'm stunned. You made a mistake walking out on me?"

"That's what I'm saying."

"You made a mistake walking out on me to move in with Colin?"

"Yes."

"What's wrong with him, then? I thought you had had enough of me, I thought we had grown apart, I thought you needed space, I thought—"

"I know. I said all those things and at the time I meant them. But… things haven't worked out as I thought. I made a break for some kind of freedom – I don't know what exactly I was looking for. I suppose with Danny going away I thought that this was it, now or never. I thought I wanted a different kind of life, but now I'm not sure I really did. I'm not sure I do."

"Well that's a shame, isn't it? You've tried it and you haven't liked it, so you want to come back to comfortable old me. Good old Rick – he'll always be there, he doesn't do anything, he doesn't change. Rick'll still be there so I'll go back to him."

"There's no need to be like that, is there?"

"Isn't there? I think there is. Every reason under the sun. Twenty-four years of marriage and you walk out on me for some twat from your school called Colin."

"He's not a twat!"

"Of course he is. Everyone in the world called Colin is a twat, and your particular Colin is more of a twat than most. He's a PE teacher, for fuck's sake!"

"I don't think that's very fair."

"Fair? Ah well, if we're talking about fairness I think I should go on a little longer. Maybe we should ask exactly how long this little charade had been going on, exactly how long you had been shagging this Colin bloke behind my back—"

"I hadn't been!"

"Well, it seems that way to me. What else had you been doing when you'd been sloping off in the evening with 'people from school'?"

Sarah looked away, head bowed, and then turned back to face me. "Look, Rick, it took quite a lot of guts to walk out when I did, to face up to things honestly, and instead of covering things up and doing nothing, to act on them. It took a hell of a lot of guts to do it and it's taken even more guts to say that I've made a mistake. So it would help if you took it all a bit more seriously."

"I'm being perfectly serious. I've never been…" Sarah was getting visibly distressed. Heads were turning. "OK," I said, calming it down. "I understand what you're saying. You made a mistake. What else are you saying? What do you want to happen?"

Sarah kept her head down and spoke with her eyes fixed on the tablecloth.

"I want to come back."

She spoke so softly I hardly heard it.

"Sorry. What did you say?"

She lifted her head. "I said I want to come back. If you'll have me."

"I thought that's what you said."

We avoided each other's eyes and sat in silence for what seemed longer than the few seconds it probably was.

"Well?" she said.

"Do you want an instant answer?"

"No. I expect you need to think about it."

Part of me wanted to reach out and forgive. Part of me wanted to forget the last two months and put them all behind us, to wipe it all out, to think about the twenty-four years of happy marriage and to see my wife's two-month fling with some loser called Colin as a temporary blip.

But there was also another part of me – another voice which started quietly but then grew in volume as it started to express its views.

What about my New Year's resolution? What about my Year of No Regrets? OK, it was a completely crazy scheme and one that I would be hard pushed to see through for a whole year. But on the other hand, wasn't there something attractive about it? So far this year (a year which was only a week old) I had done more than I had for months, and although I couldn't own up to having enjoyed it all, it was undoubtedly giving me some kind of excitement.

And why, after all, was I doing it?

To show I wasn't boring, to show that my wife was wrong to walk out on me, to show that if, like my old friend Alex, I was knocked down by a car tomorrow I wouldn't feel I hadn't given things a go, wouldn't feel that sense of wasted chances and missed opportunities.

Of course I didn't like my wife of twenty-four years not being with me. Of course I wasn't happy with what her walking out had done to me, and more specifically, the kids. But you could look at it another way and say that the whole thing had changed me, changed the way I looked at the world, and started me on a course of action which it might be interesting to see through. Besides, who was in the position of strength here? I had nothing to feel guilty about. It wasn't me who walked out. It wasn't me who had been conducting an affair for who knows how long. I hadn't walked out to live with anyone called Colin. So why not enjoy the moral high ground? Why not enjoy the opportunities it opened up? Why not see where the whole thing might take me?

I looked up at Sarah.

She looked back, her eyes full of pleading and remorse. She raised her eyebrows.

"I know it won't be easy for you," she said, "and maybe you need time…" She trailed off, looking down at the remains of her biryiani.

I leaned back in my chair and sighed. "You're right," I said. "I do need time. To be more precise, I need exactly one year. One year to think about it."

"A year?"

I nodded, and called for the bill.

"But why? Why a year? Why can't you decide before that?"

It was tempting to tell her, but I knew that would spoil everything. This was a journey I would travel by myself.

7

I woke up early on Sunday morning. Very early. I must have managed some sleep, but as I jumped out of bed at six o'clock my body sent me messages suggesting that I hadn't. All through the night Sarah's words "I've made a terrible mistake" echoed through my head on continuous loop, punctuated by the occasional sharp, percussive "take me back". All through the night I saw her familiar face looking at me imploringly through a moist glaze of tears. And all through the night I saw Maggie's face smiling up at me as she jogged up and down in a Richmond Runners tracksuit.

The two voices in my head were still conducting their debate, one wanting to forgive and forget and take Sarah back, the other telling me to forge ahead with the new me and see where this crazy resolution led me. One moment I was pleased that I had come down so firmly in favour of asking for time (and how neat that idea of a year seemed to be); the next moment I was wondering whether I had made some huge mistake and should have swallowed my pride, ditched my crazy idea, and taken her back, doing everyone, not least our two children, a huge favour.

As I hauled myself into the brand new tracksuit I had bought the previous day in an attempt to make myself look marginally less ridiculous, all I could hear were Sarah's words. Strangely, they produced no gloating told-you-so smugness, only bewilderment. Strangely, they left me feeling not so much sorry or regretful as angry. And it was this anger I tried to draw on as I braced myself for The Richmond Runners.

I jumped into the car before I could even register whether or not Maggie was about and drove down to Richmond Green, momentarily worrying whether driving was, on these occasions, the right thing to do. Maggie, presumably, jogged down, but then Maggie was fit and if I tried to do the same I knew my tank would be pretty much empty before I started any serious exercise. Compromising, I parked the car a quarter of a mile out of town, and then made my way nervously towards the green.

Walking towards the small group of runners, some of them gently jogging up and down, others stretching limbs with a terrifying flexibility and professionalism, I had no doubt that I should have said yes to Sarah, got my life back to normal, and ended this frankly preposterous scheme. While I might be able to kid myself that taking up running again was a good idea, it was difficult to convince myself that this was the way I should do it. This "social" running was exactly the kind of activity for which I had, in all my rational adult years, held nothing but contempt.

And yet here I was.

"Rick!"

The voice came from behind me.

I turned and saw Maggie jogging towards me at pace.

"So great to see you," she said, without breaking stride and without any flicker of breathlessness. "Come on over, and I'll introduce you."

She was already past me, and I realized that I was expected to follow, not by walking, but by running beside her. Already she was about ten yards ahead of me. I broke into a half-hearted jog, a little like running on the spot with a barely detectable forward motion. Maggie turned, expecting me to be just behind her shoulder. Surprised to see me still some distance away, she waved and beckoned me with hurry-up hands, but I resisted the urge to attempt any kind of increase in pace. I may have been moving slowly, but at least I still had my dignity.

"This, everyone," said Maggie, when I eventually joined the group, sweating heavily, "is Rick, and this is his first outing with us."

The group swivelled their heads towards me and I gave a weak smile.

"I won't do names, Rick, but I'm sure you'll get to know us all in time."

A fit-looking thirty-something stepped forward. He must have been fit because not only did he have sweat bands, wrist bands, and knee bands, in fact bands in every place you could possibly imagine – he also wore a t-shirt which had the words 'London Marathon' plastered across the front.

"Right, everyone," he said. "Let's warm up."

With that, everyone started to stretch and move. I stood still, expecting this leader to provide some kind of guidance, like the Green Goddess used to on morning TV, but he just launched into his own routine, so I tried to start my own. Baffled by what, exactly, I was supposed to be doing, I sneaked careful looks at what was going on around me, and did my own minimalist, energy-conserving versions of what I saw.

Maggie moved herself through her exercises to a position beside me.

"We set off in three groups," she said, "and they all do different routes, all ending back here."

"I need the slowest," I said, pretending to stretch a muscle somewhere in my leg.

"That's fine. They go at a very gentle pace, and there are some great people there."

"Great," I said, "I hope I survive."

"You will."

They called the last group the 'Gentle Group'. I could have thought of far better ways to describe it, like the fat, fucked, or better-at-talking-than-running group. There were seven of us, and all, I was pleased to see, were round about my age, if not older. The idea was for us to head through the town towards the river, to take in a bit of the towpath and then to head back. The other two groups, who clearly were not so sad as to need euphemistic labels and were known as simply Groups One and Two, would take the same initial route as us, but then would carry on when we turned for home. Given their fitness and attitude, I had no doubt that, even if they were to run a marathon, they were likely to end up back at the green before us.

There were three women and four men in our group. The three women ran slightly ahead followed by the three men with one man as the backmarker. It was no surprise to find that very early on I had become attached to the backmarker.

"I missed the name," he said.

I was running beside a tubby, white-bearded man who looked a little like Father Christmas knocked off his sleigh and running behind it trying to catch up.

"I'm Ron," he said.

"Rick."

"Well, Rick. It's good to see you here, and especially good to see you back here. I'm the traditional backmarker."

"Oh well, "I said, "I hope I don't give you too much competition. I'm not very fast myself."

"That's what they all say. They all start off with me back here and then as the weeks go by they get fitter and faster and before you know it they're off in Group Two. Some of the bastards even get up to Group One."

"Well, in my case—"

Ron held up his hand and grunted. "Don't say it. Give it six months and you'll be entering marathons."

"No, honest…"

The truth was I was finding this trick of running and talking a little difficult, even though everyone else in our group seemed to manage it OK, the group in front of us chatting brightly as they maintained their steady pace. The whole thing, at least the whole thing in this Gentle Group, seemed as much social as physical.

"So what do you do then, Rick?"

"I'm a teacher."

"Oh yes? Where?"

"Ravensbourne."

"Oh that bunch of hooligans."

"Well, some of them are OK."

"I'm sure they are, but the ones I see traipsing through the town—"

"Oh well, it's a big college, you know. It gets all sorts."

"So what do you teach, then, Rick?"

"History."

"History, eh? I never really saw the point in history. I like the here and now myself. And the future of course. You can't forget the future, can you?"

Ron congratulated himself with a huge belly laugh that momentarily slowed him down and I began to realise why so many who had started at the back with Ron had improved their fitness so quickly and moved up through the groups. Even I, a struggling novice, was tempted to increase the pace.

"So, what do you do, then, Ron?" I asked, thinking it only polite to reciprocate.

"I run a pub."

That explained the shape and the fitness – too much sampling of his own wares. Perhaps that also explained his views.

"Which one?"

"The Running Mare. Running Mare and running landlord!" He wheezed out a chuckle. "Ever been in?"

"No," I said. "I haven't."

"You must."

Ron was out of breath. He stopped talking for a while to concentrate on maintaining his modest pace and making sure we didn't fall too far behind the group ahead. As he did I tried to control my breathing while I considered whether I would be able to make it to the end of the run without needing to stop and whether or not Ron's 'You must' constituted An Invitation.

"Yeah," said Ron, when he had recovered enough breath to carry on the conversation. "You should come down. I'd love to see you."

"I'd love to," I said, still unsure whether he was inviting me.

"Yeah," said Ron, enjoying his captive potential market. "You being a teacher and all that, I'll tell you what you should do. You should get a team together and come down for our quiz. Thursday nights. It's a great quiz – we've got this bloke who does it for a living and he likes to try out some of his quizzes on us first. It's good stuff. Get a team together. We'd love to wipe the floor with some teachers. That's always good fun. So how about it? Come down and have a go."

It was definitely An Invitation.

I turned to Ron. His face was puffed and red and droplets of sweat glistened in his white beard, enhancing the Santa-running-after-his-sleigh effect.

He had definitely just given me An Invitation and I knew what I had to do.

"Count me in," I said.

"OK, then," said Ron. "That's a date, then. We'll see you down there."

We pressed on in silence. Had I been less out of condition I might have enjoyed the early morning view of the Thames, the sense of a quiet Sunday morning gradually coming to life. But then, had I been less out of condition I would not have been running at the back with Ron. Had I been fitter I would have avoided this latest invitation.

Ron's conversation was beginning to wear thin and I wondered what the etiquette would be about trying to move up to join the pair in front who looked as though they might have been doing something other than trading landlord platitudes about the state of the country, the state of the world, and, more specifically, the state of the sixth form college – which, in Ron's view – was not only connected to all the world's problems, but also in some way the cause. The more he went on, the more I wanted to get together a crack quiz team and 'wipe the floor' with his regulars, and the more I wanted to increase the pace and move ahead of him.

"I started about a year ago," said Ron, "Last thing in the world I thought I'd end up doing, but Sheila – she's a Group Two runner – she had joined and she said come along so I did. I'm not normally the running type but I thought I'd give it a go – you know, keep the weight down, that kind of thing – and I've been here ever since. It's what you should get your college students doing. Look after themselves and get fit, instead of roaming round the town taking drugs and the like. Bit like National Service, isn't it? I've always been a fan of that, and I notice now even these new Tory types are too soft. I tell you – strong government – that's what we need!"

I let Ron drone on and focused on my running. Despite the curry the previous night, despite the stress and the strain, I was, I thought, doing well. Thinking of all that could have happened – injury, stitch, a repeat of last week's early morning vomiting – I was pleased. All I needed to do now was gently increase the pace, glide away from

Ron, raise my hand nonchalantly and tell him, politely and through perfectly controlled breaths, that I'd try to stretch it a little just before we turned for home, and then move up to the shoulders of the pair ahead.

"And another thing that gets me, Rick, is these asylum seekers and all these immigrants. Where's all that going to end then? Do you know I read in the paper the other day that—"

I raised my hand gently.

"Ron…" I said.

Ron looked at me. I took another breath and prepared to shift a gear. We weren't going fast at all. My running days were not all that long ago and back then I would certainly have been moving a lot faster than this. All it needed was a gentle injection of energy to the legs, and I'd be away.

"Ron," I said, raising my hand again.

I pushed, and started to move ahead. Then, when I tried to turn to Ron to deliver the easy-breathing, laid-back line that I was moving on, I realized that something was wrong. In my left leg a sharp pain speared the back of my calf muscle, suddenly stopping all movement on my left side. I felt myself falling to the left, a gradual fall that seemed to happen in slow motion.

It seemed to take forever.

I had time to put my hands out to break the fall. I had time to think to myself that I was falling over. I had time to think that this was going to make me look very foolish indeed.

What I didn't have time for was telling Ron that I was falling into his path, and as I stumbled to the towpath, grazing my hands as they hit the ground, I was conscious of his fat publican body being unable to do anything to get out of the way. I hit the ground, felt his legs hit my side and, as I spun onto my back, I saw Ron hurtle towards the ground, a sweaty Father Christmas spinning to the ground like a mighty felled oak.

***

"I think it was cramp. Or maybe I pulled something."

I was sitting in Maggie's kitchen, my leg resting on a chair while

Maggie inspected the damage.

"Could be either," she said. "I think you'll live. Nothing's broken."

"Apart from my pride. Not to mention my dignity."

"How long were you lying on the ground?"

"I don't know. We were both there for a minute or two. The pair ahead just carried on oblivious. I suppose it wasn't until one of them turned round that they realized something had happened. Still, at least they came back. And they were very helpful."

Maggie brought two mugs to the table and sat down beside me. Inspection over, I took my leg down from the chair, rubbing it gently just to remind Maggie that, even though nothing might have been broken and even though we agreed it was nothing more than cramp or a pulled muscle, I had still hurt myself and was in need of the tea and sympathy I was currently receiving. There were, after all, enough grazes and scratches on both my knees and my hands to show that I wasn't making a fuss about nothing.

"And how did Ron take it?"

"Not too well."

Ron had spent all the time between his fall and the arrival of help cursing and foul-mouthing whatever he thought of. Given that his thoughts were mainly, at that specific moment, about me, this meant I was on the end of various torrents of abuse. The fall had been entirely my fault. This was the first time since he had taken up running with the Richmond Runners that he had ever fallen. That was the problem with beginners who were out of condition. And if he had suffered any serious injury he knew exactly who to blame.

"I'm sorry." Maggie tried to stop herself laughing but failed. "I should have warned you about old Ron. But then if I'd told you that if you ran right at the back you'd end up with the biggest bore in Richmond you probably wouldn't have turned up."

"I think you're right there."

I would also have avoided an invitation to take a team down to his wretched quiz night as well, a fixture that had assumed a needly competitive edge even before I had brought the Running Mare landlord crashing to the ground.

Maggie sipped her tea and looked up at me, her large brown eyes making me feel curiously aroused. Here I was early on a Sunday morning in the kitchen of a woman who I found very attractive. Neither of us was wearing many clothes and both of us (well, OK, one of us) was bathed in the moist afterglow of intense physical activity. I didn't need much imagination to think exciting thoughts.

Maggie got up from the table. "Can I get you anything to eat?"

"I'm fine thanks. I really should be getting back. Get myself in the bath before the kids notice what's happened."

"Why? Would that be a problem?"

"Not really. I'd just rather keep it quiet."

"It's nothing to be embarrassed about."

"I know. It's just that things are a little – strained with them at the moment."

"Why?"

Perhaps I should have stopped there. Instead I ploughed on.

"The thing is I separated from my wife a couple of months ago and things are still in the process of adjusting."

"I'm sorry. I had no idea."

"Why should you?"

"Funny isn't it?" she said. "I live right opposite you and yet I had no idea anything like that was going on. But then I'm reasonably new to the road. I'm not sure I'd even recognize her. What's her name?"

"Sarah."

"And your kids?"

"Ellie and Danny. They go back to university next week, so I'll be back to the big empty space. All by myself."

"Oh well, that'll make things easier."

What things? Like you slipping over to my place or me slipping over to yours? Like us going running next week and having breakfast together afterwards, maybe sharing a shower?

I sensed it was time to go, and struggled to my feet.

"You sure you're OK?" Maggie reached out a hand as if to stop me falling. I put out my arm and for a brief, accidental moment, our hands touched. A tingle of excitement sparked through me.

"I'm fine," I said, moving towards the door, hoping the tingle wasn't visible in my shorts.

"Well," said Maggie, "I hope you're OK for next week. If Ron's back, you might want to think of the faster group. Who knows? If the leg heals you could get out a couple of times before next Sunday?"

I smiled, shut the door behind me and headed across the road.

What was happening? Maggie was trying to convert me into some kind of runner, taking an evangelistic interest in a possible convert, an interest that I was choosing to construe in purely sexual terms. What's more, I had accepted an invitation to a quiz night at a pub run by the Richmond Runners bore, a man who I had come close to seriously injuring on my first outing.

And all this before breakfast on a Sunday morning.

8

Later that afternoon, I was lying asleep on the sofa in front of the football when the phone rang. Waking with a start, I noticed that the ice wrapped in a tea towel that I had been holding next to my calf muscle had melted and dripped onto the carpet.

"Rick, it's Jerry."

"Jerry, hi."

"Haven't disturbed you, have I?"

"Disturbed enough already, thanks."

"Sorry?"

"A joke. We used to write it under "Do Not Disturb" notices at college, remember? 'Disturbed enough already'"

Jerry sent a weak laugh down the line. "And talking of college I hope you've accepted?"

"Of course."

"Should be great. I'm looking forward to it."

"Really? I'm dreading it. Do you really want to see all those people again?"

"Well, yes, I do. See what's become of them."

"You know what's become of them. They've got older, fatter and richer. Married with kids, all boasting about how happy and successful they are and talking about how wonderful it would be to send their own kids to Balham."

"You never know – there might be some surprises."

"It's self-selecting, Jerry. The ones who have done anything interesting with their lives or the ones whose lives have gone all wrong or the ones who are miserable or poor just don't turn up."

"How do you know? You've never been to one."

"I just know – I don't have to have been to the top of Mount Everest to know it's very high and very cold up there. I just know. You went to the last one – tell me it was any different."

"I think this one will be. Now that we're all older there's less of the need to show off, isn't there?"

"You tell me. You're the lawyer, remember. I'm just a teacher. And I bet the only teachers who turn up are the ones who've become heads. It's that kind of thing. And anyway, it'll be a bit miserable, won't it, going back to where we spent three years with Alex."

"You never know, it might do us good."

"And how do you work that one out?"

"I just feel I haven't reached cl—"

"Don't say it!"

"Don't say what?"

"Closure. You were about to say 'closure', weren't you?"

"So what if I was?"

"It's a horrible word. I hate it."

"All right, forget the closure bit. I just feel unsettled by the whole thing. There are things I'm still uneasy about."

"An old friend has died – I think you're allowed to feel unsettled and uneasy aren't you?"

"I just think that going back to the gaudy will be a good thing to do."

"Look, Jerry. I'll go to the gaudy, but I can't see that it will be a very good experience. I can't see that it'll help. And besides, what if Sarah decides to go? That'd be fun wouldn't it?"

"And is she going?"

"I haven't asked her," I snapped.

"There's no need to be like that. I'm only trying to help, you know."

"Really?"

"I'm helping you face up to things."

"Of course you are. That's why I've made this ridiculous resolution isn't it? To help me face up to things?"

"Well, if you think you can't do it..."

As I sat there, nursing an injured leg, everything suddenly seemed Jerry's fault. If it weren't for him I would never have gone to the drinks party, never have met Maggie, never have gone running, never injured my leg. If it weren't for him I wouldn't be having this discussion about the gaudy. If it weren't for him I would probably have taken Sarah back and my life would have returned to normal. Jerry suddenly seemed responsible for most of what was wrong with my life.

"So," said Jerry, "Have you managed to do it then?"

"Of course I have," I replied. "I have been faithful to the resolution, faithful to the contract in every respect."

"Really? That's great. So what kind of things have you said yes to?"

I went through the list. When I got to Maggie I sensed increased interest.

"So what's she like this Maggie?"

"An actress."

"An actress? Well, you know what they say about them, don't you?"

"No, what's that?"

"Well, they… or maybe it's convent girls. I can't remember."

"Jerry, before you ask, nothing has happened, OK?"

"But remember, no backing out of the deal."

"No backing out. I promise."

"So if this Maggie asks you to—"

"I get the picture Jerry."

"And how's Sarah?"

I probably should have chosen to say nothing, but I was feeling vulnerable and I felt sleepy. Before I knew it I had told Jerry about the previous night.

"She what?"

"She said she'd made a terrible mistake."

"With Colin?"

"And she wanted to come back."

"I don't believe you. So what did you say?"

"I said no."

"Really? You said no?"

"Yes. Anything wrong with that?"

"No. I just —"

"I said I needed time. Time to think it over. Time to—"

"Say yes to every invitation that comes your way for a year?"

"You get the picture."

"Well, funny you should say that, because here comes another invitation."

"Who from?"

"From me."

***

It was a bleak day. The sky was a heart-sink grey and the air's sharp bite made us rub our hands together and stamp our feet against the cold. Entirely appropriate weather for a graveyard.

I followed Jerry as he walked along the path between the headstones.

"Thanks for the invitation," I said. "It's cheered me up no end." Jerry marched on a few yards ahead of me, like a man on a mission. "What's wrong with meeting in a pub? Or going to a football match or something?"

"This is appropriate," said Jerry. "We can go for a drink afterwards."

"I still don't see the need. We were here at the funeral."

"I just want to see him when there isn't a huge crowd around."

"It's not as though there's a lot to see, is it? A grave's a grave. A headstone's a headstone."

Jerry moved ahead, talking to the air in front of him. "I just wanted to see it, to pay him proper respects. We won't be long. I promise."

Jerry came to a halt and headed off down a row of headstones. He stopped in front of a new-looking piece of white marble, inscribed with neat Roman black lettering

IN LOVING MEMORY OF
ALEX JAMES BARDEN
RIP

"Doesn't say much does it?" said Jerry

"What do you expect it to say? It's a headstone not a novel."

"But that's it. That's his life. That's him. A name. His dates. And RIP. For someone who packed so much in it doesn't amount to much, does it?"

"What else do you want?" I said. "A couple of lines of well-chosen verse? A detailed CV?"

"That's not the point."

"No, it's not. The point is it's cold and miserable here and I'd like to be somewhere else, like in front of a beer in a warm pub."

Jerry didn't shift. "Just think of all those times we spent together, the three of us. And think of how he went. Everything fine, everything dandy and then he stepped out into the road and – bang – it's all over. It could happen to either of us any time, today, tomorrow. It could happen as we leave this cemetery. It could happen when we step outside our front door. It could happen—"

"I think I get the picture."

"The thing about Alex, though, is you never quite knew did you? He lived his life differently from us, didn't he?"

"You mean he wasn't – what's the word again – boring?"

I sometimes wondered what it was that Alex saw in us both. In Jerry's case (it was, after all, Alex who was the first to dub him Captain Sensible) it might well have been the attraction of opposites, but I always hoped he thought that I was not quite so safe and predictable. Looking back on it, though, it was clear that I had more in common with Jerry than I did with Alex. We were both ordinary fun-loving students, game for a laugh, always on for a drink or two, ready to party, ready to fall in and out of love, ready to write the occasional essay, ready to do whatever it was that students were supposed to. Alex did the same, but somehow everything he did was just that little bit more intense, just that little bit more extreme. We drank; Alex got plastered. We had a couple of steady girlfriends each throughout the three years; Alex slept around with the kind of energy and carelessness only those who lived through the pre-AIDS generation would understand. We played some low-level sport and joined a few societies; Alex joined extravagant black-tie dining affairs frequented by Etonians and managed to get his name in the University Paper's gossip columns. We worked conscientiously and steadily and came out with respectable 2nds; Alex partied right to the end, stopping only a week before finals to do some last-minute cramming and coming out with a third (and lucky to get that, according to his tutor). We went into predictable professions, me to teach, Jerry into the Law; Alex went off to join Saatchi's at the height of its fame. We married and had kids; Alex married and divorced. We were still in good health; Alex was dead.

"Are you OK, Jerry?"

We stood there, staring at the headstone, hearing, in the silence, the distant rumble of traffic, the steady rhythms of a world still going on.

"I've been thinking a lot about him, you know," he said.

"So it seems."

"And maybe I was wrong," he said.

"In what way?"

"Wrong in thinking he was always having a fantastic time. Drifting through marriage, drifting through flings, moving from ad agency to ad agency, getting bigger and bigger salaries and spending it all, going out all the time, always having a laugh. I just get the feeling that for all his freewheeling, carefree ways, I don't think, underneath it all, that he was all that happy."

"Maybe not," I said, "but if he wasn't he never really let on, did he?"

Jerry sighed. "Two days before he died he rang me. He said he wanted to talk. He sounded different."

"How do you mean different?"

"Troubled, worried."

"Hungover?"

"No. I don't think I'd ever heard him in that state before."

"So what did he say?"

"He said he was in a terrible dilemma and he didn't know what to do. He said he really wanted to talk. We agreed to meet for a drink – the day we fixed was the day after he died. But before he hung up he said, and I'm pretty sure these were the exact words, 'I'm in a real fix, Jerry, a real fix. I know I've been in fixes before but this one is of a completely different order and I really would appreciate your advice. We go back a long way, Jerry, and only someone like you can help me.'"

"That's it? He didn't say anything more?"

I felt excluded. Only someone like Jerry could help him. Not someone like me, the other old friend from college days. Had things got so bad that he turned to him before me?

"Are you sure it just wasn't Alex just being Alex. He always had a bit of the self-dramatising tart about him, didn't he?"

We stood in front of the grave, our breaths misting the air. Jerry turned to me. "The thing is," he said, "the more I think about it, the more I think it was some kind of cry for help, as if Alex was in real trouble. I know he'd been in scrapes before. I know he'd been in touch to borrow money, to ask favours, and I know he wasn't entirely squeaky clean in all his dealings, but, believe me Rick, when I heard the pleading tone of his voice I just knew that something was up. Then bang, he's gone."

Jerry turned away from the grave and walked towards the cemetery exit and I followed, walking beside him at an appropriately funereal pace.

9

When I stepped through the door after dropping Danny off in Oxford, the shell-like emptiness of the house struck me, its silence punctuated by the occasional echo of the sounds and voices of those who had left it.

I jumped when the phone rang.

"Rick? Hi, it's Jerry. How's things?"

Jerry had been ringing a lot recently, and it had always been for the same purpose. When he asked 'how's things?' what he wanted to know was not so much how I was, or how the kids were, or how I was facing up to being by myself (though he was decent enough to ask about these things, to give the illusion that he was interested); it was more a matter of finding out about me and my Invitations.

It was tempting sometimes to lie to him, to invent all kinds of offers that had come my way, all kinds of exotic, interesting, exciting invitations that would turn him green with envy and make him think this New Year's resolution was the best thing that had ever happened to me. It was also tempting on occasions simply to give up, to ditch the whole scheme, and to tell Jerry when he asked, as he did now, "How's things?" that things had been terminated, that the enterprise was well and truly over. But I was reluctant to do either. The way I had responded to Sarah in the restaurant that night, the way I had asked for time (and not just any old period of time but, specifically, a whole year), made me realise that I was more committed to the whole idea, more serious about it than I ever thought I would be. I had started, so I would finish – just like *Mastermind*.

I knew how easy it would be simply to swallow my pride, forgive Sarah her temporary aberration with Colin, recognize the fact that she was sorry and take her back. But I also knew that this would constitute some kind of defeat. Living my life according to this particular rule might be making me uncomfortable, might be scaring me witless, and I still might have no idea of where the whole thing was going to end, but I didn't want to stop. Not yet.

"Fine," I said to Jerry. "Everything's fine."

"Good. That's great. And the – er – invitations?"

"There's the quiz night coming up soon."

"Yes – and anything else?"

"Can't think. One thing, though, Jerry. You know I'm in this wretched bloody running group."

"The Richmond Runners? Yes."

"Do I still have to go this week, given my leg?"

"I don't know. Have you been invited?"

"What do you mean?"

"Well, has anyone said to you 'come along next week?'"

"I don't think so. I can't remember. They may have said see you next week or something like that, but I don't think anyone actually extended an invitation for next Sunday. I think it was just kind of assumed that I'd be there. Hang on. This is interesting. This means that I don't have to turn up to the Richmond Runners ever again. I was invited and I went."

"Sounds like it to me. You've done it. Of course, if you stop and one of them says you should come out again, then you'd have to."

"So why am I going then?"

"I don't know. Maybe you like it."

I looked down at my leg. "I don't think so, Jerry."

"So that's it then. You can have a rest this Sunday."

Giving it a miss might be for the best. I had heard that two of the group were training for the London Marathon and that several more were planning to do it next time round. What if one of them, ever so casually, invited me to join them? What if one of them turned to me as we limbered up on Richmond Green and said, "Come along and join us. I'm sure you're up to it." Or "Why don't you give it a go? We'd love you to join us in training." I would then be truly stuffed, committed to accepting the invitation, at risk of devoting months of my life to something I would never before have even remotely considered. What's more, if I gave the Runners a miss this week I would be in no danger of bumping into Ron again (assuming, that is, that he had recovered from his own injury). I might have to see him at his quiz night, but I wasn't keen to see him again on an early morning run, where I would face the prospect of either taking it easy at the back and therefore running with him again, or pushing myself harder than I should to keep up with a faster group and risking the humiliation of further injury, total collapse, or, given my luck, another bout of vomiting.

But, having begun to persuade myself that I would be far better off giving The Richmond Runners a miss this week, I felt strangely disappointed. Perhaps I was actually enjoying the exercise. Perhaps I was doing what part of me had wanted to do for some time – taking control of my physical decline and whipping myself into some sort of shape? Perhaps part of me, stung by Sarah's leaving me for Colin, wanted to turn myself into a model of PE-teacher fitness, as a prelude to offering a leaner, more exciting sexual experience? Perhaps the idea of a Marathon was not too ridiculous after all?

"We'll see," I said. "It depends on how my leg shapes up."

"Bollocks. It depends on how much you want to see that Maggie."

"Rubbish."

Was I that transparent?

"What if she asked you to – you know?"

"No I don't know. What are you talking about?"

That was the thing about Jerry and these phone calls. He was always asking about women. He had this curious notion that one of the invitations I was most likely to receive was an invitation into another woman's bed. Given that this was not an invitation I had received once in all my years of marriage I couldn't quite see how one was likely to appear now.

Unless, of course, I tried to make it happen, which was a different matter entirely. It had only just occurred to me that, although I might have no influence over what invitations came my way and although I was always going to be vulnerable to the off-the-cuff, why-don't-you sort of invitation, thrown out casually with little expectation of it being taken seriously, I could also try to exercise some control over the whole thing. I could avoid those situations where I thought unattractive invitations might come my way, but I could also put myself in other situations where the kind of invitation I might want to receive was more likely to be offered. For example, if I was more interested in Maggie than I would like to admit to Jerry, it would make sense to spend as much time as possible in her company. I could continue my Sunday morning runs perhaps, and make the post-run coffee in her kitchen a regular thing, or pop over to her house on the pretext of borrowing something. I could even invite her over to my place.

The other thing that was getting difficult about Jerry was his obsession with Alex. Not only was he taking an indecent interest in my year of no regrets, he was also developing a prurient curiosity about our recently deceased friend.

"Do you know, Rick, exactly how many women Alex slept with when we were at college?"

"Well, actually Jerry, I didn't watch him that closely. And when I did, I wasn't actually counting."

"But you know what he was like."

"Of course I do."

"The thing is I'm still puzzled."

"By what?"

"I just wish I knew what it was he wanted to talk about before he died."

"It might have been nothing that unusual. Maybe he just wanted to borrow money."

"It was more than that. I just know it. And I need to find out."

I may have been in crisis, but no one could convince me that Jerry, the respectable lawyer, wasn't in one too.

***

A few late afternoon runs when I should have been grappling with the preparation of notes on The Unification of Italy convinced me that my leg was fully recovered and that, despite all my reservations and the knowledge that I was in no way compelled to continue my commitment, I still wanted to run. This desire may well have been linked to the threat posed by the relative youth and vitality of Colin, or the attraction of the Lycra-clad Maggie, but maybe I just wanted to carry on. The extra exercise had definitely been a good thing – I was wheezing and sweating less and I got the impression that I was starting to move a little more quickly.

So when Sunday morning came round I headed down to Richmond Green confident that I would be good enough to keep ahead of Ron.

"Hi there," he said as I joined the warm-up on the green, "And who are you going to trip up this week then?"

I smiled, waving a general greeting at the others.

"How are you Ron? I hope you're OK. And, again, many apologies."

Ron jogged up and down on the spot, as if determined to prove the extent of his recovery. "I'm fine, thank you very much. And I hope you're still on for the quiz next week."

"Don't you worry," I said, noticing the glint of fierce competition in his eyes, and reminding myself that I had yet to assemble a team. "I'll be there."

Then I warmed up, occasionally looking towards Maggie, and smiling warmly whenever I thought she might be returning the gaze.

"Glad you're here again," she said.

"Well, I thought I couldn't give up so soon. Especially after such an unfortunate start."

She smiled, and gave me a quick once-over. "You look fitter already," she said.

I held my stomach in. "Really?"

"I would guess you've been out during the week."

"Would you? And why's that?"

"Because I know you have. I've seen you on a couple of occasions."

How had she managed that? Every time I had run past her house, either on my way out or on my way back, I had looked through her window to see if she was there, but I had seen no sign. Had she just casually caught sight of me from the upstairs window? Or maybe she had seen me some time later as I headed down towards the river?

Either way she had noticed me, and I liked the idea. Perhaps she was even looking out for me.

"Anyway, why don't you come over for a coffee when we get back?"

An Invitation.

"I'd love to. Maybe I'll bring some croissants with me."

"Good idea. Not for me though. I'm watching it." Maggie patted an already flat, muscled stomach and then headed off with the pack.

I started at the back with Ron, who took what he saw as familiarity as an excuse to treat me to even more of his right-wing solutions to all kinds of problems – litter on the streets of Richmond, dog crap on the towpath, the decline in literacy, global terrorism, illegal immigrants, and the Middle East.

Then I gradually increased my pace and started to pull away. I turned and gave a modest wave, and he waved back, acknowledging the fact that I was moving too quickly for him. Then I moved up to fall in behind the group of three ahead, passing a runner who had slowed down considerably and who wore the pained look of resignation of someone who had realised they would end up as a backmarker, and Ron's companion, for the rest of the run.

I trailed the group of two men and one woman for a couple of minutes before one of the men turned round and motioned with his arm for me to join them. I smiled as they moved aside to make a gap for me, and accelerated into it as smoothly and breathlessly as I could.

"Managed to get away from Big Ron then, have you?" said the man who had turned round.

"Just about," I said.

"It's Rick, isn't it?" said the woman.

"That's right," I said.

"I'm Veronica," she said, giving me a big smile.

"Andy," said one of the men.

"And Mark," said the other.

"And well done for bringing him down last week," said Veronica. "That was fantastic."

"It wasn't deliberate," I said.

“Well thanks anyway,” said Andy. “We all had a good laugh about it.”

I fell in beside them and we ran along together. They spoke as they ran, but I decided to concentrate on keeping up with the pace rather than the conversation, so I said little at first. All three were moving at a comfortable pace, Mark and Andy, both tall and elegant in their strides, finding it all quite easy, Veronica, significantly lacking in both height and elegance, finding it less so. What she lacked in height and litheness, though, she made up for in grim determination. There was something earnest and committed about her that made her face look strangely lopsided. I wondered how long she had been running. She may have looked like a well-established member of the group, but in the same way that Big Ron never looked as though he was ever going to get any quicker, Veronica looked as if she was never going to find it particularly easy.

“So tell me, Rick,” she said. “How long have you been doing this for then?”

I turned to her and saw that the double effort of articulating and running made her face look even more unbalanced. The whole of the left side of her face seemed suddenly to lift an inch, and it was difficult not to stare in amazement. I looked away, grateful that running conversations could be conducted while looking straight ahead.

“This is only my second outing,” I said.

“You’re looking good, though,” said Andy, “In fact I’d say you look like a very good prospect for Real Richmond.”

He pronounced the Real in the Spanish way as in Real Madrid.

“And what are they?” I said.

“Our five-a-side football team,” said Mark. “Do you play? We’re always looking for new recruits.”

“Hang on,” I said. “This is only my second run in about ten years. I don’t know that I’m up for any football.”

It was too long a sentence. I found myself reaching for breath that wouldn’t come.

“I wouldn’t worry about being unfit,” said Andy. “Compared to some of the ones who roll up you look in peak condition. Did you ever play?”

“Some time ago,” I said. “But…” I gasped for air.

"Come along then. We keep losing team members. It'd be good to have someone like us along to keep up the numbers."

"Like you?"

"You know, someone our age — the Sports Centre, Wednesday evening – seven-thirty, if you're interested?"

An Invitation.

First of all running, and now five-a-side football. Soon I'd be doing more PE than Colin. What was happening to me?

What was happening to me was that I was getting more and more breathless.

"I'd love to," I said. "But I think I'm going to have to slow down a little. You three go on ahead. I'll be fine."

"Great," said Andy, "but don't go too slowly or Ron'll get you."

"Don't worry," said Veronica, "I'll hang back and make sure he keeps ahead of him."

"That's kind," I said, "but you really don't have to. I'll be fine."

"No problem," said Veronica. "My pleasure."

I turned to see her flash a lopsided smile in my direction. Andy and Mark waved their hands as they pulled away.

"Next Wednesday, then," said Mark, looking at Veronica and giving me a wink that suggested they knew more about her than I did.

I fell into a gentler jog and Veronica stayed beside me. We said nothing at first and this suited me fine. But then Veronica started asking me questions – not Ron-like questions, but questions nonetheless, and I was back again to the challenge of running and talking at the same time.

"These runs shouldn't be competitive," said Veronica, "but you know what it's like. It's human nature to want to score points off each other. Everyone who starts at the back wants to get away from Ron, and before you know it, they're moving through the ranks, trying to leave everyone else behind."

"I don't think I'll be steaming ahead," I said. "This is just fine for me. I'm not the points scoring type. Unless it's Scrabble, of course."

Veronica laughed. "Scrabble! I love Scrabble."

"Yeah," I said. "So do I."

And suddenly I was thinking of those Sunday afternoon games with Sarah, the board and the Chambers Dictionary lying between us on the carpet as we lounged on the floor. We were never serious players, not the types who memorised every two-letter possibility, but we took those games seriously, to the point that the loser had been known to sulk for at least a couple of hours afterwards. It was sad to think that such games might never happen again.

"How often do you play?" said Veronica, turning to me and fixing me with another lopsided smile.

"Not too much recently," I said. "But I do enjoy it."

"I play online," said Veronica, "But nothing beats the face-to-face encounter, does it?"

"No," I said, thinking of Sarah's face bathed in the light of the Sunday afternoon fire and then turning to Veronica's strangely contorted model, "I suppose not."

"And I'm always looking for new playing partners," said Veronica, throwing me yet another look.

I kept my head fixed straight ahead, but I knew what was coming.

"Why don't you come round one evening and have a game?" she said.

An Invitation.

How could I avoid it?

"Is that an invitation," I said, "or are you just being polite?"

Perhaps she didn't really mean it. It was worth trying.

"No," said Veronica, "I'm deadly serious. Let's fix up a date now. It's not often I come across a serious Scrabble player. You need to grab these chances when they come along."

"Look," I said, "I'm really not very good."

"Let me be the judge of that," she said. "You probably said you weren't very good at running, but look at you now. So let's strike while the iron's hot, shall we?"

As we ran along, Veronica went through all possible dates. By the time we arrived back at the Green she had fixed on a Friday in a week's time. Before I left she made sure that not only did I have her address, email, and work and home phone numbers, but that she had mine. It was quite clear that she was not going to let the opportunity pass.

***

“I come out running and suddenly I’m committed to playing five-a-side football and a game of Scrabble.”

“Scrabble? Don’t tell me. Veronica’s been on to you. Be careful.”

“Why? What’s wrong with Veronica?”

Maggie shrugged. “Nothing.”

“What do you mean, nothing? You just said be careful. It’s a game of Scrabble. What do I have to be careful about?”

“I’m saying nothing,” said Maggie. “But I’m surprised you accepted. If you really didn’t want to do it, you could always have said no, or made an excuse.”

The temptation to tell her the truth rushed into my brain, but I managed to resist.

“I know,” I said, “but I didn’t want to seem – you know – rude or anything.”

“That’s sweet of you,” said Maggie, “but I think there could be another reason.”

“Oh yes? And what’s that?”

“I think you really do want to have a game of Scrabble. Especially with Veronica!”

“You’re joking! Veronica?”

It would have been cruel to mention it, but surely Maggie could see that it would be difficult to find Veronica attractive.

Maggie smiled. “Still,” she said, “it was nice of you to accept, given how easy it is to say no to these things. I’m sure she appreciates it.”

I had left the car at home and walked down to the green (another sign of my increasing fitness). Maggie had run down, but she walked beside me as we made the way back up the hill towards Afton Road. I tried to get her to say more about Veronica but she gave nothing away. It occurred to me that she might even be a little jealous, but the moment soon passed and when we popped into a small café to get the take-away croissants I knew I should, like Maggie, avoid but which I just couldn’t resist, conversation had moved back to the best way to stretch before and after a run.

At first I didn’t notice her. She was sitting by herself at a table in the corner reading a newspaper, and it was only when I glanced round the café and saw her look up and glance briefly in my direction that I realized who it was. I wasn't sure what to do. My first instinct was to turn away and pretend I hadn't seen her, but before I could she had recognized me and raised her hand in an embarrassed wave. I did the same, and walked towards her.

"Sarah!"

"Ricky! What are you doing here?"

I hoped she didn't mistake the post-run flush for a blush of embarrassment.

I opened my arms and looked around the shop. "Buying croissants," I said in a stating-the-obvious way.

"But you—" Sarah looked me up and down. "What are you wearing all that for?"

"I've been running," I said, trying to make it sound like an activity as natural as buying croissants.

Sarah looked at Maggie, who was standing beside me, and I nervously stumbled for the right words of introduction.

"This is Maggie," I said, breaking the brief, awkward silence and holding my hand out, hoping it didn't look as if I was showing off my latest acquisition. "And this," I said, moving the open hand towards my estranged wife, "is Sarah."

They shook hands. Suspicion and curiosity flickered across Sarah's face. It was obvious what she was thinking.

"Maggie moved in opposite a couple of months ago," I said. I let 'just when you left me' remain unsaid but the phrase dangled between us.

"I'd no idea you'd taken up running," said Sarah.

"Only casually," I said. "Maggie's the real runner."

"Sir?"

The man behind the counter held up my croissants. I went over to pick them up and gave another half-hearted, apologetic wave to Sarah as I walked out.

***

Back in Maggie's kitchen, I tucked into my carbohydrates while Maggie treated herself to some revolting-looking fruit and vegetable juice.

"How long ago did she walk out?" she asked, showing no trace of awkwardness or embarrassment. She seemed more familiar with these scenarios than me.

"A couple of months ago," I said.

"I'm sorry. Was it a shock?"

"Twenty four-years," I said. "Yes, it was a shock. After so long you don't expect these things to happen, not to you. They happen to other people, not you."

Maggie took a sip of her juice. I tore off a piece of croissant and nibbled it guiltily.

"It's a dangerous time, though," said Maggie. She sounded like an authority. "Kids off at university, the empty nest – it leaves you vulnerable, I guess."

Yes. So vulnerable that you take on ridiculous New Year's resolutions.

"Did you have any idea?"

"Not really. Looking back on it, I suppose there were signs, but these things are easy with hindsight aren't they?"

"I know exactly what it's like," said Maggie, sitting down opposite me and slurping some more of her strange concoction. "I was married once. But it didn't work out. He'd been cheating on me."

"And did you have any idea?"

"Pretty much. I could tell things weren't right and then when he started going out a lot with 'friends'" – she mimed the quotation marks – "I began to get suspicious."

Just like me. Perhaps it was a universal pattern.

"Eventually," said Maggie, "I followed him one night and I found out who it was."

Just like me again.

"And was it someone you knew?"

"Yeah, it was an old friend, a mutual friend as it happens. It's often the way, apparently."

"Any regrets?"

"No, I'm better off without him. I suppose I would have liked kids and I suppose it's still not too late. But it's nice to be free."

She moved a leg and it momentarily brushed mine – the contact was thrilling. There was no doubt that we were flirting. She knew that

I was by myself, I knew that she was free, and it was difficult to think of what could possibly be stopping us from getting it together there and then over the croissant crumbs.

But just as I was thinking of moving my leg more obviously next to hers, of treating her to my most smouldering smile, I thought how nonsensical the whole thing was. If something was going to happen it would surely happen, and it wouldn't be speeded up by my pathetic sixth-former attempts at seduction. If Maggie were to extend the invitation, in any form, then my response would be swift and enthusiastic, but I wasn't sure I had it in me to extend that kind of invitation myself. I had just forgotten what it was like.

"Good news, by the way," said Maggie. "I've landed a part in a play."

"Great," I said, "What is it?"

"It's Linda in *Death of a Salesman*."

"Good role."

"That's what I thought too. Shame it's in a touring production."

"Oh well, it's better to have it than not, isn't it?"

Maggie shrugged. "I guess so. It's just a drag to be away for so much of the time. And my experience of touring productions hasn't been too great. All the neurosis, insecurity and sex that goes on in any production, but with no escape for six days of the week."

"Yeah," I said, "It'll be a shame if you're away, especially on running days."

"I'll have to keep the running up, especially as I'm thinking of running a marathon next year."

A marathon.

I took a deep breath, and tried to move the conversation on quickly.

"Still," I said, "Linda, that's a good role."

"It is," she said, leaping up from the table. "And now it's shower time."

I got up from the table. Was that an invitation to join her? Had she said, "Come and have a shower with me, now, upstairs, and then we can make mad, passionate love", or was I hallucinating?

I was hallucinating.

Maggie made for the door and didn't so much as encourage me to leave as make it clear that it was probably time for me to go. Before I left, though, she took me entirely by surprise. She leaned forward and gave me a kiss on the cheek. She didn't say anything, she just kissed me. I could sense the recent exercise on her skin and I could feel the moistness of her lips. It was a definite gesture. It definitely meant something.

"Oh, I nearly forgot," she said, as I walked through the door, "there was something I wanted to ask you." I turned. "There's a production of *Death of a Salesman* on in Hammersmith at the moment. It ends soon, and I was wondering if you'd like to come along and see it with me. Maybe we could go out somewhere afterwards and talk about it?"

An Invitation.

I had no choice.

I also had no hesitation.

10

The next morning Sarah telephoned.

"Funny bumping into you like that yesterday."

"Yes. A surprise for me too."

"And you've taken up running?"

"Well, not seriously. I used to do it, if you remember."

"Of course I do. I also remember you packing it in, saying that it was a young man's game."

"Oh well, changing your mind's one of the prerogatives of old age."

An awkward silence, then she moved on to the subject that had really captured her curiosity.

"And Maggie goes running with you too?"

"We're part of a group, The Richmond Runners."

"Crikey, that doesn't sound like your kind of thing at all."

It's not. It's just that I've embarked on this crazy scheme that means I have to accept every invitation I get for a whole year.

That's what I could have said.

"After all that's gone on recently, I decided I needed to change something."

That's what I did say.

"And how long have you known Maggie, then?"

She wanted to know whether she was more than a neighbour. She wanted to know if I was sleeping with her.

"I met her properly on New Year's day at Harry's drinks."

"Harry's drinks! You never go to that. I always used to go by myself."

"Oh well. I decided to give it a go and she – Maggie that is – asked me to join the Runners. I thought it was ridiculous at first, but now that I've tried it I quite like it. I know you might find that difficult to believe."

"The reason I'm ringing is to check that everything's OK with Ellie and Danny."

What did she mean? She had their phone numbers. She knew where they were. They were doubtless in touch with her as often as they were with me. There may have been something on her mind but it definitely wasn't her kids.

"You dropped Danny off. Did he say anything in the car?"

"No. The usual Trappist monastery on wheels. How about Ellie when you drove her back?"

"Typical final year stuff. Thoughts of the Big Beyond. And the rest of course."

"The rest?"

"Wiggy. Us."

"Look, I'm happy to take some of the rap for Wiggy, but as for us, from where I'm standing there's only one person to blame and it's not me."

I heard Sarah inhale sharply. "I'll tell you why I'm ringing. I know I said this to you the other evening and I know you gave me your answer and I know there's no reason why you might have changed your mind, but can I just say again—"

"Sarah," I said, putting on my best pay-attention, sit-up-straight teacher voice, "the answer's still the same. I need some time. It's a huge thing that you did and it's made me think about a lot of things afresh. It's made me evaluate, and I need time."

"I'm thinking of the kids, Ricky. I'm thinking of all of us."

"And were you thinking of us when you shacked up with Colin?"

"Couldn't we just meet for a coffee?"

It was almost An Invitation. Almost, but not quite.

"Look Sarah. I don't think these meetings are a very good idea, not yet. The kids are away and I have some time to myself for the first time in I don't know how long. It was terrifying at first and there are times when it still is, but I think I owe it to myself to give myself that space, just to let things be for a while. If we meet, it will only complicate things again."

"We are still married, you know."

"I know, but if—"

"If what? If we were thinking of divorce?"

"I didn't say that."

"Look, Ricky. All I ask is an hour over a coffee somewhere. There are things I need to tell you. After that I promise I'll keep out of your way for however long you want – for a week, a month, two months — whatever you want. Just give me this one more meeting, a coffee, a drink, anything. Just come and meet me."

An Invitation.

There was now no avoiding it.

"OK, then," I said, "when?"

"Tomorrow?"

"Sure, what time?"

***

Sarah had chosen a small café on Richmond Hill. It may still have been the end of January, but it was just about manageable to sit outside if we kept our coats on. Our breaths misted the air, our words freezing in mist as soon as they were uttered.

She sipped her coffee and looked at me with the dark brown eyes I had gazed into so many times before under such different circumstances.

"I thought I'd have another try," she said.

"Fine," I said, "But I have nothing new to say."

"But I do, though."

"OK," I said. "Go ahead."

"I told you last time that I had made a mistake, but I didn't tell you why or how."

"Do I need to know?"

"I think you do. When I left you it was because…"

I heard the words before she delivered them.

I left you because you had become boring.

I left you because you had stopped doing interesting things.

I left you because Colin had more to offer me.

I looked at her. Her mouth had fallen open and I couldn't work out whether she had just finished speaking or was just about to start. She seemed to be looking not at me, but over my left shoulder. I turned round and saw a man standing just beside the table. I thought I recognized him from somewhere.

"Colin!"

I did recognize him.

"Colin! What are you doing here?"

Colin looked unruffled by the whole situation.

"I said I was popping into the library for some books. It's Rick, isn't it?"

As he asked, he held out his hand.

"It is," I said, getting to my feet. If blows were about to be exchanged I would rather do it from a standing position.

I shook his hand, trying to match its firmness with my own and fixing his eyes in what I hoped was a resolute, defiant stare. My mind was cloudy, and, momentarily, I found myself more surprised by the fact that he read books than by the way we had bumped into each other like this.

"Sit down, please," said Colin. "Don't let me disturb you."

Don't let me disturb you? The old college joke. Hadn't he disturbed us enough already, by shagging my wife for who knows how long before she upped and offed and moved in with him?

I stayed standing, stretching myself to full height, and still not quite meeting Colin's eye. Sarah stayed in her seat while I stood uncomfortably and awkwardly in front of Colin. I remembered him now – one of those faces from functions at Sarah's school. It was strange to be standing here, face to face (or almost) with the man my wife had left me for, strange to put physical form and shape to the man who had haunted my dreams and my waking thoughts for so many months. He looked fit. He looked young and he looked handsome. I looked from him to Sarah and then from Sarah back to him and then, although I tried to stop them, images of the two of them copulating flashed through my mind, as if projected onto a huge cinema screen. I shook my head to clear it.

Colin still stood opposite me and Sarah still sat at the table. Each of us was embarrassed in our own peculiar way, each of us uncertain what, exactly, we should do next.

"It's turned a bit cold, hasn't it?" said Colin, rubbing his hands together. "I'm surprised you're sitting outside."

Was this it? Was this the best he could come up with – his best verbal solution to this social dilemma? Of all the things that could be said, that needed to be said, was a comment about the weather anyone's idea of the most appropriate?

I looked at Sarah, trying to catch her eye, but she was deliberately avoiding my gaze. Colin was still standing there like some social retard, as if he was expecting some kind of response to his inanity.

"Well," he said, "I can see you two are talking, so I'll just get along."

Yes, I thought, why don't you do just that? It was tempting to hit him, to tell him to fuck off clearly and calmly, punch him in the face, watch him fall to the ground and walk off home, wiping my hands after a job well done. I wasn't sure, though, that I had it in me. I might have struck out, but the chances of my doing it with sufficient force to knock him down seemed remote, and I had no doubt that Colin could do far more damage to me than I could ever dream of inflicting on him.

My fist clenched only briefly before I said, "No, don't worry, I was just off."

And with that I half-raised my hand towards Sarah, made sure I gave no eye contact to Colin, and walked away from the café table. As I did, Sarah got to her feet.

"Rick!" she called. "Rick! Please! Come back! Please, Rick!"

I wanted to turn. I may have been unmanly in the way I had responded to my rival. I may have failed to stand up for myself, but I sensed that I had caused a good deal of discomfort to both of them. It would have been good to turn round and see both Sarah's pleading face and Colin's confusion, but I managed to walk away, feeling cool and controlled and, in my own modest way, quietly heroic.

11

February

The team that trundled down to The Running Mare might not have been the group of colleagues I would choose for a social evening in the pub, but I had chosen them carefully on the basis of what they had to offer. The assembled troop – Betty (Classical Music, Myths, History and anything cultural with a capital 'C'), Dave (Sport and Pop Music), Nigel (all kinds of trivia), Wayne (things that only young people know) and me (the History teacher who knows a little bit about everything and a lot about nothing) – could, I thought, give a good account of themselves, and even perhaps fulfil my real ambition of the evening which was to wipe the floor with the opposition and wipe the foolish grin off big "Santa" Ron's face.

Had I known how the evening was going to turn out I would have chosen a team better equipped in other ways.

I should have seen the way things were likely to go when Ron grabbed the mic to welcome everyone and singled us out for particular attention. "And a special welcome," he said, "to a team of teachers from our local sixth form college." I felt the heads turn, almost hearing the unuttered prejudices that Ron had aired to me on that first Richmond Runners outing. "So let's make sure we beat the teachers, shall we?" he said, laughing loudly and making an intimidating gesture with his fist. Heads turned back to tables and teammates, but I could hear the muttering and I felt as if I had walked onto the wrong terrace at a 1970s football match.

It was the familiar quiz night set-up – ten rounds of ten questions, with a joker doubling the points of any nominated round. After a brief explanation, the first round was announced as 'Opening Lines'. I took the captain's role seriously, making sure everyone got a chance to contribute, checking that we were all happy with the answer before I committed it to paper. And when there was disagreement, as happened on a couple of questions (I maintained that "Make me a deal and make it straight" was the opening line of Roxy Music's *Virginia Plain* while Dave thought it was from something by The Jam, and there was some dispute between me and Betty as to whether "Who's there?" came from *Hamlet* or a Walter de la Mare poem called *The Travellers*), I listened to the claims and made a decision, making it quite clear as I scribbled down the answer that it was the captain's call and if I got it wrong I would take any blame and any abuse they chose to hurl at me. In other words, I was the perfect captain.

The next round was a picture round, a series of buildings that we had to place in the correct city. I was less prominent here than I had been in the first round, but I held my own, and so did the team.

When the third round was announced as Pop – "Name That Group" Dave urged me to play the joker and double our points.

"Between us," he said, "We're bound to clean up."

And clean up we did.

Q. Which group took their name from a character in the science fiction film Barbarella?

A. Duran Duran.

Q. From a foreign language's rendition of "Kiss My Arse"?

A. The Pogues.

Q. From a second hand furniture store in Hull?

A. Not too sure, but when Dave suggested Everything But the Girl, I knew he was right.

Q. From a British agriculturalist?

A. Jethro Tull.

Q. From an Aldous Huxley novel?

A. The Doors.

Q. From a group in Anthony Burgess's *A Clockwork Orange*?

A. Heaven 17.

Q From a Herman Hesse novel?

A. Steppenwolf.

Q. From the name of a technique used to teach children dance and mime appreciation?

A. Unsure again, but Dave and Wayne conferred and came up with The Eurythmics.

Q. From a term in a William Burroughs novel used to describe a dildo?

A. Steely Dan.

Q. From the average ejaculation of sperm?

A. We were all baffled initially, until Betty, smiling wickedly, came up with 10cc.

Round Four: Current Affairs. We struggled.

Round Five: Sport. Dave came into his own and got most of them right.

Round Six: Language. Crossword stuff really, with a few funnies thrown in.

Round Seven: Fun Round. Every table received chocolate bars labelled from A to J. Identify the confectionery. A good deal of argument about whether sample C was a Picnic or a Topic but we seemed confident about the majority.

Round Eight: Voices. Identify the famous people speaking.

Round Nine: Connections. Ten groups of photographs, state the connection between them.

The Final Round. Names. All to do with nicknames, alternative names, original names, pseudonyms. Some doubt over what "dromophobia" was a fear of and which football club was originally called "St Jude's", but the other eight posed no problem.

The next round was another round of drinks – the fourth, or maybe the fifth, of the evening – and when Dave came back from the bar with another pint of bitter I took a few gulps and realised this was probably the most I had drunk since that fateful New Year's Eve.

Without that stupid resolution there was no way I would have been sitting in The Running Mare looking at Fat Ron lurking beside the quizmaster as he checked and counted the submitted answer sheets. Without that silly bet, I wouldn't be sitting here, drunk, wondering how I would get through the next day's teaching, and trying to hide my anxiety and worry as I waited for the results. Without that resolution, I wouldn't be thinking how great it would be to win, how fantastic it would be to have come down here with a team and beaten the best that Fascist Ron could muster, how sweet it would be to defeat him in his own back yard.

"Ladies and Gentlemen," said the quizmaster, "before the scores, here are the answers." The general hubbub subsided and all teams looked towards him. Behind him Ron looked quizzically at the sheet the quizmaster held in his hands, as if unhappy with what it said.

As he ran through the answers, we did a quick mental check. There couldn't have been too many we had got wrong. Dromophobia was a morbid fear of crossing streets, St Jude's was the original name of Queens Park Rangers and we had made a wrong call on some of the chocolate bars and the pictures, but, overall, we had done well.

"And now the scores." An expectant hush. "I'll give them in reverse order." The scores of the bottom rankers were greeted with loud ironic cheers, mainly from the teams responsible for such poor showing. As he progressed the cheers continued, but now mainly from those teams yet to be called who knew that they were still in with a chance of winning. We could now see which other tables were in contention – they were the ones who leaned in towards each other, fists clenched and eyebrows raised with expectancy as each result was announced.

"And third," said the quizmaster, "is Table Two."

Loud cheers from us and Table Ten. It was between the two of us for the winning spot.

"And the winner is…." The quizmaster paused, as if he was announcing the winner of X-Factor or the latest eviction from the Big Brother house.

We waited. I glanced across at Table Ten. Table Ten glanced back.

"And the winner is… Table Seven!"

I'm still not quite sure what I did next. I know it involved standing up and I know it ended in falling over, but I'm not too clear about what happened in between. It definitely involved a lot of cheering and whooping and there was certainly a fair amount of gesturing towards Table Ten and towards Ron the Richmond Runner.

The rest of the team were pleased and I'm sure that Betty, Dave, Nigel and Wayne were also whooping with delight, but they probably weren't whooping as loudly and as noticeably as me. After all, it didn't matter that much to them. I still didn't know why, but for me the quiz result constituted some huge personal victory. Whether it was the five pints that had unleashed a competitive spirit I didn't know I had, I couldn't tell, but I'm sure the alcohol must have been responsible for the nature of my celebrations.

"Yes! Yes! Yes!" I shrieked, leaping up and down on the spot. "Yes! Yes! Yes!"

All the hand-waving, all the hysterical affirmation might have made me seem like some kind of raving evangelical, but the language that followed made me seem less than holy.

"Fucking A! We've fucking done it. We've fucking done it Big Ron! We've fucking done it Table Ten!"

I shook my fist towards Table Ten, not noticing at first that one of their team had stood up and was waving his fist back at me.

Fat Ron continued, "So well done Table Seven – the table of teachers from the sixth form college – on your victory, by the narrowest of margins, just the one point."

The quizmaster turned off his mike and stepped down off the small platform from which he had been operating. I was still jumping up and down and whooping with delight, realizing a little too late that the rest of my team had long since stopped cheering and were sitting down, looking at me with a mixture of bemusement and embarrassment.

I turned and sat down too, but my heart was still thumping with joy.

"You were brilliant!" I said to the table. "Wait until we tell them all tomorrow."

And with that I stood up and went in search of Big Fat Ron. As I moved towards the front of the bar I saw the fist-shaker from Table Ten moving in the same direction. He looked me in the eye and came towards me.

"Unlucky!" I said. Not perhaps the wisest thing to say given the look on his face. He gave a tight smile that quickly turned into a grimace and walked past. I was sure I heard him mutter "Wanker" under his breath, but decided to ignore it as I spotted Ron seeing me approach and trying to move away.

"Ron!" I called after him, moving a little more quickly than my five-pint intake would suggest was wise. Ron pretended not to hear but I continued my pursuit, only to be blocked by The Fist from Table Ten who was standing square on to the Quizmaster and raising his voice so that most of the pub had no difficulty in hearing.

"Oy! You!" he screeched. "One of those questions was wrong."

The Quizmaster turned from packing up his gear and raised his eyes politely. "Really?" he said.

"Yes, really!" said The Fist. "And I'll tell you which one too."

"I'm sure you will."

I paused beside them. The quizmaster seemed a little upset by the assault and I thought it only appropriate that I should step forward to congratulate him on delivering such a good quiz.

"Excuse me," I said, brushing past The Fist so that I stood between him and Bamber Gascoigne, "could I just say how fantastic I thought that whole quiz was? I've been to many in my time and that must rank as one of the best – witty, challenging and, if I may say so, very stylish."

Someone had once pointed out my habit of speaking in over-elaborate, polished Queen's English when drunk. They had also pointed out that it was a habit likely to get me into trouble.

I had never really believed them until now.

"Oy!" said The Fist From Table Ten, "I'm talking. It's rude to interrupt."

"I'm terribly sorry, old chap," I said, turning suddenly into Noel Coward, "but I just thought I would offer my congratulations—"

"Congratulations my arse! One of the answers was wrong!"

The Quizmaster gave what I thought was a conspiratorial wink, a gesture of thanks and support, before he spoke. "Which question was that then?"

"It was the one about The Doors. You said they took their name from Aldous Huxley's *Doors of Perception*, but they actually took it from William Blake. That's where Huxley got it from as well, so you were wrong."

"Not really," said the quizmaster, looking as though he was quite used to dealing with complaints like this, as if he might have dealt several times with this very one. "I think you'll find that my answer is, in fact correct."

"Like fuck it is. This wanker here won by one point – and it's your wrong answer that's made all the difference."

A sudden silence fell on the pub. Heads turned towards us as The Fist's words echoed in the held breaths.

"Excuse me," I said, feeling the need to say something to fill the void, "are you calling me a wanker?"

"Yes," he said, "I am."

"And why is that?"

"Because you are."

"And in what sense of the term am I, precisely, a wanker?"

He moved towards me and I stepped back, fearing the appearance of The Fist's fist.

"Look, all I want is this quiz bloke to admit he got the answer wrong, that's all. If he does that it'll all be OK. We'll have won and you, wanker, will have come second."

"Sorry, did you just call me a wanker again?"

The Fist stared me down. "Yes," he said, "do you want to make something of it?"

"Look here, old chap." Quite where the 'old chap' came from I had no idea. Or rather I had a very good idea – from five pints of bitter. Every time I opened my mouth I sounded like a P.G. Wodehouse character. "Look here, I think it far more likely that Jim Morrison was influenced by Aldous Huxley's deliberate mind-altering experiments with mescaline than he was by the early Romantic poet's mystical visions, wouldn't you agree?"

"Are you taking the piss?" The Fist moved forward suddenly and I could have sworn his fist was drawn back ready to deliver a killer blow.

The quizmaster stepped between us.

"Relax," he said, "it's only a quiz."

"What do you fucking mean, only a quiz? You make your living out of the fucking things!"

"I meant," said the quizmaster holding his hands out as if separating a couple of boxers, "that there's no need to get so upset about it."

"I'm not upset, I'm fucking furious!"

"OK," said the quizmaster, "why don't we call it a draw? You can split the money."

"What's all this?" Suddenly Reindeer Ron had joined the fray. "Is this man causing you any trouble?"

I looked to see how The Fist was going to respond and then realised, with a shock, that Ron was looking at me. He thought that I was the one causing all the fuss. Still reeling from his Richmond Runners humiliation perhaps, or maybe just exceedingly pissed off that I had brought a team down here and won.

"No, Ron," I said. "You don't understand. It's not me causing the fuss. It's this complete arsehole here—"

"What did you call me?"

"A complete arsehole."

The combination of Bertie Wooster formality and crude colloquialism finally did it for him. This time he came straight for me. I was already moving backward and both Ron and the Quizmaster were quick to intervene, so he didn't get too close.

"You may be a fucking teacher but you don't know everything, wanker!"

"Cool it, arsehole!"

As if once wasn't enough I was choosing to repeat it.

"Outside!" he screamed.

"What?"

"Outside! Now! You and me!"

"Sorry, I don't quite understand."

"I'm asking you outside to settle this. Now."

"Oh I see! You're asking me outside for a fight!"

He snarled, threw off his jacket, and rolled up his sleeves, jerking his head towards the pub doors.

"Too fucking right I am. Now!"

And then, as if from nowhere, as if such a response had become so deeply ingrained in me that it was now mere instinct, I said to myself – An Invitation.

And without any more hesitation I replied, "Of course I'd like to come outside to have a fight. How could I possibly refuse?"

The rest is all a little hazy. I remember The Fist walking to the door and me following. The whole pub was by now on its feet and as we walked to the door a corridor formed. I could hear cries of "Sort him out Gary!" (a surprise to me that he wasn't, after all, called The Fist) and "Fucking have 'im mate. Calling you an arsehole? In your own manor? Who does he think he is? Fucking teacher!" But I could also hear the voices of my colleagues and teammates, Betty, Dave, Wayne and Nigel, saying all kinds of sensible things which occasionally made themselves heard above the buzz in my head – "Rick, don't be stupid!", "Rick what's got into you?", "Cool it, Rick", "This isn't a good idea!"

In my head all I could see was the word "Invitation" flashing brightly and the word "Yes" lighting up beside it. In front of me all I could see was Gary's muscular back and shoulders.

The door opened. Gary walked through. I followed, the noise of the crowd behind me.

Outside Gary turned and faced me.

I stood still.

He pulled back his arm.

And then I ran.

I don't know how far I ran and I don't know how fast. All I know is that I got away. I didn't look behind, but I sensed that Gary had taken off after me and I imagined that he had the whole of The Running Mare locals running with him, like a pack of hounds in some human fox hunt. I had no idea where I was heading, but I knew I had to just keep going. All at once I seemed very sober, acutely aware of just how embarrassing my behaviour had been, but strangely proud that I had, in the midst of such a crisis, kept faith with my resolution.

The Fist had extended me An Invitation, and I had accepted it. I had, admittedly, not stayed very long with him, but I had followed him out, and it was definitely the right thing to run away. As I pounded the pavements, heading for what I hoped was the town centre where I would pick up the first taxi or minicab I could find, I realised how it could not have ended any other way. Or rather it could, and that was the worry. Either he could have hit me, causing me a lot of damage, possibly breaking parts of my face and body, or I could have hit him. Unlikely I know, but it was definitely a possibility, and it could have led to all kinds of things – like a proper fight, or prosecution.

I was out of breath. My recent outings had given me enough fitness to get this far, but I knew I could go no further. What if Gary and his mob had got into cars to follow me? What if they were just round the corner, a lynch mob ready to string up the teacher outsider from the nearest Richmond tree? What if I stopped only to hear the screech of tyres and Gary's voice giving me another invitation that I would just have to accept?

I pounded on, seeing the lights of the town centre coming closer and keeping an eye out for a passing cab. Thankfully, I was now running downhill and was in a more populated area. Even if Gary were to come upon me now there wouldn't be much he could do to me without a considerable number of witnesses. Who knows? I might even have been getting closer to the police station.

It wasn't until I reached the train station that I found a cab. By this time I was sweating considerably and starting to sober up. The five pints were now a distant bad memory, and so was the whole sorry episode, as if it had happened to someone else on some other evening. I slumped in the back seat, making it quite clear to the driver that I didn't want to engage in conversation, and then rang Dave on the mobile.

"Where are you?" he said. "What the hell are you up to?"

"I'm fine," I said, "I'm in the back of a cab heading home."

"You made a complete embarrassment of yourself," said Dave. "And of us."

"I know. I'm sorry, but I got away, didn't I?"

"You might have got away for the moment, but I think that bloke still wants you. I'd tread carefully."

"I will, Dave," I said. "I will. Say hi to the others and I'll see you tomorrow."

"I don't think you'll be able to keep this one quiet, Rick. Everyone's going to know. And everyone's going to want to know what happened."

"I'll deal with that tomorrow. Oh – and Dave?"

"Yeah?"

"Well played. We beat the bastards, didn't we?"

When the cab pulled up in Afton Road I was desperate to get inside, have a shower and go to bed. Getting out of the car, though, I saw another cab pull up in the road and Maggie climb out. She paid the driver, turned, and smiled when she saw me.

"Hi Rick, had a good night out?"

"Well, let's just say that I hope you had a better time than me."

"Why? What's happened?"

I laughed helplessly and shrugged. "You wouldn't believe it if I told you."

"Try me."

"I wish I had the energy."

"Well why don't you come and tell me over a cup of coffee?"

Oh no.

"I couldn't," I said, "not now. Very kind of you, but I really am too tired. School tomorrow and all that, so I can't."

She seemed disappointed, genuinely disappointed. Maybe she wasn't just being polite. Maybe she really did want me to come over and have a coffee. It unnerved me a little. But the strange thing about the whole situation was how odd, how wrong it felt for me to come out with words that constituted a refusal. Not long ago it had felt strange to say yes. Now it felt strange to say no, so strange that I felt the need to correct myself immediately.

"Actually, Maggie," I said. "What I meant to say was yes – I'd love to come and have a coffee. I don't know what I was thinking."

"Well that's just great," said Maggie, jangling her keys and leading me to her door. "You can tell me all about it."

I followed her, feeling a strange mixture of emotions – happy and relieved that I had kept faith with my New Year pledge, excited and apprehensive about being in Maggie's house so close to bed time, grateful that my face had not been mashed by The Fist in The Running Mare car park, and bewildered and baffled by the mess I seemed to have got myself into.

We sat down in the kitchen and Maggie set about making the coffee. My mind and my body were in too much turmoil for me to see things straight, but I got the impression that the air of sexual tension and anticipation that I had expected had not quite materialized. Was it that I was too exhausted, too focused on the warmth and comfort of my own bed to long for the excitement and passion of someone else's? Or maybe it was because tonight of all nights, now of all nows, was probably the time when I would be least equipped to make the leap? Mentally and physically I just didn't feel up to it. That could be the only reason that at some deep level I was making myself read all Maggie's actions as innocent of any possible sexual reading. Whereas before I thought of flirtation, I now thought of avoidance.

"You look tired," she said.

"I am."

"I'm sorry. Has the evening been particularly – strenuous?"

On other days I would have seen this as a come-on and I would have been excited.

"I was in a quiz."

"Crikey, it must have been some quiz, you look like you've been running."

"Well, yes, I have actually."

"Very commendable, we'll have you running a marathon yet."

Oh no. A marathon.

"I don't think so," I said. "No, I had to run to get a cab—"

"Really?"

I just couldn't tell her. I made something up about needing to get home quickly and luckily I wasn't asked to elaborate further. I moved the conversation on to *Death of a Salesman* very quickly, making a few subtle observations about Linda's relationship with Willy Loman.

"Willy," said Maggie. "I've always had a thing about Willy."

Another time, another place I might have been urging her to have a thing about my own, but not tonight.

She was even leaning towards me when she said it, even raising her eyebrows seductively.

"And by the way," she said, "I've got tickets for the Lyric production.

Put the date in your diary." She leaned forward and whispered. "March 28th, a date?"

"A date," I said.

I got up to leave, making my excuses and thanking her for the coffee. As we stood at the door I leaned towards her, thinking a polite kiss on the cheek would be appropriate. I was surprised when she took the initiative by leaning towards me and even more surprised when she kissed me not on the cheek, but on the lips, and even more surprised than that when she put her hand on the back of my neck, pulled me closer towards her and prised my lips apart with her tongue.

This was it, I thought. This was what I had been waiting for. This was what I had been anticipating for some time. This was why I had carried on running.

But I knew I wasn't up to it.

Now wasn't the time and I knew that I had to go. I pulled out of the kiss, smiled, said goodnight and headed off across the road.

***

It was Jerry's idea to meet for a drink. As he had so correctly pointed out, he was inviting me, not asking me, so I had no choice. It was also his idea to make it in town (as he liked to put it) rather than the suburban delights of either Richmond or Purley, and that explained why we were sitting opposite each other in a loud Mexican bar on the South Bank.

"Jerry this is absolutely crazy. I'm getting into all kinds of trouble."

"Why?" said Jerry, leaning forward across the table. "What kind of invitations have you been getting? I want to know all about it. Come on, you can tell me everything."

He was like some kind of stamp collector, keen for new additions and categories. When I told him about Gary's invitation "outside" he wanted to know every detail, as if he wasn't quite sure where to put it in his album.

"So what exactly was the invitation then?"

"He asked me outside."

"Sorry?"

"Outside as in outside for a fight. Are you telling me you've never heard the phrase before?"

"Of course I have, I just couldn't hear you properly."

The truth was he had never heard it before. His life had always been sheltered. You could tell at college what he was like, and marriage, kids and life as a lawyer living in Purley had done little to change him. In recent weeks I had been more than usually tempted to make everything up, to invent my invitations, to fabricate the details that I knew would give him a thrill. I hadn't though. This evening, for example, all I had done was add a few embellishments here and there to make my squaring up to Gary a little more defiant and my running away a little less pathetic.

But when he asked about Maggie I found myself leaving things out rather than adding them.

"So how's it going with the sexy runner, then?"

"Who? Maggie? Fine. Did I tell you she's invited me to the theatre?"

"No? What are you seeing?"

"Death of a Salesman."

"Fantastic. You're not far from shagging her then are you?"

There was definitely something sad about Jerry's prurient interest. Even the word 'shagging' seemed inappropriately laddish for someone of his age and dullness. It was OK for me to use it, but Jerry was far too old. We may have technically been contemporaries, but that didn't stop him being older than me.

Age was about more than years.

"Don't be ridiculous, Jerry."

"I'm not. And just think, Rick, all these things, all these experiences you're having wouldn't be yours if it weren't for the bet, would they? Just think of all that's happened since Sarah left – or rather since New Year's Eve."

Jerry's involvement was beginning to wear thin. He may have started me on this particular road, but I didn't see why he had to make the journey with me and I also didn't see why he had to behave as if it was he himself who was accepting invitations. A small vicarious thrill was one thing, but I got the sense that he almost believed it was happening to him.

Maybe that was why I decided not to tell him about the kiss. It might have been too much for him to bear.

Jerry leaned towards me again. "Let me ask you something, Rick."

"Fire away," I said. "As long as you don't accuse me of being boring."

"Have you been – or rather were you ever – unfaithful to Sarah?"

"We've been through all this, Jerry. You know I wasn't."

"And if this Maggie, let's say for the sake of argument, did invite you, you'd have no hesitation at all?"

I sighed. "It's like any invitation isn't it? It's like you asking me to this wholly inappropriate bar so you can ogle girls far too young for both of us."

"I'm not ogling girls!"

"Of course you are. You've been eyeing everything up all evening. Your eyeballs have been popping!"

"Bollocks! And what's inappropriate about this bar?"

"Forget it," I said, shaking the cocktail umbrella to one side of my glass and finishing off my second Tequila Sunrise. "And don't worry, if anything happens with Maggie, if I get any invitation, I'll make sure you're the first to know."

Jerry sighed, beckoned the waiter over, and ordered more drinks. "Sometimes I think Alex had everything exactly right. All that shagging around..." I winced at the word. "While I was building a life for myself in – in Purley. Do you know, Rick, I've never, ever, in all my years of marriage to Caroline, been unfaithful. I've never strayed, and what's more remarkable, I've not even thought of it, never been tempted."

"You must have," I said. "Surely you must have at least thought of it."

"Never," said Jerry, "until Alex died, and until our New Year's Eve drink together. And speaking of Alex, I've found out some more. I got in touch with a couple of his friends."

"Yeah? So what have you found out?"

"Just that he had taken up with a woman and it was serious, but no one seemed to have met her."

"Hardly the greatest of discoveries is it?"

"But I've got more people I can talk to."

"You're not obsessed by this at all, are you? I mean, you're going to a lot of trouble trying to track this down."

"I've just got this instinct, Rick. Trust me."

And then I said what I knew I shouldn't.

"You know when you suggested I was boring on New Year's Eve?"

"I didn't actually say that, Rick. What I said was maybe she left you because she *thought* you were boring. There's a difference."

"Whatever," I said, frightened at how easy it was to talk like one of my students. "The point is I'm getting a little worried about you."

"Me? I'm fine. You're the one with the—"

"I'm the one with the problem? I don't think so, Jerry. I think you're far too interested in what I'm doing."

"What do you mean too interested? I'm just checking that you're keeping up the bet. You're just saying that."

"And why would I do that?"

"So that I stop checking up, so that you can give it up. You don't like me getting in touch all the time because it keeps you to it, keeps you doing something you might otherwise stop."

He couldn't be further from the truth. Having started this I was, as the great Magnus would put it, going to finish.

"And," I said, "I think this whole Alex thing is also symptomatic."

"Symptomatic? You're talking bollocks. Symptomatic of what?"

I smiled at my memory of him using that very word on New Year's Eve.

"That you need to get out more. That you need to get a life."

"But look at me," said Jerry, tossing back his drink, "I am out! And I have got a life!"

He shouted the words and a few heads at neighbouring tables turned and smirked.

"Jerry," I said, "maybe you should think about getting back."

He looked at his watch and, as a hen party in sombreros took to the karaoke platform, nodded his head in drunken agreement.

"Get back," he said, "now that sounds like a good idea."

And with that he got to his feet, and headed for the door, shaking his head slowly as if saddened by the out-of-tune karaoke performance or stunned by the philosophical implications of the words "get" and "back".

12

March

As the weeks passed, I became sensitised to the whole idea of Invitations in a way I would never have imagined. In the past I had been programmed to avoid the things as much as possible, and the more I avoided them, the fewer came my way; invitations had not featured prominently in my life. Now that I had started to accept them, though, the more they seemed to appear, and the more they appeared, the more I tried to find ways of handling them.

One evening I found myself hovering, walking up and down a quiet street on the road towards Sheen. I knew the house number and I knew the time I needed to be there and I knew that I had no choice. Even so, I had no real desire to ring the bell, and was trying to think of a way of avoiding it, when the door opened and the woman who I had spoken to in Richmond High Street the previous Saturday called to me.

"Yoo-hoo," she said. "We're in here."

And soon I was in there with them.

A group of ten men and women, all the wrong side of sixty, sat in a circle, cradling dainty cups of tea, some of them gently nibbling on a biscuit. The woman who had called me in, and whose house this clearly was, sat down on a chair slightly higher than the others and motioned for me to sit on the one spare seat. I took my place, delivering half-hearted smiles to my neighbours – a seventy-ish man clasping his hands together forcefully and muttering under his breath and a blue-rinsed woman whose face was fixed in a wide-eyed smile.

The woman held her arms out to her sides as if she was trying to take off. As she did, the gentle chatter subsided.

"Welcome, everyone, to this week's meeting, and welcome especially to Rick." She held her arms out, palms upwards, towards me, as if offering me as some kind of sacrifice. I smiled awkwardly and nodded my greetings round the circle.

"Maybe," said the woman, "before we begin properly, perhaps Rick could tell everyone why he's here."

"Well, everyone," I said, clearing my throat, "it's like this. I was walking through Richmond last Saturday morning, when this lady…" I pointed at the woman.

"Rose," she said.

"Well, Rose stopped me just by Smith's and asked me if I would have a word with her and, well, I'm not the sort of man who turns down an invitation." I paused to let the polite laughter subside. "So I said, yes, I'd be happy to have a word. And then she asked me if God was in my life and I said no, at least I think I said no."

Rose leaned forward in her chair. "You said you were having a trial separation, but you were still good friends."

I laughed. Looking round the circle I saw that no one else had joined in. Everyone looked faintly embarrassed.

"Ah yes," I said. "Maybe that's what I said. But, anyway, then you said would I like to come along to talk about my relationship with God amongst a group of like-minded people. And, again, not being one to turn down an invitation I said yes I'd love to."

Rose leaned forward again. "You asked me if it would be with people whose mind was like mine or people whose mind was like yours."

"Did I?" I laughed again. "Well, as you can see, here I am."

"Well," said Rose, "it's good to see you here, welcome. And what I'd like us all to do now is bend our heads in silent prayer, asking God to come down and be with us here, asking the Almighty to guide us and help us this evening. And then when any of you are ready, just talk. Talk about your relationship with God and what he means to you."

I bowed my head and panicked, kicking myself for the thousandth time that day for having caught Rose's eye outside Smith's instead of walking on. I should have seen it coming. I should have realised that any kind of High Street stop-and-chat was likely to lead to An

Invitation. Surely, though, now that I had said 'yes', now that I had met the terms of my resolution, I didn't have to endure any more?

The silence continued.

Then I had the idea.

"Sorry," I said, breaking the silence. "I'm very sorry."

The heads were raised and expectant eyes turned towards me.

"Rick is sorry," said Rose. "Tell us, Rick, exactly why you're sorry. Tell us and tell God."

I reached into my pocket. "It's my mobile," I said. "I put it on silent. I should have turned it off. I'm sorry. But I'd better take it, just in case." I pressed a button and gave as good an impression as I could of a man listening to someone on a phone.

"What?" I said. "I don't believe it! Where? Oh my God!"

I turned to the group. Several of them repeated "Oh my God" as if it was the lead-in to a prayer.

"Is everything all right, Rick?"

"I don't believe it, Rose. It's my wife. She's had an accident. She's in hospital."

I tried to give a suppressed sob, tried to colour the words with a tinge of shock and repressed emotion.

"I think," I said, "that I may have to go."

I got up from my chair. As I did, the group fell to their knees. Several crossed themselves and started to pray.

"God bless you Rick," said Rose as I headed for the door, "and God bless your wife."

And then I was out.

***

It was also a mistake to stop-and-chat to Fred in the road one morning. All he did was raise his arm in friendly greeting and all I needed to do was raise my arm back and move on. Instead I indulged in the kind of low-level banter I had avoided for so long.

"Fred," I said, pausing, "how are you? How's it going? How's the writing?"

"Fine," he said, and then he was walking across the road towards me, looking up to the sky and making comments about the weather.

I now had no choice but to stay and talk. Walking away from him when he was crossing the road to speak to me would just be rude, and, although I might not have been the most sociable animal for many of my recent years, rudeness had never been my intention.

"How's school?" he asked.

"Fine," I shrugged. There was never anything interesting to say about school apart from reminding people how long it was until your next holiday.

"I expect you'll be breaking up for another holiday soon."

"One's never far away," I grinned.

Fred shook his head as if struck by some wonderful insight. "I sometimes envy you, you know."

"Don't be silly," I said. "I'd much rather be doing your job. Staying at home and writing. Sounds great. I've always wanted to do that. In fact I've got about five novel beginnings locked away in some bottom drawer somewhere."

"Doesn't everyone," said Fred. "That's not to belittle yours of course," he added, "I'm sure they're great."

"No they're not. They're crap, which is why they're locked in a bottom drawer."

"Maybe that's what I should have done with mine."

"Don't be silly," I said, "they're great."

I had only managed to finish one of the Dickie Peters series and hoped he didn't push me for further critical evaluation.

"The thing is," said Fred, "I'm stuck – completely blocked. I've a crime I can't solve, let alone Private Eye Dickie Peters. Every time I read out a bit at the Writers' Circle I realise how terrible it is."

"Writers' Circle?" I said. "Sounds interesting."

"It's a kind of support group, and a good place to test out new ideas. Why don't you come along?"

"No, really," I said, holding my hands up and stepping back.

"Go on. Come along and read something of yours. Unlock that drawer and dig out one of those novels. We're all very friendly, and it's always good to have some new blood."

An Invitation.

And I had been lying about the bottom drawer. I hadn't written anything creative for years.

There was no doubt that it had been An Invitation and no doubt that the Invitation was not just to turn up but also to read something out. It was a terrifying prospect and I spent the next week like a recalcitrant school kid moaning about difficult homework.

Where to start? The obvious place would be the beginning of a novel. That, after all, was what I told him I had and that would make most sense. Poems, of course, would be shorter and less likely to attract hostile criticism (from my memory of these things people were less likely to criticise poetry simply because you just never knew what, exactly, it might be trying to do – if you didn't get it, there was always the chance that you just weren't clever enough).

I tried a few poems but ended up writing a string of obscene limericks that, on reflection, probably weren't the right kind of thing at all. Besides, I wasn't even sure that poetry would be allowed and to keep my resolution I needed not only to go there, but to read as well. Then I tried some novel openings, but that didn't work either. They were all horribly clichéd, making even Private Eye Dickie Peters look like the creation of a Booker Prize winner.

I tried everything: romance, thriller, fantasy, gritty urban realism, even all that tricky, post-modern stuff where you weren't even sure who was telling the story, or that magical realism thing where the whole story was the work of a parrot or something. I even turned my hand to pornography, but that effort was so disgusting, so revealing of dark parts of myself which I didn't know existed, that I not only deleted the file immediately but also shredded the print-out, just in case anyone ever found it and connected it to me.

What I needed was something that was simply acceptable. It didn't need to be brilliant, but on the other hand it shouldn't be so awful that I disgraced myself by reading it out in public and that I led my novel-writing neighbour to believe that I was an illiterate philistine without a creative bone in my body.

Eventually I hit on what I thought was a pretty elegant solution.

***

"And who would like to read next?"

I looked around. Fred was looking in my direction, nodding and raising a pair of your-turn eyebrows

I hesitantly put my hand up.

Fred had read the latest chapter in his blocked novel, a woman called Marge had read a chunk of clearly autobiographical childhood misery about growing up in Romford, and a man had given us part of a school story in which a group of unruly pupils kidnap the head teacher and hold him to ransom, threatening to dismember him limb by limb unless their demands are met. Now it was my turn.

I cleared my throat and began.

"I was a small boy in a small town, growing up with what can only be called small dreams. That I should have ended up so big, a big man in a very big house is just one of those ironies that life likes to throw at us. I'm certainly not complaining. And here, as I sit at my desk in the early evening, watching the sun go down over the bright Mediterranean sea, I count my blessings for all that I have managed to achieve. I also keep my ears trained for the slightest sound – the footstep in the drive, the lifting of the latch, the creak of the stair, the whispering of my name – and occasionally reach for the gun I always carry in my pocket, wondering whether they might ever catch up with me..."

And I was off. I made no great claims for it, but thought it would do the job. It wasn't fancy, and it may have been horribly close to cliché, but it was clear enough and, I hoped, engaging enough to make my reading a passable, if not valuable, contribution to the evening.

Soon I was nearing the end of my opening pages.

"... I put down my pen, lifted my head and listened. It had definitely been a footstep on the gravel. There was another. And another. Someone was walking towards me. I reached for the gun and turned, expecting one of the many faces that had sought mine for so long, and preparing myself for the worst. 'Take away pizza?' said the delivery boy..."

I trailed off and lifted my head, signalling to the group that this was the end of my piece.

There were a few mutters and general nodding of heads, and then everyone started to make encouraging comments.

"Nice pace," said one.

"Good dialogue," said another.

"And how does it go on?" said a sour-looking bespectacled woman in the corner, who had said nothing all evening.

"Ah," I said, "I'm not exactly sure. That's only the beginning."

"And have you got a title for it?" she asked, expressing what I took to be unusual interest.

"Not yet," I said.

"Well, I have a suggestion for you if you want one," she said.

"Please do," I said. "I'd love some ideas."

"How about 'No Hiding Place'?"

And then I realised my mistake.

It was desperation that had led me to Oxfam the day before and I had thought the old sixties paperback I had fished out of a basket was surely obscure enough not to be recognized by anyone, let alone anyone with enough literary pretension to be a member of Fred's writing group.

"You," said the woman, "have just read out the opening of one of my father's novels!"

All heads turned.

It was like one of those Bateman cartoons. I looked round the group, my mouth open in disbelief and embarrassment. Heads were turning to each other and shaking in muttered disapproval. I avoided Fred's eye and tried to think of a way out of it.

"Are you sure?" I said to the daughter of the author of 'No Hiding Place'.

"Of course I'm sure. I can remember every word poor Daddy ever wrote, especially that one. It's the one he dedicated to me!"

And then she started to cry. She didn't just sob, she cried – huge convulsive sobs and big noises. The other writers rushed to her and Fred came over to me.

"I think," he said, "it might be better if you went."

"I can explain," I said, "honest."

Soon I was through the door, embarrassed and humiliated perhaps, but at least secure in the knowledge that I was unlikely to be invited back.

***

I made only one appearance in Andy and Mark's five-a-side team. It was clear from the start that I was nowhere near the standard of everyone else on the pitch. After five minutes I feigned injury and was put in goal, where I managed to let in every shot that came my way (apart from those that hit the bar or the posts). There was nothing deliberate about my pathetic display, but it did bring with it the advantage of never being invited to play again.

"Shame about your leg," said Andy after the game over a drink in the bar. "Goalie's probably not your best position, I'd bet."

"Yeah," I said, "never mind, though. You're all too good for me, I think."

It was the perfect opportunity for either Andy or Mark to leap in out of politeness and tell me just how wrong I was, reassuring me that I was just as good as all of them and that they very much hoped I would become a regular member of the Real Richmond squad. Neither took it, though.

"I think," I said, "that I might just stick to running."

Again, neither of them leapt in. Instead they both nodded, as if this seemed a good idea.

"And talking of running," I said, "is there anything I should know about Veronica?"

"Veronica?" said Andy. "What about Veronica?"

"Maybe I'm being silly," I said. "It's just that she's asked me round for a game of Scrabble, and I mentioned it to Maggie and..." I broke off. Andy and Mark's faces were creased by broad, unnerving, knowing grins.

"What's the problem?" I said.

They said nothing. It may have had something to do with the way my performance in goal had contributed to their worst defeat in living memory, or it may have been their sense of humour, but there was something about the way they both shook their heads slowly and sucked in their breath through pursed lips that made me entertain serious second thoughts about Veronica's scrabble invitation.

***

I had been told to turn up at about six o'clock. It seemed a strange time – too late for tea and too early for dinner – the kind of time that leaves you very unsure what to expect and even more unsure about what to bring. Veronica had mentioned nothing about dinner, but a bottle of wine still seemed appropriate. What could be better than a bottle of wine shared over a Scrabble board?

I turned up at her flat off Upper Richmond Road just after six, brandishing a respectable ten-pound bottle of red, and was greeted by a Veronica unrecognizable from the podgy track-suited Richmond Runner. Her hair hung loose and so did her jeans, giving her a more flattering appearance than the body-hugging Lycra, and her blouse was undone just enough to reveal the beginnings of a generous cleavage.

If her appearance, enhanced by generous make-up and the scent of perfume, failed to give me the sense that Veronica may have had an agenda other than a good game of Scrabble, the living room left me in no doubt. Subtle candlelight illuminated the room, at the centre of which stood the Scrabble table. A vase of flowers sat at one side of the board, an open bottle of wine at the other, a tall wine glass standing to attention beside each of the empty letter racks.

"How good of you to bring wine," said Veronica, taking the bottle and admiring the label. "That's two bottles now."

"My goodness," I said, adjusting to the subtle lighting, "you shouldn't have gone to all this trouble."

"I like to make my Scrabble games special," she said, pulling back a seat for me at the table.

"So I see," I said, smiling and nodding my head in approval.

"Have a seat," said Veronica, "and let's get started."

She looked much more appealing than she had done running along the towpath. There was equally no doubt that she still looked rather strange. There was nothing obvious about it, just a combination of her short stature and her face, which, despite the make-up and the flattering lighting, still had that look of someone who had just been told bad news, the edges of the mouth turned down in a permanent expression of sadness. It was an unhappy face, one that looked even more unhappy the more it tried to break into a smile.

"I'm so pleased you were able to come," said Veronica as she poured the wine. "It's so great to find another Scrabble fan. Maybe we could make it a regular thing."

I had only just arrived but I felt my enthusiasm for the game suddenly dwindling. This was why Andy and Mark had given me such strange looks. This was why Maggie had tried to warn me. I should have listened to them, and I should have broken my ridiculous Invitation resolution. Look where it had led me – into the den of a clearly unhinged woman who looked as though she was about to either seduce or execute me.

"Who goes first?" she said, rummaging in the bag and pulling out a 'B'.

I reached in the bag and pulled out an 'X'.

"Looks like it's me," she said, putting her letter back and pulling out seven new ones. I followed, arranging my letters in front of me, and shifting them around the rack as I waited for her to go.

Suddenly, Veronica started to laugh. Then the laugh turned to a smile and then the smile turned to a whimpering giggle accompanied by a doe-eyed stare over the top of the wine glass.

"Oh, dear," she said in a way that made me feel very uneasy.

Any unease I felt was confirmed as I saw her first word spread itself, letter by letter, across the double word score. The first letter down was an 'F'. This was followed slowly and deliberately by a 'U' a 'C' and a 'K'.

I looked at it, oddly (and ironically, given that this was a game of Scrabble) lost for words.

"Oh dear," she giggled. "It looks like I've started with a rude one!"

I could think of no appropriate response, so I just nodded my head. I hoped I looked unembarrassed and, more importantly, unexcited.

She sipped her wine, looking up at me with eyes that were explicit rather than suggestive.

"Oh well," I laughed. "It's in the dictionary, isn't it?"

"I can check if you want," she said, reaching across the table, and delivering another whimpering giggle.

Had this been planned? Had she in some way managed to fix it so that she was able to put down on the board what was so clearly on her mind, what, it now appeared, was clearly the purpose of this visit? And was 'FUCK' really the highest scoring word she could come up with?

I looked at my letters. 'POMEQNV' seemed very unpromising. Strangely, the only words that came to mind were 'POKE' using the 'K of 'FUCK' and 'COME' using the 'C'. What was going on here? I looked for other words, but none appeared. Was Veronica some kind of witch, capable of jinxing a game of Scrabble so that both contestants could come up with only words that had a sexual meaning? Suddenly I saw the solution and put down 'PUN', not a particularly high score, but one that at least saved me from giving the wrong impression.

As the game went on, I tried to develop an exit strategy. Veronica clearly thought this game would lead somewhere, most likely the bedroom, and this was not something I was prepared to consider. There was nothing wrong with her, but it just didn't seem the right thing to do. My life was complicated enough as it was without adding this unnecessary twist to it. The important thing was to get out without offending her and get out before she said anything that could remotely be construed as an invitation.

A couple of things soon became very clear. The first was that I was very unlikely to win the game. In fact, I would be lucky to get over 150. The second was that whenever possible, Veronica would put down a word that, if not explicitly sexual, carried some sexual connotation. Why else would a game which began with the word 'FUCK' also feature 'PRICK', 'SHAG' and 'BUM' Even innocent-looking words like 'UP', 'IN' and 'GO', when accompanied by Veronica's simpering giggles and wide-eyed stares of seduction assumed frightening power.

I knew I had to get out.

I had said 'yes' to the invitation and I had turned up. That, surely, was enough. I could have tried some other avoidance strategy when Andy, Mark and Maggie had hinted that coming here for a game of Scrabble might not be a good idea. But I had kept my word and I could leave now with no resolution broken and with my secret code of honour still intact.

Veronica was now onto the second bottle of wine and nearing the end of the game. When this game ended, would she ask for another one, or (and this seemed more and more likely) would she suggest some other kind of game?

I didn't want to hang around to find out.

"Veronica," I said, "I think I need the loo."

As I sat on the toilet, trying to piece together more of Veronica's life from the photos on the walls, I searched desperately for a solution. Suddenly I had it.

"My God," I shrieked as I rushed out of the loo, "I have to go!"

"What?" said Veronica, "What's the problem? Time for another game surely?"

"I'd love to, but I've forgotten something very important and I have to go."

"What is it?"

I paused, giving what I hoped was a good impression of someone who was reluctant to reveal a truth.

"What is it?" repeated Veronica. "Maybe I've got whatever it is here."

"No, you don't understand," I said. "You see – it's medication. I normally bring it with me whenever I go out. And it's really important I take it."

"Medication? I see…." Veronica looked thrown, as if she had suddenly lost control of her carefully manufactured seduction. "Medication for what?"

I paused, all kinds of medical conditions running through my mind. It had to be something serious, but at the same time it shouldn't be too alarming.

"I'd rather not say," I said, "but believe me it's absolutely vital that I get this medication quickly. I can't believe I left home without it."

"You can tell me," said Veronica. "Maybe I can help."

"No really," I said. "I must go." I put my hand to my throat as if I was about to turn from Jekyll to Hyde at any moment and headed for the door.

***

As the weeks passed, I began to realise just how many casual daily contacts involved invitations of some sort and I became more and more adept at dealing with them. If anyone called at the door who was likely to come out with anything sounding remotely like an invitation ('Excuse me sir, but I'd like to invite you to think about Third World poverty', 'I'm inviting you to switch your power supplier now and experience fantastic savings', 'Come and join us in our effort to stop the new Sainsbury's') I shut the door in their face before they reached any of the telling words. I was also wary of opening any odd-looking emails. As soon as I had responded to an invitation to try out Viagra at 'special rates' and I had visited a web page offering 'Girls who would like to meet you' simply because I was addressed by name and asked to, I realised that emails had to be treated with the same ruthless attitude as doorstep callers. Anything that looked as though it might contain an invitation of any kind was deleted before it was opened. In the same way any junk mail was thrown straight into the bin.

It would have been tempting to cheat. I could easily have feigned deafness on certain occasions, or simply pretended that what was clearly An Invitation had been something else. I could have pretended a packed social calendar led to unavoidable clashes, making me strangely unavailable on certain days. I could have said yes to invitations I liked and something equivocal or non-committal like "I'll try" to those I wasn't sure about.

I could have done all these things and no one would have ever known. It would have been easy to lie to Jerry and, more importantly, it would have been easy to lie to myself. But through all those months I kept the faith. I may have twisted the rules a little on a few occasions, I may have developed a few coping strategies, but whenever I was invited, wherever, whoever, or whatever it was, I always said yes.

13

When Ellie first went off to Bristol, Sarah and I made a point of visiting her once a term. We dropped her off and picked her up at the beginning and end, but we also felt it right to make one more visit, bringing her provisions and taking her out to lunch. Ellie may well have hated it all, may, as I had in my time at college, have dreaded the parental visit, but if she did, she had the good grace, as I hope I also had, to not let it show. And when she asked whether she could bring someone along to lunch, and when that someone turned out to be Wiggy, we too tried to keep our true feelings hidden, asking her newly acquired boyfriend polite but unsearching questions, smiling at his attempts at humour, and ignoring his extraordinary dreadlocks and piercings. We would rather have seen our daughter by herself, but we were both sensible enough to realise that what we were going through was just one of those stages – like the first tooth, the first word – and although we might have preferred another First Serious Boyfriend, we kept up the termly visits and the awkward lunches.

When Danny went off we expressed our intention to do the same with him. That was, of course, before Sarah's walk-out, before we faced the problem of having to arrange separate trips, of increasing both the number and the awkwardness of these visits from home. I had visited Danny once in his first term, shortly after he heard about Sarah's walk-out, a time, I assumed, when he would need some comfort as well as some explanation. I'm not sure I provided him with either and I have no idea whether Sarah, who visited him a couple of days after me, provided any more.

This term, when I dropped him off, I said I would visit but I was fairly vague about it, leaving it loose and open-ended so that he felt he wasn't being put under any undue pressure. I don't know what Sarah told him, but I thought I would give him a touch more space and was quite happy not to pay him a visit, or to let him come back for a night or a weekend in his own time if that was what he wanted.

I was a little surprised, then, to get a phone call from Danny a couple of weeks into term and An Invitation.

"I thought you might want to come and visit me this term."

"Of course I would. I thought I'd leave it to you to say when."

"Well, that's what I'm doing now. Why don't you come up Saturday week?"

"That's great. I can't see a problem. Hang on, I'll just check."

I reached for my diary. It wasn't something I had been in the habit of doing over the last few years, but in my new life I was finding it increasingly necessary. I was sure there was something about that weekend.

"Sorry, Danny, I can't do that. I'm at the theatre."

"You're where?"

"The theatre."

"But you never go to the theatre. What are you seeing?"

"Death of a Salesman."

"I wouldn't bother, if I were you."

"Why not?"

"He dies. That's all you need to know."

"Is that what they're teaching you up there?"

"What else do you need to know about it? And, more importantly, why go to see it in the theatre?"

Because I've been invited by Maggie, who has already snogged me and who is definitely going to take it further with me soon, possibly on that very night when we get back from the theatre.

"How about the next Saturday then?"

"That's fine. Let's go out for lunch or something."

"OK, then."

"Great. I look forward to it."

"Yeah, so do I."

Had I heard him correctly? Had he just said that he was actually looking forward to having lunch with me? I was thrown, and what followed left me even more unsettled.

"It'll be good to talk," he said. "There are things I need to speak to you about."

As I hung up his words echoed round my head. Things I need to speak to you about? What did that mean? It sounded serious, urgent almost, as if this was far more than a casual invitation.

As the *Death of a Salesman* date drew closer I began to prepare for it as if I was cramming for an exam. I went out to buy a copy of the text, sat down and read it in one sitting and then, still being a little uncertain about what I was supposed to make of it, I went out again to buy as many sets of Literature-Made-Easy notes as I could find. That made everything a little clearer, but to add a little intellectual sophistication I had a look at Miller's autobiography as well, and even went online to discover some state-of-the-art feminist criticism. By the day before the theatre trip I felt I could tackle pretty much any angle, but I was particularly expert on Linda Loman, figuring that the chances of Maggie, being an actress, wanting to discuss anything other than her own performance were pretty remote.

But my preparation was more than academic. I now had no doubt that the evening would end up with me in bed with Maggie, and this prospect meant I had to prepare myself fully in other areas.

Sex with Sarah had been comfortable. Predictable might be another word to describe it. I knew what she liked and she knew what I liked. At times I thought we could do with a touch more variety, a little more experimentation, but she had never complained and neither, I suppose, had I. Now Sarah was up to who-knew-what with Colin the PE teacher, a man considerably younger, and fitter, than I was, and unless things took an unlikely turn, I was about to end up in bed with Maggie, a woman who was on the verge of running a marathon. It may have been exciting, but I would be fooling myself if I didn't own up to finding it absolutely terrifying as well.

I knew such things were about more than the merely physical, that, if all these women's magazines were to be believed, a sense of humour, a good laugh and a kind smile were all you needed to touch a woman's right buttons, but I already knew what Maggie's body would be like: taut, lean and trim – in short it would be the kind of body you had when you ran as regularly and as obsessively as she did. I also needed no mirror to realise what my body would look like: the kind of body you had when you had only recently started to take serious exercise after years of abuse and neglect.

I had yet to make a return to The Richmond Runners, largely because I didn't relish the prospect of talking either to Ron about the Running Mare Quiz Night, or to Veronica about our aborted game of Scrabble and my serious medical condition. Every time I saw Maggie I dreaded her saying anything that amounted to an invitation to come back and join them on the next Sunday morning and if I sensed a running reference looming I tried to steer the conversation in other directions. But I did carry on running, going out by myself after school and at the weekends, trying to push myself just that little bit further, trying to shed the pounds that prevented me from being the lean, toned attractive hunk that I knew lived within me. Every time I got back from a run, I flirted half-heartedly with a sequence of sit-ups and muscle stretches that I had read about in some Sunday supplement, and looked at myself in the mirror, seeing what I looked like if I held my stomach in as tightly as I could and speculating (in a way I hadn't done since the middle of my teenage uncertainty) about how my size might compare to other men, or, more specifically, to other men who Maggie might have slept with.

Whenever I thought about actually doing it with Maggie I started to feel a little queasy. It wasn't a moral difficulty. It wasn't a feeling that what I was doing was in any way wrong. After all, it had been Sarah who had done it first, neatly relieving me of any feelings of guilt or betrayal; Sarah had been screwing Colin all that time, so here was my chance to do something I was perfectly free and, perfectly permitted, to do. It was more a feeling of being unprepared, of having some crippling lack of confidence about the whole thing.

Maybe my anxiety was a simple case of transference. Maybe I was taking my worries about Sarah, about Ellie and Danny, about my crazy New Year's resolution, and I was loading them all onto what I thought would happen with Maggie. And why not? It seemed a perfectly reasonable thing to do. And it wasn't as though I was fantasizing or being unrealistic in my expectations. She had kissed me that evening. She had kissed me long and hard. And she had pulled me towards her in a way that left me in no doubt. She was there for the taking. But if that was the case why had I not taken the opportunity then? Why had I rushed back over the road as if I was terrified of the whole thing? It wasn't because I didn't fancy her, it wasn't because I didn't want to, and I don't think it was because I feared I might disappoint her as a lover.

The only conclusion I could reach, and this is a crazy thing to admit to, was that I didn't do it then because she hadn't actually invited me to.

The more I thought about this, the more I realised that it was probably the truth. And the more I realised it, the more I began to doubt my sanity. Could I have become so committed to the whole resolution that I would only go to bed with Maggie if she specifically invited me to? Was I really waiting for her to say it with words, to formalize it, to ratify the whole idea by the terms of my enterprise? Did I want this to happen only if it was something I could tell myself I had no choice about, if I could justify it or rationalise it as an unavoidable result of my crazy scheme, of the way I was now living my life? If she had uttered the words "Come upstairs" or "Would you like to come to bed with me?" would that really have made all the difference?

It was as if I had surrendered control of my life to the whim of The Invitation god.

The last thing I needed before I went over to pick up Maggie was a long telephone call from Jerry. But that's what I got.

"I've made progress," said Jerry. "Real progress."

"Progress with what?"

"On the Alex front."

"Really?"

"You don't sound very interested."

That's because I'm not, you idiot. I'm going out this evening and I really don't want to talk about this.

"Sorry, Jerry. It's just that I've got other things on my mind."

"What? Invitations?"

"No," I lied, "it's been very quiet on that front. I've hardly had any."

"Really? Well, I guess it'll pick up. That's the way it goes sometimes. But listen, I spoke to two people last week about Alex. I spoke to Natalie – remember her?"

"Of course I remember her – I was at their wedding." Natalie was Alex's first wife.

I could tell that he wanted me to ask about what she said. But I refused to play the game.

"Guess what she said?"

"I can't, Jerry. You'll have to tell me."

"She said that he spoke to her about three days before he died – because they had always been on speaking terms and had kept up a kind of best-friends relationship."

"So what did she say?"

"She said he seemed really strange, really troubled. She said she hadn't heard him like that before."

"And that's progress?"

"What do you mean? It confirms exactly what I thought – that there was something going on his life, something huge."

I sighed and strummed my fingers on the table in the hope that he might hear my impatience and cut the call short.

"But you knew that already, Jerry. I don't see how this has moved your investigation..." I paused, ironically undermining the word with some implied quotation marks "...any further. You knew that already."

"OK, but you haven't heard about the other person I saw." Again, I didn't ask. "Someone from his last ad agency. I tracked him down. And do you know what he said? He said exactly the same as Natalie but he also said that the day before he died Alex had gone out for a drink with him at lunch time and said that he was in a fix." He paused, and although I was in a hurry to get out, I must admit I did want to hear whether there really was any discovery about to be revealed. "Alex told him that he was involved with a woman but it was very complicated. It went back a long way and it was the thing in his life about which he felt most guilty."

"OK," I said, "and did he give any names?"

"No names, but Alex did say something along the lines of 'I know what it's like to do the dirty, but this one's in a different league, and I feel really really bad about it.'"

"He was just exaggerating. He always did."

"No, Rick, I think there was something going on that we need to know about."

"Why?"

"Why what?"

"Why do we need to know about it?"

Jerry went silent for a moment and I wondered whether he was finding it difficult to answer the question. Maybe he was beginning to realise that his fascination with what was happening to Alex before he died, together with his obsessive interest in whether, and how, I was keeping to the terms of my bet, suggested that there was something seriously missing in his own life. Maybe he had realised the truth of what I had said to him that evening in the Mexican restaurant – that it was *him* who needed to get the life.

"I just think we owe it to him, don't you?" said Jerry.

The truth was I didn't. And the truth was that Jerry's weak clichéd response did little to allay my suspicions. He too was nearing fifty. He too was married with two kids also off at university. He may have been Captain Sensible at college and he may have been similarly anal for most of his adult life, but he too was clearly in some kind of crisis.

I looked at my watch. Across the road Maggie was waiting. "Look, Jerry," I said, "you may be right, but the thing is—"

"It's important to me. It really is. I don't know how to say this but things here aren't too great at the moment."

So I was right. My old friend was about to launch into some long bottled-up confession about an unhappy marriage, about how beneath his calm dull suburban life lurked all kinds of demons that were suddenly making themselves known. It would make cutting the call short even more difficult.

"It's Caroline," he said. "She doesn't like what I'm doing."

"What are you doing?"

"Nothing special. I'm just going out a bit more, I suppose."

"Why?"

There was a long pause. "You see the thing is, Rick, I told her about you, about your bet, about what you're doing."

"You what!"

I couldn't believe it. I had pledged secrecy and I had assumed that he had done the same. It felt like the biggest betrayal imaginable.

"I couldn't help it. It just slipped out. We were having a row and—"

"I thought it was a secret. I thought it was just between you and me!"

I felt my temper rising, the intensity of my anger taking me by surprise. I knew this thing had become important to me, too important perhaps, but I wasn't prepared for how much Jerry's revelation shocked me.

"I don't believe this, Jerry," I shrieked, "I don't fucking believe it!"

"It's all right. She hasn't told anyone else."

"I should fucking hope not!"

"The thing is we were having this row about whether or not I was going out too much. I didn't think I was. I was just going down to our local pub a bit more often, nothing special. But Caroline got annoyed so I started talking about how it's important to get out and do things, otherwise you can end up in a rut."

I couldn't believe this was Jerry talking. Jerry liked ruts. He was comfortable with them. The word 'rut' could almost have been coined with him in mind.

"And," he said, "to illustrate it I told her about our bet."

Quite why it seemed like some act of blasphemy, some deeply wounding spiritual betrayal, I couldn't work out. But I definitely felt as if something that had become special to me had in some way been sullied. I could just about tolerate Jerry's phone calls, his insatiable appetite for updates on, and intimate details about, my latest invitations, but this was of a different order entirely.

Maybe it was because I was in a hurry to pick up Maggie. Or maybe it was because all of a sudden I felt I'd had enough of Jerry.

Whatever the reason, what I said next came to me from nowhere and surprised me as much as it surprised him,

"Well," I said, "I've got some big news for you."

"What's that?"

"You can tell Caroline it's all over."

"What do you mean?"

"What I mean is I've stopped it. I've stopped the bet. You've won."

"But you can't do that!"

"Why not?"

"Because you agreed. It was a bet, a New Year's resolution."

"I know, and I've lost the bet. I've broken the resolution. If I'm honest it's a bit of a relief."

"So I was right," said Jerry, "you are chicken!"

"It's not that."

"You're chicken and you're boring!"

"You don't understand, Jerry. It's not like that. It's not that simple."

"Seems simple enough to me."

"You weren't the one who was doing it."

"But it was doing so much for you. You were a changed person. You were going out. You were meeting people. You were getting over all that misery last year. It was working!"

Now Jerry seemed the one betrayed.

"The thing is," I said, "it was taking me over and that was dangerous. I was following it so faithfully. I was keeping it so well that it was running my life. If I'm honest, Jerry, it was becoming a bit of an obsession."

Jerry suddenly had no comeback. He spluttered down the line.

"I'm disappointed," he said, "really disappointed."

"Why?"

"I just am."

"I just couldn't keep it going Jerry. It was taking me over. I know you enjoyed our phone calls. I know you enjoyed tracking my progress, but I have to be honest, I couldn't keep it up – not for a whole year. I was kidding myself. I could have pretended, but I thought it best to tell you."

"I'm glad you have," said Jerry.

"I just thought it best to tell you the truth," I said.

Some of what I was telling him was true. It had definitely become too important in my life and it had definitely started to take me over, but the rest was lies. I had no intention of giving it up. All I wanted was Jerry off my back. He could talk to me as much as he liked about his Alex theories but I wanted his interest in my Year of No Regrets to stop. I would carry on, but I would carry on alone.

I left the house, headed over the road, and started speculating about a night at the theatre and any Invitation that might follow.

14

There was a time when I was a regular at the theatre, when I would have been one of the first to take in the latest offering at The Bush, The Royal Court or The National. It was, though, a time long gone. As I moved towards stopping going out altogether, my theatre-going was one of the first things to disappear, and it was easy to see why. First the hassle of getting tickets, then the hassle of getting there and then, worst of all, when you did get there, being unable to avoid other people who thought it worthwhile to indulge in the same activity, a self-selecting bunch who weren't slow to establish in their whole manner, and more specifically in their loud comments at the interval bar, just how significant and important they were. Once I stopped going, whenever I read a bad review, or whenever I heard anyone in the staff room or on the bus or tube, talking about "shows", I knew I hadn't been missing much.

Now I was about to go back on the circuit, but for very different reasons. The purpose of this trip to Hammersmith's Lyric was not to reacquaint myself with the electrifying oxygenating atmosphere of live performance, nor was it to experience again the tragedy of Willy Loman, low man by name and low man by nature, victim of mid-20th century capitalism and casualty of The American Dream (as my copy of York Notes had so succinctly put it). The reason I was there was that I was with Maggie, ostensibly to give her some perceptive insights into the role of Linda that she was about to play on tour, but in reality to sleep with her when we got back home.

As we headed to Hammersmith on the tube, I felt an exhilarating sense of liberation. Jerry had only himself to blame. He was the one who betrayed the confidence, who told his wife about my New

Year's resolution, and my response had been both swift and entirely appropriate. How clever it was to tell him I had given the whole thing up ("What? But it's only March!"). I knew now that, whatever happened tonight, I would, at least, be spared Jerry's prurience.

And I knew that what I had told him was definitely untrue. I would see this thing through, and when it was over I would tell Jerry exactly what I had done, show him that despite what he might have thought, I definitely did have the guts and the courage and, yes, the sheer nerve, to fulfil the terms of my bet.

At the interval, I deployed some of my reading to telling effect as I told Maggie exactly what I thought of the production and, more specifically, of the interpretation of Linda Loman.

"You're a harsh critic," said Maggie.

I smiled and raised my glass. "I'm sure you'll do it better," I said. "And I hope I get to see you doing it."

"On one condition."

"And what's that?"

"That you're not as harsh on me as you've been on her."

"I thought you wanted my views, my honest views."

"I do."

She smiled the kind of smile that said later she would be all mine. I finished my drink quickly and, finding it difficult to cope with the excitement, thought about another. Once Willy Loman had killed himself and Linda had cried over his grave I would be heading back to Maggie's bed. It would be a struggle to stop myself cheering as Willy smashed himself up in the car.

It was then that I saw him.

At first I didn't notice him in the crowd; he was just another theatre-goer out with his wife or his partner, sharing a quiet intimate drink in the corner, leaning close and seeming very much together. It was only when I passed him on my way to the gents and saw him close up that I realised what I had stumbled on.

There, in the corner of the Lyric theatre bar, was Colin having an interval drink with a woman. And he wasn't just having a drink. They were all over each other in that embarrassing way you used to be when you were young. Not only were they clasping each other's hands and looking lovingly into each other's eyes, they were also periodically leaning into each other and exchanging kisses that would definitely have become full-on snogs had they been somewhere more private. They looked as though they might ditch the second half and slope off to a local hotel room to finish it properly – that's how intimate they seemed.

What took me by surprise, though, was the fact that, although I had no doubt that the man involved was Colin, I equally had no doubt that the woman he was with was not Sarah.

Colin, the man my wife left me for, was out flirting outrageously with another woman. My wife had betrayed me and now, it seemed, she was being betrayed herself.

My first instinct was to rush over, haul him off and start telling him exactly what I thought. Or maybe just to haul him off and smack him in the face. It only took a moment's reflection, though, to realise that this was a pretty complicated scenario which needed careful handling. So I forgot the idea of physical assault and rushed into the gents, unsure where my sympathies should lie in this sophisticated network of infidelities. What, exactly, should I do? Should I tell Sarah? And, more immediately and problematically, should I let Colin know I had seen him?

I had no answer to the first question, but I quickly settled on a course of action. Under no circumstances should Colin know I was there. Knowledge, as great philosophers had a habit of saying, was power.

"What's wrong?" said Maggie when I reached the bar.

"What do you mean?"

"You walked across the room in a very strange way."

I turned round, as if Maggie might have been addressing someone behind me, turning back sharply when I realised that doing so had exposed me to the risk of discovery.

"Yes," said Maggie, "You kind of leaned away and turned your collar up. Like you were in some kind of spy movie."

"Did I? I can't think why."

"Are you all right, Rick?"

"I'm fine. Honest."

I looked round the bar as if trying to prove that nothing in the whole room, in fact nothing in the whole world, was at all wrong. As I turned my head towards Colin and Lover I saw them stand up and move across the bar towards me. I looked away quickly.

"There!" Maggie's voice was a loud told-you-so. "You've just done it again!"

"Done what?"

"Gone all mysterious."

Throwing a quick glance sideways, I saw Colin walk past and into the theatre.

"I'm absolutely fine," I said, downing my drink and gesturing towards the auditorium. "Time to get back, I think."

I walked away from the bar, keen to see exactly where Colin and Lover were sitting.

"Hang on," said Maggie, picking up her bag and following me. "What's the hurry?"

The hurry was wanting to find out where Colin was sitting without him knowing I had seen him. There was always the chance, given that he had only seen me a few times before our recent meeting in Richmond, that he wouldn't recognize me, but I didn't want to take the risk.

I knew that I had to pay attention to Maggie, keeping it all sweet and easy and ensuring that the prospects of post-theatre action remained bright, but I also knew that I had to keep an eye on Colin. I had to keep more than an eye on him, I had to work out what, exactly, was going on and what it meant for Sarah. It may have been her who had walked out on me and she might therefore have deserved everything coming her way, but I was surprised to find that I still felt strangely protective. After all, I knew only too well what it was like to be betrayed.

As we sat down in the stalls I started a subtle sweep of vision round the theatre.

"Well," said Maggie, "I'm looking forward to more of your expert literary analysis of Linda."

And I'm looking forward to later, I thought, carefully scanning the rows of seats.

"I can't work out whether she's a doormat or a heroine," said Maggie, "but if you play her as a doormat you're in danger of losing sympathy."

"Well," I said, "however you play it I'm sure you'll get sympathy. I bet you've never played anyone really bad, have you?"

"What do you mean?"

I turned my head to the right, trying to locate Colin, then swivelled it to the left. "I mean," I said, "I bet you've never been cast as a villain or as a baddie."

"Well, funnily enough, I haven't."

"And do you know why that is?" I asked, wondering whether Colin might be up in the gods.

"No. Why?"

"You're too nice, that's why."

Maggie turned towards me at the very moment that I decided to turn round to look up into the circle. I realized too late that she was about to give me a friendly peck on the cheek and, as I turned, our heads clashed, my forehead making a neat smacking sound as it connected with her cheekbone.

"Fuck!" She jumped back, holding her face. Heads turned in the direction of her loud expletive and as they did I caught sight of what I had been looking for – Colin and his woman high up in the circle. They were holding hands and laughing and looking even more together, even more physically intimate, than they had seemed in the bar. While Maggie uttered a series of loudly whispered "Fucks" and held the side of her face, Colin turned briefly away from his woman and looked down in our direction. I turned back sharply.

"You've hurt me! Are you listening, Rick?" Maggie was reaching in her bag for a mirror.

"I'm sorry," I said.

"Sorry about what? That you've just nutted me in the face or that ever since the interval you've been behaving like some kind of halfwit?"

"It was an accident," I said. "I didn't expect you to..."

"To what? Give you an affectionate kiss on the cheek?"

"Well, no."

"What if it's bruised?"

Typical actress vanity. The chances of a bruise were minimal, yet that was clearly why she was still hunting for the mirror

"I barely touched you," I protested. "It won't be bruised."

"You bashed me in the face. And you bashed me hard."

"It was an accident."

"I don't care. It hurts and it might bruise."

There was real venom in her hissed words, and I got the sense that the evening had started to come off the rails. My enthusiasm for the second half of the play had disappeared entirely and my attraction towards Maggie was going in the same direction.

I reached towards her cheek. "Let me look," I said.

"Don't!" She jumped away and pulled a mirror out of her bag. Snapping it open she held her face up to catch the dim theatre lights and started to examine her cheekbone.

Then the house lights went down.

"Shit," she said, "I'll have to go."

"What?"

"I'll have to go."

"You can't. The play's about to start."

"I need to check my face is all right."

"Your face is fine. It's still lovely."

"Rick, this is no time for that kind of shit."

"I'm sorry. I'm sure it's fine. Is it hurting still?"

"Yes, it is. It hurts like fuck!"

The lights came up on the stage and Willy and Linda were in the kitchen having breakfast.

I leaned towards Maggie and put a reassuring hand on her arm. "I'm sorry," I said, "I really am, but it'll be OK."

"Why did you turn your head like that anyway?"

I shrugged.

"And," she said, "why were you acting so strangely in the bar?"

"Ssh!"

The noise came from behind and it was followed by another from our right.

"Do you want to go?" I tried to make it a quiet whisper but another "Sssh!" followed it immediately, this time from our left.

"Let's stay," said Maggie. But the warmth has gone out of her voice and I knew the evening had been ruined.

All through the second half my mind was elsewhere. Linda could have taken off all her clothes and leaped into the front row of the audience, Willy could have made a miraculous return from the grave before the final curtain and I wouldn't have known. As the tragedy unfolded in front of me on stage I was more conscious of the real-life one going on in the seats. Behind me Colin was betraying my estranged wife while beside me Maggie was worrying about the damage I might have done to her face. As the minutes passed I could feel her growing colder and colder, could sense the idea of post-show sexual activity heading for a salesman-like death.

As soon as the play ended, Maggie headed off to the ladies to get a good look at her face and I was left lurking in the entrance. I had already worked out that Colin was likely to leave by the same exit and I kept an eye out for him, still keen that he shouldn't realise I had seen him. When he came through the exit I turned sharply away but sneaked a glance back just to check that he had safely left. It was with a sense of horror that I saw him pause and point his lover towards the ladies. Looking through the crowd heading for the street, I could see that Colin was now doing exactly what I was – standing on the other side of the aisle waiting for his partner to emerge from the loos.

The crowd started to thin. Soon we would be standing opposite each other with nothing between us to obscure the view. I kept myself turned towards the wall, an eye trained on the ladies door, praying that Maggie would come out first. I made sure that my head remained turned away from him, that my eyes were truly averted.

His voice took me by surprise.

"Rick?"

I kept my head turned. Maybe if I didn't respond he'd think he was addressing someone who looked like me but who was in fact called something other than Rick.

"Rick? Is that you?"

Why was he being so brazen about the whole thing? If I was in his shoes I would have been trying hard to keep myself hidden. Was he about to pretend that he wasn't with the woman he had been manhandling all evening? Would he have the nerve to pretend that he was entirely innocent?

He was moving across the hall towards me. I had no choice but to turn.

"Colin! What are you doing here?"

As stupid questions went it was up there with the stupidest. He had just been to see a play, the same play as me, and looked very much like he was waiting for someone to come out of the loos.

"What did you think of it?" he said.

It was enough of a surprise to see him. To see him try to initiate some kind of critical discussion left me speechless. He might, at least, have had the decency to look sheepish. He was the man my wife had run off to live with. He was the man my wife had been sleeping with during my 'boring' years. And here he was with another woman, giving every appearance of being about to go home and sleep with her. And yet he seemed not at all ruffled.

"Fine," I shrugged, not wanting this confrontation to dwindle into an Arts Review discussion. "I thought..."

"Maggie!"

As soon as I saw her come through the swinging door I leaped towards her as if she was emerging from twenty years in the jungle rather than a quick pee.

"Thank goodness you're here!"

Maggie, not for the first time that evening, looked at me as if I had lost the plot completely.

"Of course I'm here. I've only been in—"

"And how's the face?"

I moved towards her, took her arm, leant up close to inspect her cheek as if looking for any minute signs of damage, and started to steer her past Colin towards the door.

"Rick," said Maggie, "what are you doing?"

I moved my mouth to her ear and whispered. "I'll explain later."

"You're doing it again."

"What?"

"This spy shit. What's going on?"

By this stage we were sweeping past Colin. As we did he turned to the loo door to see his woman emerging.

"Rick," he said, swivelling his head between the loo door and our receding backs, "wait, let me introduce you."

"Sorry I can't stay Colin. Got to dash!"

And with that I swept Maggie through the doors out onto King Street, fuming at Colin's nerve. Not content with stealing Sarah he wanted to introduce me to the woman he was cheating on her with. How could someone be such a callous scheming bastard? How could anyone have such nerve? How could anyone find it so easy to attract, and cheat on, women?

Such thoughts were racing round my head when Maggie stopped beside me and put her hands on her hips in an I-mean-business fashion.

"I think," she said, "I'm owed some kind of explanation."

"I'll give you one," I said, "I'll give you one when we get home."

She didn't even smile at the innuendo.

I was beginning to doubt whether tonight, after all, would see the consummation of our relationship. She had asked me in and made me a cup of tea but there had never seemed a moment when she was likely to utter the words which would seal the whole thing. It was as if that brief snog had never happened.

All I needed were a few simple words. My night would be complete if she offered an invitation.

But the words just didn't come.

At the moment she was definitely more interested in things other than taking me to bed. A few simple words, the merest hint of the invitation, were all that would be needed to lead me upstairs to her bed, but all she could talk about were the two big events of the evening, neither of which involved *Death of a Salesman*.

The first was the way she nearly damaged her jaw.

"Look, I know I overreacted, but I really did think I had done something serious. It was like a headbutt. If only you'd told me you'd seen this bloke."

"I'm sorry," I said, "but I don't think that would have made any difference to when I turned my head, would it?"

"No, but it might have explained all that James Bond stuff."

The second was Colin.

"No wonder you were in a state. Just goes to show, doesn't it? You can't trust anybody nowadays, can you?"

At least she had the decency to be as outraged as I was.

"It must be difficult for you."

"It is," I said. "Sometimes I just need a little – I don't know – comfort."

No harm in a little reminder.

"Comfort! Of course you do, silly me! And here I am offering you tea or coffee. There's some whisky somewhere. Fancy that?"

"I was thinking of..."

I raised my eyebrows in what I thought a carefully cultivated suggestiveness.

"I know what you're thinking of," she said, and she reached out and took my hand, "and I sense you might have been thinking of it for some time."

This was it.

It was about to happen.

"Do you want to come upstairs?"

An Invitation.

"Yes," I said.

15

Never before had I felt so guilty. Whatever my motives, whatever my justification, I knew, as I woke up in Maggie's bed, that this just didn't feel right.

I crept across the road after breakfast like a sixteen-year-old school kid, and went up to bed, burying my head under the duvet as if something huge was about to come crashing down on me.

Even Jerry could not have imagined just how dramatically keeping the terms of his bet had extended my sexual experience. Even he could not have anticipated the kind of invitations that had followed the move upstairs.

I wasn't imagining it.

The whole thing had really happened. I was lying in my bed on a Saturday morning, having, for the first time since I got married, slept with another woman. And I couldn't decide whether or not it had been a pleasurable experience. I suppose I had expected something more straightforward to mark my first ever adulterous act. If this is what everyone having affairs got up to I could understand why the comfort of fidelity had remained so attractive for so long. If Maggie and her antics were anything to go by, it was a big bad dangerous world out there, a world in which you could be shocked, surprised, and even actually tied up, all in the pursuit of pleasure.

That stuff, surely, wasn't normal? Or maybe it was. Maybe this was what Colin and Sarah got up to, what Colin and The Woman got up to. Maybe this was exactly what had been missing in our lives for so long?

It all brought me back to that New Year's Eve when Jerry had asked me about my sex life. Had I been naïve in imagining for so many years that there was no need to do anything different? Was this what the whole world was up to and was this what following the trail of Invitations had led me to discover?

Never had I felt more like giving the whole thing up, doing for real what I had already told Jerry I was doing. How could this way of living be any good if it had led me to this position, lying in bed and feeling miserable?

It was that thought that made me ask Jerry to come over.

It was only on my third pint that I felt able to discuss the intimate details of my session with Maggie.

"The thing is, Jerry, I feel awful, absolutely awful."

"Why? Wasn't it any good?"

"It's not a matter of whether it was any good, it's a matter of how I feel."

That wasn't strictly true. It was entirely a matter of how good or how bad it had been. It certainly hadn't been a disaster. I had managed to fulfil each of Maggie's increasingly bizarre invitations without, I hoped, appearing as though I had never been involved in anything like it before. I had done what she requested with the handcuffs (the truth was I had never even seen a pair of handcuffs before. I had seen the proper ones, the ones that policeman use, but never this variety, the kind they sold in shops that I had never had the nerve to enter). I had cleverly decided to await instructions from Maggie, as if that was my particular pleasure, asking her specifically what she wanted me to do, and doing nothing until she told me. It may have made me seem a masochist to her dominatrix but it seemed to work. I did the same with the cream and with the leopard-skin number and with everything else that Maggie demanded of me before she reached her climax with what I thought were rather over-theatrical cries strangely reminiscent of Linda Loman wailing over her husband's grave. It may, of course, have all been one big performance on her part but, bewildered as I was by her sequence of bizarre requests, I found it difficult to judge.

As for my performance, well at least she didn't complain. I may not have been the youngest or the fittest, but my running had at least got rid of the excessiveness of the flab – and all that was left seemed respectable enough. I couldn't compare to Maggie's slender trim tones, but I did the best I could with what I had, feeling a bizarre mixture of relief, fear, guilt and bewilderment, and sensing that my lack of noise and drama might have made me a disappointment to her.

Jerry skewered the last chip with a fork and held it up in front of his mouth. "So, tell me, then, how do you feel?"

"I feel shit. I feel like I've done the worst thing imaginable."

"You've done nothing wrong, though. Just think of what Sarah did to you."

"I don't know, Jerry. Maybe I should have taken her back and got things back to normal."

"Normal? What's normal? There's no such thing."

"There was, though, Jerry, about six months ago. That was normal."

"You can't think like that. You can't turn the clock back. You've got to look forward. You'll get used to it."

"I don't think I'll get used to Maggie."

"You never know. You might."

"Oh, well," I said, "At least I've stopped trying to keep that ridiculous resolution. Who knows where that might have led?"

Having told Jerry I had given it all up, I was determined to maintain the illusion.

Jerry took a sip of his drink and shook his head. "I'm disappointed in you," he said, "really disappointed. I still think you should have carried on with it."

"That's easy for you to say, you didn't see where it was leading me."

"Yes I did. It was leading you to sex with Maggie. Don't pretend that if it wasn't for the bet, you would have ended up doing what you did last night."

"Maybe," I said, "I'd have been better off without the whole thing."

Jerry snorted. "Rubbish! It was doing you good, I could see it."

I sighed. "It might have looked good from your side, but I was seeing it differently. It was like – I don't know – some kind of drug."

I wasn't used to lying, and it didn't come very naturally, but now that I had started I knew I had to carry on. I had to make my reasons for giving the whole thing up sound convincing.

"A drug, eh?" said Jerry.

"Not that I've ever taken any – or many. But the thing is, it was kind of compulsive. It sort of took me over. At first I felt really uneasy about the whole thing but the more I tried it, the less uneasy I felt; the more I tried it, the more I actually started to enjoy it. The thrill of not knowing what the next invite would be, not knowing where it would come from, not knowing what the hell it might lead to, and that knowledge that your answer would always be yes, that you wouldn't even have to think about it. It was all kind of liberating but it was also scary, addictively scary. Just like with drugs you think you can control it, but you can't. Eventually it gets control of you. There was a time when I thought I could control it – if I got myself in certain situations and if I said certain things I thought I could engineer them, I thought I could get the sort of invitations I really wanted, but it didn't work like that, it really didn't. You ended up needing it and wanting it, but you didn't end up controlling it."

I could see that Jerry believed every word I was saying, and that was probably because every word I was saying was true. I might have been giving him reasons for why I had stopped, but I knew, as I spoke the words, that they were compelling justification for why I had chosen, privately, to carry on.

"Jerry," I said, "you might not believe me. You might think that none of this could apply to that harmless bet you made on New Year's Eve, but it's true. It really was getting to me and I think I stopped because I was frightened about where it might lead – genuinely frightened. I'm not sure I can explain it properly. There's no way I can get you to understand."

Jerry leaned forward and touched my arm gently. "I do, though. I do understand."

I shook my head. "That's easily said, Jerry, but I really don't think you do."

"I do, honestly, believe me."

I shook my head again, more slowly this time. "Look, I know it was your idea and everything, but this thing is really really very weird. It's…"

"What? Changed your life?"

"Well, no – well yes, I suppose it did. Or it nearly did. But what I'm just saying is that you can't really understand it unless you've done it."

Jerry grinned.

"I know."

"No, Jerry, you see—"

"And that's why I understand."

It took a few seconds to sink on. "Hang on. Are you saying..."

He nodded.

"I've been doing it myself. Every invitation."

My mouth dropped.

"What? You mean you've been doing the same thing as me?"

Jerry nodded.

"But why the fuck didn't you tell me?"

"It didn't seem relevant."

"Of course it was fucking relevant. The whole thing was your idea in the first place. Why didn't you tell me?"

"I didn't think you'd be interested."

"How long have you been doing it?"

"That's the thing. I only started when you told me you'd stopped."

"But why?"

Jerry took a deep breath and leaned back in his chair. "It occurred to me that everything I said to you on New Year's Eve about your life having become dull and boring actually applied to me as much as it did to you. And when you said that it was actually me who needed to get out more, me who needed to get a life, it struck home. I realised that everything you were saying was true."

My God. Jerry had realised he was boring. After all these years he had finally owned up to it.

"And when I saw you doing it, I thought it was – I don't know – exciting. That's why I was so interested in how it was going. I know things are different for me. I know that, unlike you, I'm happily married, or at least I was happily married."

"What do you mean 'was'?"

"OK, I still am. I'm still married. It's just that since I've started this invitation thing I've realised anything could happen."

This was all proving too much. Captain Sensible, after all these years, had finally taken leave of his senses.

"Jerry, you're mad. You're crazy. You don't need to do this."

"So you think I'm not boring then?"

"I didn't say that."

"So you do think I'm boring then?"

It was a strange reversal of our New Year's Eve conversation.

"I didn't say that either. What I mean is you don't need to do this."

"Well neither did you then."

"But I did – because Sarah walked out on me and I needed something to change me, something to give me a kick up the backside and get me doing things again. But I've stopped. I've given it up."

It was all very weird. I suddenly felt possessive about it, as if no one else had any claim to my resolution. It was my thing, and Jerry, despite the fact that it had been his idea in the first place, had no right to it.

"The thing is," said Jerry, "I've always been the boring one. There was Alex the wild one and there was you – not as wild as Alex but not as, I don't know – safe – as me. I guess I've always been predictable. And I guess that up until last year I've never really worried about it – wife, kids, partner in a law firm, nice house, nice everything. Then what happens? Alex gets knocked over by a car and Sarah walks out on you. All these things were signs, signs that nothing lasts for ever – and it made me think. You're a clever bloke Rick. You don't need me to tell you that I suggested the resolution to you because, deep down, it was what I wanted to do. You knew the score. You said as much to me – you accused me of getting a vicarious thrill and you were right. Why did I ring up so often to find out how it was going? It wasn't to check up on you, it was to live through you. And then when you said you'd given it up, I thought OK, the field's clear, let's see what it's like."

I was still annoyed that he had moved onto my turf, still irritated that he was staking some claim to what had been exclusively mine. But very quickly the annoyance gave way to curiosity. I wanted to swap notes.

"So tell me, Jerry, where has it led you?"

Jerry laughed uneasily, as if about to deliver a sad and tragic tale.

"The funny thing is, Rick, it hasn't taken me very far. For the first three or four weeks I didn't get one invitation, not one. If you live a predictable life I guess that's what happens. But things have started to look up..."

"How?"

He shrugged.

"A few drinks invitations at work that I'd normally say no to. A couple of local things." He seemed sheepish, as if there was something else.

"There's a woman, isn't there?"

He shrugged again.

"You're mad, Jerry. If you've got something good, don't throw it away. Don't ruin it."

"But you've done it and Alex did it the whole time!"

"But it's different for me. I didn't do it first and it's different for Alex because he was always like that."

"But maybe I want to. Maybe, after all these years, I—"

"Don't do it, Jerry, please. It's not a good idea. It's dangerous."

"But you did it. If it's not a good thing why did you do it?"

"Because it was a bet, because you dared me to, because it was a New Year's resolution. Besides, I've stopped, and why do you think I've stopped? Because I saw just how dangerous the whole thing is."

"You enjoyed it, though, didn't you?"

"OK, perhaps I did – bits of it at least – but Jerry, you can't live your life like that. It just doesn't work."

"It's working for me OK."

"It might be now, but just you wait."

Jerry looked away, as if weighing up the temptation. "But don't you," he said, "sometimes think you've lived your life so safely, that it might be time to break out, to bust loose, to take a risk of some kind before it's all over?"

"Of course I do, but I'm not sure this is the right way to do it. This way you lose control of things. You have no choice."

Jerry laughed.

"But as you said before, sometimes no choice is exactly what you do need."

Had it all come to this? Two fortysomething men, married with kids, having the kind of what's-it-all-about existentialist discussion you thought you had left behind at college, and having it loudly and in public?

What would anyone say if they knew the truth – that I was trying to dissuade my friend from a scheme (an absolutely fucking crazy scheme) that I was myself involved in, but which I had told him I had stopped? A scheme, which I had thought preposterous and had wanted to avoid, had suddenly taken over us both.

It was mad and it was dangerous, and it had both of us in its pocket.

***

Perhaps it was a mistake to call Sarah when I got back. As soon as I heard her voice, I felt awful. First of all there was the overwhelming guilt of having slept with Maggie, then there was the knowledge that Colin, the man she left me for, was playing around with someone else.

"Sarah," I said, sensing I didn't really know what to say to her, "how's things?"

It was a stupid question. Things were clearly not right, nor had they been right for quite some time. Why else would she have asked to come back? Why else would she admit to having made a huge mistake? Why else would Colin be going to the theatre with another woman and snogging her in the bar?

Maybe I should tell her that I knew about it. If that was the reason she wanted to come back, perhaps she would feel better if I let her know that I knew the truth. But what if she didn't know? What if she had no idea that Colin had been playing away? I needed to tread carefully.

"I wondered if you'd heard from Ellie and Danny recently."

"Why? Haven't you?"

"Well… yes. I just wondered—"

"Rick, this isn't a good time, can I call you later in the week?"

"Sure," I said, and hung up.

Not a good time? What did that mean? Had she just discovered Colin's betrayal? Or did she not want to talk because I was proving to be a heartless bastard?

Suddenly I felt sorry for her.

OK, she had been unfaithful, but then, ever since last night, so had I and it didn't make me feel any better. If I was being truthful, it made me feel a hell of a lot worse. I hadn't enjoyed it. Making love to Sarah may not have been exciting in the eyes of those who indulged in Maggie-style excess, but at least it had been comfortable. And at that moment, as I hung up on the woman I had lived with for so long, the woman with whom I had fathered two children, I longed for a bit of that old security.

I longed for it so much that I almost picked up the phone to ring her back, to tell her about Colin, to tell her about me and Maggie and to say that if she hadn't changed her mind of course I would take her back and was, in fact, on my way round to pick her up at this very moment.

But the moment didn't last long.

I had started so I would finish.

And now that Jerry was doing the same thing, I was even more determined to see it through.

16

April

I paused outside Danny's door. Behind it I could hear female laughter, and it made me feel strangely nervous. What if I had come at the wrong time and he was not just with a girl in there, but actually *with* a girl in there? Would my knock on the door lead to farce-like grabbing of trousers, a hasty rearrangement of the bed, and an embarrassingly long wait before anyone answered? I paused and, checking that no one was coming up the staircase behind me, put my ear closer to the door.

I could now hear Danny's voice, but I could also hear more female laughter, this time a different kind of laughter. There were at least three people in the room, which meant I must be safe. Unless…

I stopped such ridiculous thoughts immediately and knocked.

"Danny," I said, speaking to the door. "It's Dad."

This announcement was followed by more female laughter, this time both of them together, and I was sure that I could hear Danny quietly saying something that provoked even louder laughter. Was I being over-sensitive to think that he had just made some comment about me?

He pulled the door open and beckoned me in.

"Hi," he said, as coolly as ever. He had grown out of hugs and my recent efforts to initiate manly Soprano-like mafia embraces had met with little approval. "Come in. This…" He pointed at one of the two very attractive girls sitting on the bed, "is Hayley."

I nodded my greeting, thinking briefly about offering a handshake but deciding against it.

"And this," said Danny, holding his arm out in front of the other very attractive girl, "is Caroline."

I wondered which one, if any, might be Danny's. He could, of course, be just good friends with both, but any hot-blooded male (and, though I had no evidence and wouldn't want to probe the issue, I somehow assumed that Danny was) would have had no objection to getting to know either Hayley or Caroline on intimate terms.

"So," said Hayley, "you're Danny's Dad."

I nodded. "Yes," I said, "that's me."

I smiled and looked round the room. The girls on Danny's bed looked at me and I looked back at them, unable to shift my idiotic grin and unable to stop imagining the pair of them without clothes on. My night with Maggie seemed to have unlocked some strange emotions.

"We've heard all about you," said Caroline, tossing back her shiny blonde hair.

"All good, I hope," I said, reaching for the nearest cliché. The girls smiled and said nothing. I turned to Danny. "What have you been telling them, then?"

He shrugged. "Not a lot."

"Rubbish," said Hayley, "he's been telling us loads of things."

Like how his mother walked out on his family but his Dad was big enough to stay?

"He hasn't told us anything directly," said Caroline, "but he has said a few things in his stand-up."

"Really?"

My son was using me as comic material. It should maybe have surprised me more.

"Well, thanks girls," said Danny, carrying a cup of coffee towards me. "Maybe my dad doesn't want to know about my comedy act. Maybe I have deliberately not been telling my dad things about my comedy act – ever thought of that?"

Caroline held her hands up to her mouth. "Shit," she said, "have I put my foot in it? Should I go before I say something else you don't want him to hear?"

Danny shook his head. "Don't bother," he said, "it's the risk you run when your parents come to visit, isn't it? Or rather… parent…" He left the word hanging in the brief embarrassed silence that followed. "Tell you what though Caroline, you let me know when yours are coming, won't you? And I'll make sure I'm in your room when they arrive. I can think of a few things they might like to know."

I caught the look Caroline threw Danny. It was half-smile, half-frown. Was this the kind of look that existed between lovers? Did they have a history, or were they maybe a current item? Or maybe it was Hayley? I couldn't stop myself speculating, couldn't stop myself thinking of these women, no girls, not just young enough to be my daughter, but younger than her, in a totally inappropriate way.

"Tell me," I said, turning to both the girls, "what else could you tell me that Danny might not want me to hear?"

"I could tell you more," said Hayley, "but he'd never forgive me."

Caroline leaned towards me. My heart jumped. "But you'd be better off coming to hear him perform. He's really good, you know. You'd be amazed at what you'd discover."

"I bet I would."

Danny moved between me and Caroline, as if trying to cancel the whole conversation.

"Please, Caroline!"

"Why not?" she said.

"Because I don't want you to talk about it."

"He should come, though, shouldn't he Hayley?"

Hayley nodded her agreement. "He's good, seriously good."

"Which isn't a bad achievement for a comic," I said.

They ignored the joke.

"So come along," said Caroline

"Are you inviting me?" I said, laughing privately.

"Yes," she said, "I am."

An Invitation.

"Ignore her, Dad," said Danny, "they're joking."

I laughed. "No Danny, *you're* joking."

I must have been nervous. Why else was I coming out with pathetic attempts at humour?

"Very funny, Dad. Maybe you should take it up yourself."

I turned to the girls for support. "The thing is," I said, holding my arm out in Danny's direction, as if presenting him as some kind of exhibit, "he doesn't tell me much about what he's up to, so I really have no idea."

Danny moved forward, waving a pair of game-over hands. "Leave it, Dad, please. Let's go out."

"OK," I said, standing up.

That, after all, was why I had come to see him. There were, in his words, things we needed to talk about.

Hayley and Caroline stood up to leave. As they did, Caroline leaned towards me. I thought for one absurd moment that she might be about to give me a kiss.

"Remember," she whispered, "come and see him when he's next on."

An Invitation.

I had no choice.

***

As I sat opposite Danny over a pizza, I kept hearing Caroline's softly whispered words. It was definitely An Invitation and, given the way the conversation with my son was developing, it was definitely an invitation that was going to present me with more than a few problems.

"Look Dad," said Danny, wolfing down the last bite of his American Hot and rubbing his hands together as if he could manage another, "I don't really want to talk about my comedy act, if it's OK by you."

"That's fine," I said. "It's your thing. I don't want to intrude."

"And I know Caroline invited you but she was just being polite. She's like that."

"She's very nice, isn't she?" I said.

Danny gave a non-committal nod. I prayed he had no idea of the inappropriate thoughts that had once again started to flash through my head.

"But look," I said, hurriedly trying to fill the silence and to stop seeing the nubile Caroline naked on my son's college bed. "I quite understand. It's great to hear that you're going down well, but if you don't want me to come..."

"It's not that I don't want you ever to come. When I'm ready I'll let you know, honest. Just ignore what Caroline said, just forget it, OK?"

I nodded, pondering the impossibility of ignoring the imperatives of an invitation.

"OK," I said, wondering how easy it would be to disregard Danny's feelings, and what might be the best way to do it.

We sat in silence, Danny looking occasionally at me, but more often at other parts of the restaurant, while I finished my pizza. Then I decided it was time to be brave.

"You said on the phone that there were things you wanted to talk about," I said.

"Did I?"

"It sounded as though there was something specific on your mind."

"Something specific other than Mum walking out on you like that, you mean?"

"Well, I'm obviously happy to talk about that. I just thought..."

"Why did she do it, Dad?"

The question came out sharply and urgently, as if long-suppressed resentment was close to eruption.

"Why?" he said again.

I had no new answers to give him, so I trotted through the clichés that he had already heard.

"We still talk to each other, you know," I said. "And we both still care about you. We both still love you."

"Please, Dad!" Danny looked round the restaurant. "Not that sort of shit, not here."

"But it's true."

Danny looked at the tablecloth in silence. Then, without lifting his head, he said quietly and calmly, as if he was delivering some dreadful secret or intimate confession, "Actually, Dad, there is something I want to talk to you about."

I waited, holding my breath. He kept his head down, saying nothing.

"What is it, Danny? Whatever it is, you can tell me."

Danny lifted his head and looked at me full-on, his eyes brimming with intensity.

"The thing is," he said, "I want to..."

Another pause. It might have been difficult for him, but it was also hell for me. I had no idea what was coming as I leaned forward, raising my eyebrows in encouragement.

"Yes?" I said.

"I want to leave."

"What?"

"I want to leave."

"That's fine. I'll just get the bill."

"No. You don't understand. I want to leave college, I want to leave Oxford."

I tried to seem cool, nodding my head slowly as if it hadn't shocked me or surprised me in the slightest.

"OK," I said.

"What do you mean 'OK'?"

"I mean OK," I shrugged, "as in I understand."

"But I'm not sure you do, Dad. I'm not sure you understand at all."

"Try me," I said.

None of it made sense. He hadn't even done a year and yet here he was thinking of chucking it all in, throwing away a place he had worked so hard to get, a place many would have killed to secure.

"Just tell me," I said, "tell me why."

"I'm... I'm just not enjoying it," he said, looking as though his face was about to crumple into tears.

"Which bit?" I said. "What, exactly, aren't you enjoying?"

"Look, Dad, this isn't particularly easy for me. I didn't know how to tell you and, to be honest, I wondered whether I should tell you at all. Maybe it would have been easier if I had left and then told you after the event. At least then you wouldn't have had to go through all this."

He was just about keeping it all together, but he was definitely on the edge.

"Take your time," I said. "You don't have to tell me anything if you don't want to."

Had something terrible happened to him? Was I about to hear some sickening revelation? Was he on drugs? Was it girls? Had he slept with Caroline, perhaps, and made her pregnant? Or was it just that his Mum had walked out on us and he was feeling completely fucked up?

Danny took a deep breath. "I just haven't settled and, I don't know, I just can't see the point of it all."

So he was a student who couldn't see the point of it all. Even in my day not seeing the point of it all came with the territory. Do a bit of work, go out and get drunk, fall in and out of bed with all kinds of girls, fall in and out of love with some of them, and worry about the point of it all.

"That's perfectly normal," I said, "I remember..." And then I stopped myself just in time. I was banned, by mutual agreement, from uttering any sentence that began with "In my day..." or "When I was at college..." I changed direction. "Is it anything to do with Mum and me?"

"Maybe. I don't know."

"So if we were still together, you'd..."

"I'd what? Not want to jack it in? It's not quite that simple, Dad. Are you saying that if I said I'd stay if you two got back together you'd do it? Do you really think I'd go in for that kind of emotional blackmail?"

"No," I said, "of course not."

If only he knew the truth. If only he knew how easily it could be arranged, that Sarah had already asked to come back and I had said no.

"I know how unsettling it must be," I said. "It's difficult enough leaving home for university – all those readjustments, all those new people. And then to get a phone call like that after a few weeks. It must have knocked you for six."

"Knocked me for six. Yeah, I suppose that's the right kind of cliché. Yeah it did knock me for six. Over the boundary and right out of the ground if you want to continue the cricketing metaphor."

"You know what I mean," I said.

"Yeah, I know what you mean." He paused, and sighed, as if some great revelation was on its way. "But that's not the reason, not the only one."

"What else is there?"

"There's no list. I just don't see the point."

"Maybe there is no point."

"Exactly."

"No," I said, shaking my head. "I don't mean it that way. What I mean is it's best not to look for points. Sometimes it's just best to, I don't know, do it."

"I will just do it, jack it in. That's doing it, isn't it?"

"Is it the work?"

"That's not the issue. I read books. I talk about them. I write essays."

"But everything seems to be going so well," I said, "and your comedy seems to be shaping up, if Caroline and Hayley are to be believed. I'd say you've got a couple of fans there."

"What are you talking about?" he said.

"They think you're good," I said, "that's all."

"Maybe I am," he said, "and maybe that's one of the reasons for it."

"For what? For feeling crap?"

"No, for wanting to jack it in. I'd like to give it up and give the comedy thing more of a go."

"What do you mean?"

"If I wasn't doing this, I could get on the circuit and get my name known."

So that was it. My son wanted to drop out of Oxford and go to Clown School. I paused, gathering myself, knowing that the first thing I said would be important. But the longer I paused, the more difficult I found it to think of any sensible response.

"Well?" said Danny. "Haven't you got anything to say?"

"I'm not quite sure what I… I mean…" I opened my palms and shrugged, "I suppose the first question to ask is can't you pursue the comedy thing while you're still here? It's probably a pretty good place to be if you want to get your name known, isn't it?"

"What, even if it makes you unhappy?"

"I thought most comedians were unhappy. Goes with the territory."

I knew it was the wrong thing to say.

"Well, in that case my parents have certainly done their level best to turn me into a good comedian, haven't they?"

"No," I said, "I didn't mean it like that." I wanted to go further. I wanted to say that if he was in the business of blame then it was parent in the singular. What had I done – apart, perhaps, from being a little boring? "What I mean is I think it's great that you want to give the comedy a go, but giving all this up," I waved my arms around as if he was giving up a job working in Pizza Express, "might not necessarily be the best solution."

"Maybe you don't think I'm good enough. Maybe that's it."

"That's not it at all, though since you haven't let— since I haven't been to see you, that's a difficult call for me to make."

What was I saying? No matter how good he was at standing up in a small sweaty room above a pub trying to make people laugh, he was probably a damned sight better at reading books, talking about them and writing essays. Sticking it out for three years at Oxford would put him in a far better position than spending more time in sweaty rooms above pubs. It was, as Danny's generation might like to put it, a no-brainer. Did he really want to do it, or was it some kind of cry for help, some kind of retaliation for what his parents' cracked marriage had done to him?

"All I'll say, Danny, is try to give it time. Don't do anything hasty. We're all trying to come to terms with what's happened. Me. You. Ellie. Mum."

"You're assuming that it's all to do with that. Maybe it's not. Maybe it's what I would have wanted to do, even if you were still together."

I smiled sympathetically. "You don't want to do anything rash, anything you'll regret. Give it time."

"I've given it time."

"Give it longer – at least finish the year. Then, if you need to chuck it in, you've left the door open to come back."

"Who spoke about coming back?"

"You never know what you might want," I said. "All I'm saying is give it a year. Whatever you do, make sure you come out of it all with no regrets."

The irony of the words suddenly hit me. Give it a year. No regrets. It was the scheme I was on, the scheme that Jerry was now on, the crazy, ridiculous enterprise that seemed to be destroying everything. Who was I to advise anyone, let alone my son, on what to do with their lives when I was making such a spectacular mess of my own?

Maybe, if I had taken Sarah back, if I had been adult and mature, understanding and forgiving, none of this would have happened? What was it in me that felt the urge to continue with a New Year's resolution, a bet undertaken in drunkenness and embarked on in stupidity? Surely it was time to stop it now? If I was going to stop in a year why not stop now? What would be the difference?

I cleared my throat, trying again to hit the right balance between gentle concern and down-the-line common sense. "Have you spoken to anyone else about this?"

Danny shook his head.

"Not yet."

"Not Caroline or Hayley?"

Another shake of the head.

"I've told them I'm not happy, but not about wanting to leave."

"And how do they feel?"

"What do you mean?"

"I mean are *they* happy? As I say, quite a lot of people go through this."

"What are you talking about, Dad? What does it matter whether they're happy? We're talking about me here. Forget about Caroline and fucking Hayley." I thought of fucking Hayley, wondering whether it was something my son had already done, and wondering, ridiculously, what it might be like for me. "It's nothing to do with Hayley and fucking Caroline."

The film in my head suddenly changed its cast.

"It's nothing to do with anyone apart from me."

"And me, perhaps?" I said. "And your mother?"

"If it makes you happier to think so, then yes, but what I'm going through isn't all down to Mum walking out. It would have happened anyway."

Maybe he was right. Maybe I *wanted* it all to be the result of Sarah's walk-out. Maybe I *wanted* him to be the victim of our broken marriage, of her unforgivable betrayal.

"How about giving it a year and then deciding?" I said. "And I really think you ought to speak to someone. Don't you have a tutor or something? A moral tutor – isn't that what they're called? They must be used to this kind of thing."

"'This kind of thing'? That's right, belittle the whole thing why don't you?"

"I didn't mean that," I said. "I mean they'll be better than me. They'll have a better perspective, and talk to Caroline and Hayley. They seemed – you know – nice."

And then, for reasons I found difficult to understand, I started to think not about Caroline and Hayley, not about whether Danny was sleeping, or had slept with, either or both, and not about what it might be like if, preposterously, I ever had the chance to do the same. No, I started to think about Caroline's invitation. She had asked me up to see Danny's comedy act. Danny didn't want me to go and yet if I was to be true to my resolution I had to accept.

This, surely, was the perfect moment to scrap the whole scene, to come to my senses and to get my whole life back on track.

In front of me, my son, close to tears, was thinking of dropping out of college to try to make it as a comedian. Opposite him sat his father working out how he could accept an invitation to see him perform without him finding out.

And, bizarrely, his father was serious about the problem, so serious that he thought he had stumbled on a way of solving the dilemma.

He would come, but he would come in disguise.

17

When I left Oxford late that night I had, I thought, persuaded Danny to think about it more, to talk to people, to give it a year. All evening the words "no regrets" and "give it a year" had haunted me, and they still danced through my mind as I headed down the M40, listing all the things currently on my mind:

1. My wife had walked out on me for a man who, I had recently discovered, was cheating on her.

2. My son was thinking of dropping out of college to pursue a career as a stand-up comedian.

3. I had embarked on an affair with an actress with strange sexual tastes (and had started to entertain ridiculously inappropriate thoughts about attractive young students).

4. I was keeping a crazy bet/resolution that I could quite easily stop but was very reluctant to.

5. My old friend had recently started to keep the same resolution.

Only the first two were unrelated to my resolution, and yet it was, without any doubt, these that were the most significant. These were the ones over which I had least control; nothing I could have done would have stopped Sarah walking out (apart from being boring, perhaps) and nothing could have stopped Danny preferring comedy to college. 3 and 4 I could stop tomorrow if I chose to, and while 5 was also a problem over which I had no control, it somehow didn't seem quite as significant.

But the more I thought about it, and the closer to London I got, the less problematic the list seemed to be. I could, if I wanted, do something about number 1. Sarah had, after all, asked to come back, and if I took her back maybe the number 2 might disappear. Maybe if I called her when I got home and told her to get her things and move back in Danny might decide not to drop out and the first two problems would have disappeared entirely. And that would leave 3 and 4, both of which I could remove overnight simply by deciding to stop the charade and behaving sensibly. And, who knows, that might even have some effect on Jerry, neatly removing number 5 and eliminating each and every one of my current problems.

Looked at that way, things didn't seem so bad.

So why, as I pulled up outside the house, did I find myself thinking of the best methods of disguise?

***

The next day I braced myself for what I knew would be a difficult call.

"Hallo."

It was a man's voice, Colin's voice.

"Ah, is that Colin?"

"Speaking."

Death of a Salesman rushed back.

Maybe I should do it now, chuck at him the full venom of my anger. First you steal my wife and then you cheat on her. You fuck me up and then you fuck her up. You fuckwit! You scumbag you maggot you cheap lousy faggot! You—

"Could I speak to Sarah, please?"

What a coward. Not only did I not confront him, I didn't even tell him who I was. I even changed my voice slightly so that if he thought he knew me from the way I said "Is that Colin?" he might have been less sure when he heard my next words.

"I'll just get her," he said, calmly.

If he did know who I was he was wise enough not to let on.

When Sarah came to the phone I tried to be as business-like as possible. I asked her how she was and then moved on to Danny, asking her when she last spoke to him and then telling her that I was just back myself from a flying visit.

It was when I paused a little too long that she suspected something was up.

"Has something happened to him, Rick?"

"No. He's fine. Well, when I say fine…"

And that was it – she started asking more and more urgent questions, becoming increasingly hysterical as I told her as much as I could, trying to keep it all very factual and unemotional.

"I think he'll be fine," I said.

"But this is awful, it's a disaster!"

"I asked him to finish the year and I'm reasonably optimistic."

"Reasonably optimistic!"

"It's quite a common thing, Sarah. A lot of kids go through it."

"What! A lot of kids chuck in a place at Oxford to be a stand-up comedian?"

"No," I said, trying to stay calm, "a lot of kids have doubts and uncertainties. Can't you remember what it was like when you were nineteen?"

And then she started to cry. All I could hear coming down the line were huge convulsive sobs. God knows what Colin was doing in the background, but he certainly wasn't doing anything to calm her down. I kept repeating her name, saying the kind of things I thought might smooth things over.

But I had little effect.

And then I heard the words I didn't want to hear.

"Will you come round, Rick? I really want to see you."

"What?" I said. "Now?"

"Why not?"

I needed to clarify this one.

"Sorry Sarah, are you inviting me round to see you? Now?"

Another huge sob.

"Yes, Rick. Please. I need to."

"But what about…?"

Another huge sigh.

"What about Colin?"

"He's going out."

I'll bet he is. And do you know where he's most likely going?

"Please, Rick. Come round."

It seemed I had no choice.

***

It was the first time I had been in Colin's house and it felt very strange. As soon as I walked through the door, I was looking for the tell-tale signs of their cohabitation – those little things that told the story of their life together. And when I saw them – the chairs they sat in, the food they cooked, the television they watched, the music they listened to – it was tempting to come out with what I knew about Colin.

But I wasn't a bastard.

Sarah had already owned up to her mistake. She had already asked me to take her back. I may have been annoyed and I may have been angry, but I couldn't bring myself to kick my estranged wife when she was clearly down.

"I don't believe it," said Sarah, dabbing at her eyes with a tissue. "I was so proud that he got there."

Yeah, so proud that you walked out on us four weeks later.

"It's not definite," I said. "I think I managed to persuade him to see out the year."

"Just like you then."

She sobbed again.

"What do you mean?"

"Seeing out the year. That's what you asked for when I said I'd made a terrible mistake."

"Look, Sarah, let's not confuse issues here, shall we. We're talking about Danny dropping out of college."

"You can't separate it. It all runs into each other."

"It doesn't have to. Danny asked me to tell you and I have. I thought a phone call would be enough, but you were obviously upset, so I've come round."

"I know, thanks, I do appreciate it, I really do. I'm sorry, it's just that everything seems so mucked up I sometimes don't know what to do."

Looking at her across the kitchen table, seeing her tears and seeing her distress was almost too much for me. OK, she had screwed up, OK, she had walked out, but the man she had moved out for was being unfaithful. Could I sit here and let it happen or should I do something?

"Sarah," I said, trying to make her name sound like a prelude to something weighty and significant, "how's Colin?"

She started "What do you mean how's Colin?"

"I just wondered how things were between the two of you."

"Why do you want to know that? You've never been interested before."

That was before I knew what he was up to.

I took a deep breath. It was time to put my wife out of her misery.

"It's just that I saw him the other night."

"Saw him? Where?"

"At the theatre."

"Really?"

"You didn't know he was there, did you?"

"Which theatre?"

"The Lyric."

Sarah shrugged unconvincingly, desperate to make it all seem perfectly normal.

"We... we don't do everything together."

"That seemed to be the case."

"And what does that mean?"

What was the best way to put it? *Was* there a best way to put it?

"Nothing, I just expected to see you with him. I was surprised that you weren't."

Here was her chance. All she had to do was ask whether he was by himself, whether there was anyone with him, and I'd be able to introduce the whole thing.

But she said nothing, just lowered her head as if in defeat.

"Did you talk to him?" She spoke softly, almost whispering, and she kept her head bowed, as if bracing herself for bad news.

"No," I said, "I think he may have seen me, but we didn't have the chance to talk."

She lifted her head and her voice seemed to brighten. "Oh," she said, "I assume he wasn't by himself then."

Here was my chance.

"No he wasn't – and that was why I was surprised."

She started sobbing again. I reached out and put my hand gently on her arm. It felt just like the old days, as if we were making up after some petty, unimportant family squabble.

"Who was he with then?"

"I don't know who it was."

"But it was a woman?"

I nodded.

"So you know then."

I nodded again. It was all out in the open. I knew that Colin was cheating on her and she knew that I knew. The circle was complete.

"I know," I said, "and I wanted to tell you."

"Such a mess," said Sarah, reaching for another tissue, her shoulders beginning to heave. "It's such a mess."

"At least I know," I said. "But tell me, how long has this been going on?"

"What?"

"The whole Colin thing."

Sarah shook her head as if she had been asked an impossible maths question.

"It's always been like that. That's the whole point. It's always been this way."

This was getting confusing. I thought I had got somewhere, but suddenly she was making no sense again.

"What do you mean it's always been like that? You mean he was up to that kind of thing all the time?"

"No, I don't mean that."

"Is that why you wanted me to take you back, because you realised that Colin's been sleeping with other women?"

"No that's not it, that's not it at all."

"It sounds like it is to me. It must have been horrible finding out that you were with someone who was having it off with someone else. Imagine going through that, eh? Well, maybe it might have done you good to find out what I felt like."

"It's not like that at all, Rick, it really isn't!"

"Oh no? Are you trying to tell me that isn't why you asked me to take you back? That's what you meant by you'd made a terrible mistake, wasn't it? Colin's shagging around so take me back!"

Sarah looked around the room as if there was something she might find which would make it easier to explain. "There's not much more I can say that would make it any easier. Maybe we should get back to Danny."

I laughed.

"There's not much more to say about Danny, but I get the idea there's a lot more to say about – Colin." I said his name as if I was spitting.

"You mustn't blame Colin."

"What?"

"You mustn't blame him."

"What else am I supposed to do? Of course I fucking blame him. If it wasn't for him we wouldn't be in this fucking mess, would we?"

"It's not his fault."

"Not his fault! Not his fault that he was knocking you off behind my back all that time and not his fault that he's moved on to having it off behind your back as well!"

"Rick!"

"Just because he's a fucking PE teacher! Just because he's fit and works out. In fact he's so fucking fit, he probably can do it behind his back! He's probably a fucking contortionist, he's so fucking fit, Mr PE teacher! Maybe if I'd been fit enough to do it behind my back you'd still be with me!"

Sarah looked at the ground, hanging her head in what I hoped was shame. "I asked you round," she said, "because I was upset about Danny. I didn't expect this." She wanted me to apologise, but I couldn't bring myself to. "I don't know what else I can say," she said. "You know I've made a mistake. I've asked to come back and you've said no. You now know that things aren't as they seem with Colin." She paused. In the silence I could hear her quick breaths. "You don't know how I felt all those years," she said calmly.

"And which were those? My boring years? The ones when you went out and I stayed in. Well, I can tell you one thing. That's all changed."

"I never said you were boring."

"No, but you felt it. You didn't need to say anything."

Sarah laughed.

"I really don't know what you're talking about."

I knew now that I had to go before I told her everything. It was just on the other side of my lips and I knew I was in danger of letting it all slip.

"Just give me until the end of the year," I said, turning for the door, "that's all I need."

I opened the door.

Sarah stood in the kitchen doorway. "And what happens then?" she said. "What's so special about the end of the year? How's that any different from now?"

I shrugged. "I just need the time, that's all."

18

When I pulled up outside the house, I made sure Maggie's light was off before I got out. Ever since that night, the night on which I had sex with another woman for the first time since I got married, I had been trying to avoid her. It wasn't that I didn't want to repeat the experience – it was more that I wasn't keen to repeat it too soon. While it was good to have the whole sex-with-another-woman thing out of the way, I was still a little uneasy about it. Maybe it was just her taste, or maybe it was her appetite – whatever it was I didn't find myself wanting to rush back for another course. One thing could so easily lead to another, especially when you had to say yes to every invitation.

I had tried very hard to keep out of her way, knowing that if I saw her I would be in danger of ending up back in her bed. A casual invitation for coffee would surely lead to other invitations and before I knew it I might be in even less familiar sexual territory, the kind of off-piste sexual terrain where handcuffs and domination were the mere nursery slopes. If only I could hold out until she went on tour, everything would become a little easier. She would start shagging Willy or Ben or Happy as she did her Linda Loman round the provinces, and on the few occasions that she would be back in the house opposite, she might well have other things on her mind than resuming the affair with her neighbour. That was why I checked her house for lights before I got out of the car. When I saw they were off I moved briskly to the safety of my front door.

It was only when I got in that I realised that, in my hurry to get to Sarah, I had forgotten to bring my mobile. I picked it up to find two missed calls and two voice mails from Jerry. And he had also left a couple of messages on my landline.

"Hi Rick. It's me. I've tried your mobile and I'm getting nothing. So I thought I'd try this. Where the fuck are you? I need to talk."

It had been a long day and a tiring evening and I didn't want to hear what Jerry had been up to in his attempt to follow the Invitation god. But I knew any avoidance could only be temporary, so I picked up the phone and rang.

"Jerry, not too late I hope."

"No, it's fine. I'm glad you called. Hang on a minute, Rick, I just need to close the door." He put the phone down at his end and I heard him walk away. I also heard a distant voice that sounded like his wife's.

"It's for me, love," Jerry called, "someone from work."

It was unlike Jerry to lie.

"Rick?" he said, coming back to the phone.

"Hi."

"Sorry about that."

"What's up Jerry? Why all the secrecy."

Jerry sighed.

"This invitation thing," he said, "it's amazing."

"What are you talking about?"

"The thing, the bet, the resolution – it's fantastic."

"Why what have you done?"

"Nothing yet, Rick, but I'm about to."

I shuddered. I could still remember how uneasy I had felt about starting the scheme, how full of doubts and fears. It certainly wasn't something I had willingly embraced. Yet here was Jerry jumping at it, and it all seemed wrong. It was, after all, my thing. I was the one who had been challenged. I was the one seeing through a crazy New Year's resolution and Jerry had merely jumped on the bandwagon.

"Are you sure you know what you're getting yourself into?" I sounded like an older, more experienced addict warning against the dangers of that first puff, that first tablet, that first injection.

"Well not exactly," said Jerry, "but that's the whole point, isn't it?"

"But Jerry, think about it. You're in a different position from me."

"What do you mean?"

"You're married, happily married."

"Yeah, well about that—"

Now wasn't the time for Captain Sensible to treat me to the state of his marriage.

"And you've got two lovely kids," I said. "Think about it. Look, Jerry, it's late. I know you want to talk but maybe we should do it some other time. All I'm saying is think before you do it. I know what it's like. I know what it can do to you. It becomes, I don't know, a compulsion. Be careful." I paused, "That's why I stopped. Because it's dangerous."

"It's what I need though, Rick. All my life I've been saying no to things, when what I should have been doing is saying yes. So every Friday when some of the girls at work, the secretaries, are off to some bar somewhere they always ask me along. It's out of politeness because they know I'll turn it down. But when I decided to do it, I said yes and I went and, Rick, it was terrific. I should have been on the train home to Purley, back to Caroline and back to a weekend of shopping in the supermarket and a bit of gardening. I know what you all called me at college – Captain Sensible – and you were right. But it's changing, suddenly I can feel it all changing."

It pained me to listen and I had no idea what to say.

And then it came to me.

"Jerry," I said, "what are you doing tomorrow?"

"Why?"

"I was wondering if you could do something for me."

"Sure, happy to help. What is it?"

"I'd like you to come round here… could you do that?"

"Come round to see you? Sure, no problem."

"There's something else though."

"What's that?"

"When you come round here I'd like you to do something else for me."

I paused.

"OK," said Jerry, "what is it?"

"I'd like you to come round here and… suck my dick."

"Sorry? Did you just say suck your—?"

"Suck my dick. I'd like you to come round here tomorrow and suck my dick. I'm asking you round. I'm *inviting* you."

"Don't be silly."

"I'm being serious."

"No you're not."

"How do you know?"

"Because you're not like that. You're—"

"Maybe I've changed. Or maybe I've always wanted it but been afraid to ask."

"Don't be ridiculous."

"I'm not being ridiculous. It's a serious invitation. I'm asking you round here tomorrow to suck my dick and while you're here, lick my arse too. And then when you've done that why don't you—"

The line went dead. Jerry had gone and so, perhaps, had his resolution. Unless he turned up the next day ready for action.

He rang in the morning.

"That was very funny yesterday, Rick."

"What was funny?"

"All those joke invitations."

"Who says they were jokes?"

A pause.

"You mean you were being serious?"

"Of course I was. I was showing you how ridiculous it is. When I invited you to come round and suck my dick, I thought you'd realise that you can't live your life accepting every invitation that came your way. It just won't work. When you hung up on me I assumed that was what you'd realised."

"I was tempted."

"What do you mean? You mean you…"

"I thought about it, yeah."

Maybe Jerry's crisis was bigger than I thought. Maybe there were things about him I had never known.

"So if you thought about it, why did you hang up like that?"

"I hung up because Caroline was listening and I didn't want her to know about it."

"Know about what? About coming round to suck my dick?"

"No, about the whole invitation thing. I didn't want her to hear me talk about invitations in case she realised what I'm up to."

"What do you mean – what you're up to? You're not still doing it, are you?"

"Of course I am."

"But you can't!"

"Why not?"

"Because you didn't accept my invitations. If you had you'd have been round here kissing my arse and sucking my dick."

"Get ready. I'm on my way round."

"What?"

"I'm on my way round as soon as we finish this call. Get yourself ready, my friend."

"You're joking!"

"Of course I am. And so were you last night. They were joke invitations, they weren't proper invitations at all."

I felt my anger growing. He couldn't change the rules like this.

"Jerry," I said, trying to hide my annoyance, "you can't discriminate like that. An invitation is an invitation. It doesn't matter who says it or whether you think it's a joke, it's an invitation. All invitations are equal. Some invitations aren't more equal than others. You have to follow the rules!"

It wasn't as if he had cheated at cards, or called a tennis shot in that was clearly out. This was serious.

"Did you follow the rules, then, when you were doing it? Did you accept every invitation?"

"Of course I did!" I snorted. "It's the only way to do it and that's why I gave it up. I didn't want to lick anyone's arse or suck anyone's dick."

"Why? Did anyone ask you to?"

"That's not the point."

"What is the point, then?"

I knew I shouldn't have been getting so angry, but then there were many things I knew I shouldn't have been doing – like the scheme itself, like telling Jerry I had given it up when I had every intention of carrying on, like giving him ridiculous invitations in an effort to get him to stop.

"The point is, Jerry, that it's a dangerous thing if you do it properly."

"And what about if you don't do it properly? What if you just take the invitations you like and don't bother with the others?"

"You don't get it, do you? That's what everyone does, that's normal, that's how you end up doing nothing and having your wife leave you."

Jerry paused. The lawyer in him wouldn't let the argument go. "What if," he said, "you try to control the principle rather than let the principle control you?"

"Because then it stops being a principle, and it stops being dangerous, and that's not the idea – that's not the idea at all. Do it, or don't do it – there's no halfway house."

"We'll see," Jerry grunted. "We'll see."

It was difficult to tell whether or not I had got through to him, but it felt like some kind of victory.

***

Later that day, as I tried on disguises in front of the bedroom mirror, I congratulated myself on having dissuaded Jerry from continuing to do the very thing I had convinced him I had stopped. He could, if he chose, fall into ill-judged affairs and threaten the stability of his life in pursuit of his half-hearted, half-cocked version of our bet. He wouldn't, like me, be doing the real thing.

But as I stared at myself in the mirror, wondering how best to make myself look unrecognizable, I asked myself whether such smug self-congratulation was in order. Who, after all, was the mug here? Was it Jerry, who was aiming to give himself some kind of thrill while maintaining control? Or was it me, standing in front of the mirror trying on hats and coats and sunglasses and thinking of false moustaches?

Facing the thin array of shirts, jackets and jeans that constituted my wardrobe, I realised that I had nothing of any use when it came to dressing up. Whichever items I selected from the range in front of me, in whichever combination I chose to wear them, I ended up looking unmistakably me – not quite the effect you're looking for when you're going for disguise.

I might not have had many suitable clothes but I did, at least, have a few ideas – like a hat, for example. So I started with that, trying on the only one my wardrobe offered – a blue and white striped woollen thing that in my youth I had called a bobble hat, but in these bobble-less days was simply the kind of hat, a beanie or something like that, that you wore to football matches. I tried this on, thinking it would immediately make me less recognizable, but it had little effect. It looked like me wearing a blue and white striped hat.

With sunglasses, though, it might all look different, so I rummaged for a pair in the bedside drawer and shoved those on to see if they made any difference.

They didn't.

Perhaps what I needed was another style of hat, so I headed into Danny's room. If my wardrobe couldn't provide much help, my children's surely could. Danny had taken most of his clothes with him to Oxford and the clothes he had left seemed as useless as my own when it came to disguises. I did, though, manage to find an old baseball cap and when I tried that on things began to look much more promising. It covered all of my hair and overshadowed most of my face, and made me look not unlike those football hooligans you see orchestrating riots. Almost as good as a hoodie, I thought, adding that to my mental list of possibilities. If it was good enough for criminals trying to avoid the gaze of CCTV, surely a hoodie would be the very thing for a fortysomething man trying to avoid recognition by his son at a student comedy gig?

The most important principle, I decided, was to keep most of my head covered, and there was no doubt that the cap, or even better a hoodie, would do that job well. The sunglasses were probably too much, but a pair of some kind, with plain lenses perhaps, might not be a bad idea. And then there was always facial hair – for a man who had spent his whole life resolutely clean-shaven a beard or moustache could be just what was needed.

It was just after I had the facial hair idea that I remembered something else, something from my distant past. I remembered reading that the easiest way to recognize anyone is by their walk. Conjuring up a small sample of people and seeing if I could recall their walk this fact began to seem undeniable, and before long I was trying different walks in front of the bedroom mirror. A limp would be too obvious, and likely to draw attention in a way that defeated the whole purpose of disguise, but varying the stride length, together with a slight change of posture might make the right sort of difference.

Half an hour in front of the mirror, though, left me uncertain about the whole enterprise. Small steps, large steps, straight back, arched back – whatever I tried just didn't feel right, and when I tried it with Danny's baseball cap I just looked stupid. It all seemed so extreme. All I needed here was something that would enable me to sneak into the back of Danny's comedy gig without him looking in my direction and saying, "Dad, what the fuck are you doing here?"

It didn't need to be elaborate, it didn't need to be the kind of thing that would defeat scrutiny from a close-up examination. It wasn't as though I needed to get past a police inspection or passport control or anything. I had no intention of standing near the front or getting close enough to Danny to give him a chance of recognising me. I just needed something that would work.

***

It was a long time since I had been in Party Fun, but then it was a long time since I had been to a fancy dress party. Not since Boy George had seemed quite fashionable – that's how long ago it had been.

"And what kind of beard is it you're looking for, sir?"

The young assistant was clearly used to dealing with people wandering in with no idea of exactly what they wanted.

"Something that'll make me look very different."

"Oh I see, so you're not going *as* anyone, then?"

I laughed.

"*As* anyone? No. This is just…" I could hardly tell her the truth. "This is just a come-in-disguise party. The idea is to come so that no one can recognize you."

The assistant raised an eyebrow. "Really? I've never heard of one of those before."

I felt defensive, as though she didn't believe me. "Yes," I said, "it's the latest thing, and some people go to extraordinary lengths."

"I bet they do," she said. She clearly thought it was something very kinky, some kind of fetishists' convention.

"Yes," I said, regretting the way I had moved the conversation in this particular direction. "Some have masks made, some wear wigs, some even change their skin colour…"

What was I doing? All I needed was a false moustache or a false beard. There was no need for any of this.

The assistant responded enthusiastically and soon I was faced with a range of possibilities: Father Christmas beards, pirate beards, Fu Manchu beards, mutton chop whiskers, handlebar moustaches, Hitler moustaches and straggly hippy beards.

"I'll take one of these," I said, picking up a modest full-set moustache and beard that seemed unlikely to attract attention and placing it next to a pair of dark-rimmed glasses that I had already selected.

"Very good sir. And have you thought of a mask at all?"

"A mask?"

"Very popular, just what you might need for this kind of party."

I followed her to a stand and she held out her hand, showing me the range. Tony Blair, the Pope, a monkey, a pig, a nun...

I shook my head. I didn't want to look silly.

"Come and try a few on," said the assistant.

An Invitation.

I had no choice. And, yes, I did look very silly.

Half an hour later I was walking back up the hill from town, wearing the false beard and glasses together with a big hoodie that I had bought from one of the shops I would usually not be seen dead in. It felt great. Assuming another personality was proving to be a liberating experience and it was with a new bounce in my step, as well as a slightly more hunched posture, that I turned into the road.

As I did, I saw something that I had been trying to avoid for some time – Maggie had just left her house and was walking towards me.

I nearly stopped, wondering whether I could turn and walk away before she recognized me.

But then I remembered. I was in disguise.

I walked on, deliberately staying on the same pavement so that Maggie would have to walk past me and tilting my head slightly downwards. She walked towards me, her eyes looking straight ahead. I moved down the road, keeping my steps small, my posture a little more bent than usual, and my head firmly under the hood.

Maggie stopped a few yards ahead of me.

I carried on.

"Rick!"

Shit.

I still carried on.

"Rick! What on earth are you doing?"

I carried on further. If I didn't respond to my name and walked straight ahead maybe I could get away with it. But there was nowhere to go.

Maggie stood in front of me, hands on hips, looking at me as if I was a naughty schoolboy. She was blocking the pavement. There was no way through.

"Rick, what the hell are you doing?"

I looked up at her from beneath the hood. She reached out and pulled the hood down. "I don't believe it!" she said, breaking into hysterical laughter. "You look ridiculous!"

"I can explain," I said. "Really I can. It's not what it seems."

Maggie laughed uncontrollably, as if she had never before seen anything quite so funny. "I don't even know what it seems. Have you been out robbing people or something?"

"Of course not. I'm just…"

Maggie reached forward, pulled off the glasses and started to reach for the beard.

"Please, no," I said, holding on to the hair. "I'm just trying out a disguise, that's all."

"I could see that," she said. "But it's not very good, is it? I spotted you a mile off."

"Why? How?"

"Your shape."

"My what?" OK, so she had seen my shape on intimate terms quite recently, but surely it wasn't so noticeably awful that it shone through a false beard, glasses and a hoodie.

Maggie laughed.

"It just looks like you in disguise. I'm an actress, remember. I know all about disguise. But you still haven't told me – what's going on?"

"It's a long story," I said.

"I've got a lot of time," she said. "Why don't you come in and have a cup of coffee and you can tell me at leisure?"

Shit.

"It's a what party?"

"A come-in-disguise party."

I sipped my coffee and looked at her across the kitchen table, worried that an invitation upstairs was just about to fall from her lips. For someone into theatrical sex all this talk about disguise was probably acting as a huge turn-on.

"I've never heard of those," she said. "What's the point?"

"I don't know," I said, "I've never been to one either."

The whole thing was ridiculous. Maybe I should just tell her the truth. I didn't need to tell her the whole truth, just the bit about wanting to see my son perform but not wanting him to know I was there.

"OK," I said, "It's like this."

And then I told her.

When I had finished, Maggie seemed sympathetic. "I think that's very noble," she said, "wanting to see your son perform like that, though, as an actress, part of me thinks you should respect his wishes and if he doesn't want you to be there maybe you should stay away."

"It's not that simple."

"I know that if I said that to someone, I'd want them to respect it. So for example if I said I wanted you to come and see me on tour then it would be great if you could make it. But if I said stay away, I'd rather you did."

"I understand," I said.

"And while we're on that subject why don't you come and see me on tour?"

"Is that, er, an invitation?"

"Yes, it is. I'd love you to come."

I tried my best to smile.

"Well, thanks," I said, "that's great. Any particular place?"

"Bristol," she said. "I was thinking you could come down and see me in Bristol. Lovely city, not too far and it's where we open."

I nodded again, still trying to look enthusiastic, and thinking immediately of combining it with a trip to see Ellie.

Maggie put down her coffee cup and leaned towards me across the table. "But now," she said, "why don't I give you a little help?"

"Help? How?"

"I'm an actress," she said, "And I know all about disguises. I've also got a lot of them upstairs. Why don't I show you?"

She took me by the hand and led me away from the table towards the door.

I followed, not knowing whether to laugh or cry.

19

May

A few weeks ago I had never been unfaithful to my wife. Now I had been unfaithful wearing a Superman cape and a Mickey Mouse mask. Not at the same time, admittedly, but even so, this was clearly a giant leap beyond what I might, in my days before that New Year's resolution, have regarded as my comfort zone, and although there may have been no handcuffs this time, it all felt very far from liberation.

At the end of the session I had learned a good deal, though, not only about the strange variety of Maggie's appetite, but also about how to disguise yourself in more conventional situations. With a proper beard and moustache, glasses, padding that made me even more bulky, and clothes of a colour and style I would not normally be seen near, I could, I thought, make myself difficult to recognize. And although there might be no need for an altered step, if I threw one of those in as well I reckoned I could make myself pretty impenetrable.

I was now ready for the trip to Oxford, but I was keen to try it out before then just to make sure. I was also, if I'm honest, a little excited by the whole thing. Knowing that people couldn't see you was strangely empowering, turning you into someone with superhero attributes, as if you were genuinely invisible or able to fly.

At first I took it all gently, just taking my disguise out with me, putting it on in some store's toilets and walking round for a while in the town centre before changing back. But as the date of Danny's stand-up grew closer, I wanted to stretch the whole thing a little further.

I suppose it was only natural that I should be drawn to the prospect of spying on Sarah and Colin, but I did feel strange on those nights when I took to walking past their house in the hope that someone might emerge. I didn't lurk on the opposite side of the street with my hoodie pulled up and I didn't stake them out with binoculars or anything like that, but I did get in the habit of putting on the kit and walking down to their part of town.

Once I followed Colin. He came out of the house by himself just as I was turning into the road and headed off towards the town centre. I trailed him at a distance, and watched his every move.

I saw him talk on his mobile. I saw him go into a shop and buy some sweets. I saw him pick his nose. And I dare say that if I had persevered I could have even got to see Colin heading off for another illicit shag with his other woman, that is his second other woman. Playing the detective, having that kind of power over Colin, felt great, but I knew I shouldn't follow him for too long. The more I watched him, the more I might be unable to resist the urge to sneak up on him, call his name, and then, when he turned, hit him over the head with a blunt instrument and kick him unconscious as he lay on the ground.

***

The next few weeks passed quietly. The house was empty and, with term in full swing, I managed to get myself back into some kind of pre-New Year's Eve routine, almost returning to some of the old predictability. I called the kids a couple of times a week and they did the same, Danny carefully avoiding any mention of his plans to drop out, and Ellie saying nothing about either Finals or the world beyond Finals. I also phoned Sarah at least once a week. Most of our conversations became a discussion about Danny and ended with me making it clear that the more pressure we put on him, the more likely he was to carry out his threat. Sarah was keen for us to visit him together to show how much we cared, but I managed to steer her away from the idea, suggesting that neither of us should go up until asked, and reassuring myself that my impending trip in disguise clearly didn't count.

The most significant factor, though, in my brief return to routine was Maggie's absence. With her away on tour, there were no prospects of invitations to taste more of her strange sexual offerings, and that came as a huge relief. Knowing that I could step outside my door and walk past her house without the fear that she might appear and offer me An Invitation lifted my spirits considerably and made me reconsider how much I had actually enjoyed any of our sexual encounters, and realise how little I looked forward to the next one.

Driving down to Bristol on a bright May Saturday morning I knew that the next one could be that very night. After lunch with Ellie and an afternoon in Bristol, Maggie's Linda Loman lay in wait and I knew that after that evening's performance another one might lie in store. I would have been more than happy to drive back to London after the play, but I knew that all Maggie needed to do was utter any words which might constitute An Invitation and that would be it – I could end up wearing God knows what chained to some bed in a Bristol hotel.

Ellie greeted me with a kiss and a hug, and I followed her down the hall of her terraced Bristol house, giving everything an evaluative once-over as I went. I wasn't sure what I was looking for – evidence, perhaps, of the kind of student activity of which a respectable parent was supposed to disapprove (despite the fact that he did the very same thing in his day). There was little sign of squalor and filth – the result of her sharing with two sensible, responsible, final year girls – and there was nothing to suggest excessive consumption of substances, legal or otherwise. I wasn't naïve enough to think there hadn't been a massive tidy-up in anticipation of a parental visit, but, even so, it was reassuring to think that Ellie's lifestyle was no cause for concern or, at least, that with a quick tidy-up, she could make it seem so.

"So," I said, sitting down at the kitchen table, "it'll soon be over."

Ellie flicked on the kettle.

"Yeah," she said, "That's what I'm worried about. It goes quickly, doesn't it?"

"Everything goes quickly," I said. "And three years at university is nothing in the grand scheme of things."

Ellie sat down opposite me.

"And talking of the great scheme of things," she said, "how are they?"

"What do you want? The short or the long version?"

"The true version."

"The true version is – they're fine," I said, smiling. "And anyway I'm sure you've spoken to your mother about it." Since Sarah had walked out she had become 'mother' rather than 'mum'. "And I'm sure you've spoken to Danny as well."

"I still don't understand it, Dad."

"Maybe you shouldn't try to."

"That's ridiculous," said Ellie, throwing up her hands in disbelief. "I have to understand it, and to do that you need to talk about it, don't you?"

"I don't mind talking about it," I said. "I don't mind at all. It's just that I've been over things again and again and sometimes it seems there's very little new to say."

I had only been in the house a few minutes and already we were into the awkwardness I had wanted to avoid.

"And Mum's happy with Colin, is she?" said Ellie, getting up to make the coffee.

"Why do you ask?"

Had Sarah said something? Or was Ellie just being her usual perceptive self?

"I've said it before, but when I saw them together, they just didn't seem right."

What she meant was Colin was far less attractive than me, far less witty, far less handsome and far less fit.

"I can't judge these things," I said.

"No, but I can."

I reached across the table and squeezed her hand.

"That's very nice of you," I said. "But there's not much I can say, is there? It was your mother's choice. And what I want you to do is not worry about it. Concentrate on yourself."

I hoped it was unnecessary advice. She was, after all, still a student. Thinking and talking about yourself were part of the syllabus.

"In a few months' time," I said, "this will all be behind you and there'll be no going back. You owe it to yourself to give it your best shot."

It would have been easy to tell her about Colin, to let her know that her suspicions were absolutely correct, that her mother was, as she thought, unhappy, and that the reason for her unhappiness was that Colin was cheating on her. It would have been an easy way to make me feel better about the whole situation, and I was seriously tempted.

"Have you spoken to Danny recently?" said Ellie, sounding like she wanted to change the subject.

"Only the other night. Why? Have you?"

"Yeah. He rang me last night."

"Was he OK?"

Ellie shrugged.

What did that mean? Had he told her he was thinking of dropping out? And if he hadn't, should I tell her?

"I think so," said Ellie, "but then it's difficult to tell with Danny isn't it? He likes to keep things – I don't know – bottled up. Ironic isn't it? That someone who gives so little away should be a stand-up comedian."

I coughed.

"And did he have any news?"

"Yeah, he did actually. He wanted to check I was still coming to see him perform."

"And are you?"

"Yeah, I think so. It's before my exams, but it'll be good to get away and I'd really like to see him. It takes a lot of guts to do stand-up, you know."

I nodded.

"Did Danny mention anything else at all?"

"What do you mean? Anything about you and Mum?"

"Not necessarily. Just – anything."

"I can't remember absolutely, but I think he said something about everything at home being 'fucked'. Yes, I think 'fucked' was probably the word he used."

"I see," I said. "Nothing else?"

"That was it. He didn't say anything else. It was mainly about his stand-up. And I think I'll definitely go."

My disguise would have to be good.

"I'm worried about him," I said.

"He's fine, Dad, he's fine. It's not been easy but he's fine. We're both fine."

"I don't mean the home thing. I mean something else."

I hadn't meant to tell her, not like this, but it suddenly seemed the natural thing to do.

"What is it?" said Ellie. "Has something happened?"

"He's thinking of leaving college, of jacking it all in to be a stand-up comedian."

"You're joking!"

I laughed.

"That's almost very funny," I said, "but I'm being serious, I'm afraid."

"But why?"

I shook my head and took Ellie through a re-run of my Oxford conversation. Ellie shook her head throughout as though she didn't quite believe it.

"What can I do?" she said when I had finished. "I mean, is there anything I could do?"

"You could talk to him, I suppose," I said.

"What should I say, though? I mean, should I let him know that you've told me?"

"Just say you're worried about him and that you get the sense that he hasn't quite settled and see what he says."

"And what if he doesn't mention it?"

"Then leave it."

Ellie threw her hands up in the air, as if everything had become too much.

"This is brilliant, isn't it? As if I haven't got enough on my plate!"

Then the front door opened and Ellie's housemates came in. Soon the three of them were in girlish conversation and I was a casual eavesdropper trying to piece together from the crumbs of their conversation what my daughter's student life was actually like. And as the three of them spoke, I found myself looking at Ellie's friends in exactly the way I had looked at the girls in Danny's room just weeks before. Quite where this had come from and quite where it was likely to go I had no idea, but it seemed entirely and unnervingly inappropriate and I was pleased when the sound of the door bell snapped me out of it.

At first I didn't recognise the man's voice in the hall. Then, as it came closer to the kitchen, I realised that I did. And when he walked in behind Ellie my fears were confirmed.

There, standing beside Ellie in a way that suggested they were back on fully intimate terms, was Wiggy. He beamed at me.

"Mr Matthews!" he said offering me his hand.

"Wiggy," I said, trying to keep it polite but failing to convey any enthusiasm. "What a surprise."

Ellie had said nothing, but I could see from the way she looked at me, as Wiggy sat down at the table and made himself comfortable, that she felt guilty. After all that fuss of separation, after all that barely suppressed glee on behalf of her parents that she and the awful Wiggy had, at last, decided to go their separate ways, here they were back together.

Was this her way of getting revenge?

"So, how are you?" said Wiggy, fixing me with a huge, smug grin.

I could have told him exactly how I was at that particular moment, that I was horrified to see him again, and even more horrified to think that he might have got back together with my daughter.

"I'm fine," I said coolly, catching Ellie's eye and sensing her reluctance to catch mine. "How are things with you?"

The last thing in the world I wanted to hear was how things were with Wiggy, but some politeness reflex made the words come out instinctively.

"Good," said Wiggy. "Things are good."

I bet they're good. You're back in bed with my daughter, that's why they're good.

"Well," I said getting up from my seat, "Maybe I'll catch up with you later. We're heading out for lunch, aren't we Ellie?"

I looked at Ellie who looked from me to Wiggy and then back again. For one horrible moment I thought she was going to ask if Wiggy could come with us too, but she shot him a see-you-later smile that made me even more convinced that they were an item again, and followed me to the front door.

"See you later Mr Matthews," said Wiggy, as he settled into a sofa and flicked on the TV. "I'll probably be here when you get back."

I had no doubt that he would. Daytime TV, a big fat joint and a little snooze. Studying philosophy was tough.

All through lunch we avoided certain subjects. Neither of us wanted to say too much about Sarah's walk-out and her shacking-up with Colin, and I certainly didn't want to start a conversation about Wiggy's return. Ellie avoided him too, so we spent some time talking about Danny's plans – both the stand-up and drop-out variety – before turning to Ellie herself. But even when we were talking about her she still seemed guarded. She didn't want to talk about finals (apart from needing reassurance that she was doing enough work and that it didn't matter what she ended up with) and she certainly didn't want to talk about jobs and careers and prospects.

It soon became clear that what she wanted to do was talk about Wiggy or, more specifically, to leave the restaurant as soon as possible and get back to Wiggy. I didn't want to do either, so I just let things drift along in the way all our recent conversations had seemed to, with both of us polite and pleasant, but neither of us talking about what we really wanted to.

After lunch we wandered around town long enough for Ellie to get me to buy her what she called 'essentials' but what seemed to me to be anything but, and then headed back to the house. As expected, Wiggy was slumped in front of the TV, looking as though he hadn't moved since we left.

I sat in a chair beside him and half-raised my hand in greeting, hoping he wouldn't take it as an invitation to engage in conversation. He did.

"Good lunch?" he said in his middle-class estuarised vowels.

I had forgotten how much they grated.

"Yeah," I said, "very nice."

"Where did you go?"

"Oh, I can't remember the name. Somewhere near the centre, I think."

"It was Pollyanna's!" Ellie called from the kitchen.

"Nice one," said Wiggy. "We like going there, don't we?" He called into the kitchen as if he were some sitcom husband addressing his wife. "And it's right next door to where I play pool. Do you play at all, Mr Matthews?"

I had forgotten how the way he called me that irritated. It was that public school politeness lurking below the affected urban chic that did it. Every time I heard him call me Mr Matthews I wanted to scream, to take him by his dreadlocks, tweak one of his piercings, and shout, "You're not real, you fucking tosser. You're not real and you're shagging my daughter!"

So far, luckily, I had resisted the urge.

"Pool?" I said. "I like pool. Snooker's more my game, but I don't mind a game of pool now and then."

Wiggy sat up in his chair, unusually animated. "That's cool," he said. "Tell you what – why don't you come down and have a game some time?"

It took a second or two to realise exactly what Wiggy's words constituted.

"Sorry?" I said.

"I said come down and have a game some time."

An Invitation.

I hesitated, momentarily tempted to make Wiggy the reason I gave up on the whole thing. And then the words were out.

"Do you know what?" I said. "I'd love to."

"What? Really?" Wiggy was now sitting up in his chair, his face a mixture of wonder and disbelief, as if I had just provided some blinding insight unafforded by two years studying philosophy. "That's cool," he said, "that's really cool! Ellie! Ellie!"

"What is it?" said Ellie, coming in with a tray of coffees.

"Your Dad's just said he'll give me a game of pool! How cool is that?"

First he slept with my daughter, now he thought I was cool. Things were getting worse.

"Really?" said Ellie, looking from me to Wiggy as if she were the victim of some kind of practical joke. She knew I didn't like Wiggy. She had seen her parents' unconcealed joy when they had split up and she had seen my face fall earlier that day when I saw that Wiggy was back on the scene. Yet here I was offering him a game of pool.

"I didn't know you played pool, Dad."

"Well, I don't very often," I said. "Or at least I haven't for some time, but I'll give it a go."

"That's great," said Wiggy, smiling at me and chewing excitedly on one of his dreadlocks. "How long are you down for?"

"Well, as it happens I'm staying for the evening. I'm going to the theatre."

"The theatre?" said Ellie. "You didn't tell me. What are you going to see?"

"Death of a Salesman."

Ellie looked puzzled.

"Why do you want to see that?"

Wiggy turned to her and said, "You mean apart from the fact that it's one of the seminal works of twentieth century drama, a powerful, searing and moving indictment of American capitalism?"

First Wiggy thought I was cool and now he was sounding clever. I preferred him slumped in front of the telly.

"Well obviously," said Ellie, "but apart from that?"

"I know someone who's in it," I said. "She's a neighbour."

"A neighbour. Which one?"

"Maggie, she lives opposite."

I've slept with her several times, and she has very strange tastes. Kinky. If I'd said it, I would doubtless have seemed even more cool to Wiggy.

What I did say was, "She's playing Linda Loman."

Ellie nodded.

"So what are you doing before the theatre, then?"

I shrugged.

"I was going to let you get on with it. I'll go for a stroll, see the city."

"That's great then," said Wiggy. "We can have a game this evening!"

"Well, OK, then," I said, "as long as I'm not taking you away from anything."

Like my daughter, for example.

"Who? Me?" said Wiggy. "You're joking!"

"If you mean work, Dad, I wouldn't worry. Wiggy doesn't need to, he'll get a first through sheer brilliance. I have to study, but he can do it playing pool every evening."

"Right," said Wiggy, who had pulled a piece of paper out of his jacket pocket and was drawing a map, "here it is, The Chalk Tip. Six o'clock all right? It's close to the theatre so we should have time for a good session."

He held the map towards me.

"And how about you?" I said, taking the map and turning to Ellie. "Are you coming?"

"I'm fine here," she said, "I'll leave you two boys to it."

I kissed Ellie goodbye and headed into town, trying to remind myself how to play pool and bracing myself for an evening of questionable bonding.

***

Maggie had left the ticket for me at the box office. There was a note with it:

> *Rick - so pleased you could make it. Hope you enjoy it. Meet me at the stage door afterwards and come out for a drink. Any problem - my mobile is 07704987286. See you later.*

It was hardly a surprise. The chances of my getting out of Bristol without receiving another Invitation from Maggie were as strong as the prospects of my beating Wiggy at pool. I had anticipated as much and I had come prepared, knowing that I might very well not be able to head back to London until the next morning, but I didn't anticipate what might happen with any real enthusiasm.

Whether it was Maggie's strange appetite for sexual dramatics or whether it was a nagging feeling of doubt and guilt, a sense that I was in some way betraying Sarah, I knew that if the Invitation came (and I was determined that I would not initiate it – nothing would happen that evening unless a clear, unambiguous Invitation made it impossible to avoid it) I would definitely reach for one of my Invitation strategies.

It was something I found myself doing more and more. It wasn't cheating – I was clear about that – but it may well have been a reflection of the fact that as I neared the mid-year mark of No Regrets I was getting a little tired of the thrill. I no longer approached it with the youthful enthusiasm of the convert, no longer threw myself at the mercy of the god of Invitation with such willingness and wonder. It was a little like losing my religion.

Faced now with an evening of three invitations, (pool with Wiggy, *Death of a Salesman*, and a drink with Maggie and what it might lead to) I was already working out how best to deal with them.

I took out my phone and punched in Maggie's number.

"Maggie, it's Rick."

"Rick, where are you? Are you here?"

"I'm in the car on my way down. I was ringing to ask a favour."

"You're still coming, aren't you?"

"Yes I'm still coming, but I was just wondering if you could do one simple thing for me. Could you give me a call at about six-thirty on this number?"

"Do I get any explanation?" she asked.

"I'll give you one later," I said.

She laughed.

"I bet you will," she said, and hung up.

20

The Chalk Tip was not the kind of place I would normally frequent. It wasn't just that I was the oldest person there by about twenty-five years or one of the only two white men (Wiggy was the other) – it was more the fact that I was crap at pool. I hadn't lied when I told Wiggy that I used to play, but I should, perhaps, have made it clearer at the outset that I was never actually very good. Maybe then he wouldn't have extended An Invitation and maybe I wouldn't have ended up losing two games in very quick succession – in fact, in about four minutes. I broke and Wiggy cleared the table. Then Wiggy broke, I cocked up my shot and Wiggy cleared the table again.

"You're cool, you know that?" said Wiggy as he racked up the balls for the third game. "When I asked you for a game I was kind of joking. I didn't expect you to say yes."

"Oh well," I said, trying to adjust to being thought cool by a boy I still thought was a complete tosser, "I like surprising people."

"Yeah," said Wiggy, "so do I."

"I bet you do," I said. "You certainly gave me quite a surprise today when you walked in."

I hadn't meant to say anything like it. I had vowed to myself as I nervously entered the Chalk Tip to avoid any conversation about anything serious, and at all costs to avoid talking about Wiggy's relationship with my daughter.

"Yeah," said Wiggy, calmly potting another stripe, "and why was that then?"

I couldn't back out now. I couldn't pretend that he had surprised me for any other reason than the fact that he was there and I had thought it was all over.

"I just thought that you and Ellie…"

"You thought it was all over between us?"

I shrugged.

"Well, I suppose I did think that…"

"Mr Matthews." I flinched. "I'm back with Ellie because she called me up and said she wanted to see me and things have kind of developed from there." He paused for breath while he struck another stripe neatly into a centre pocket. "I'm sure I don't need to tell you that she's had a lot to deal with recently."

He looked up from his cue and it suddenly all seemed my fault: my fault that Sarah walked out; my fault that Ellie was back together with Wiggy; my fault that Danny wanted to go to Clown College.

Just then the phone rang, bang on cue.

"Hallo?" I said.

"As requested," said Maggie.

"Really?" I said, trying to sound genuinely surprised.

"What?" said Maggie. "What are you talking about?"

"Oh no!" I said, raising my eyebrows at Wiggy who stopped clearing the table and looked at me, hearing the concern in my voice.

Maggie's voice came down the line. "What's going on Rick?"

"That's terrible," I said.

"What's terrible?" said Maggie.

"I'd better come. I'll be right back."

Maggie raised her voice. "Rick, what the fuck are you talking about?"

"OK," I said. "I'm on my way."

I hung up and turned to Wiggy.

"Has something happened?" he asked.

"It has," I said, "and I'm really sorry, but I'm going to have to go."

"That's a shame," he said, "we've only just started. You haven't even warmed up."

I shrugged.

"I think I'm about as warm as I'll ever be and I really must go."

"What is it? What's happened?"

"It's my son," I said. "I have to get back."

"A shame. You'll miss the theatre."

I shook his hand.

"I guess so," I said, "but good to see you again, Wiggy."

And with that I headed for the Chalk Tip door, no closer to seeing anything to be pleased about in Wiggy's unexpected return, sad that I had been unable to sink more than one ball in the entire session, but pleased to at least have honoured his Invitation.

As I walked towards the centre of town, though, I began to wonder whether arranging Maggie's phone call like that had been a legitimate strategy. It may not, technically, have been against anything in my commitment to the Invitation game but was it, and other strategies like it, strictly in its spirit? Was it a sign that I was going soft, going down the Jerry route of wanting the whole thing on my terms? Maybe I was cheating? Maybe I was finding ways of ducking out? Maybe I was losing my nerve?

Perhaps it was time to reassert myself, to say to myself that I would accept the next Invitation immediately and without hesitation.

It was still too early for the theatre so I decided to walk round the city. Despite my frequent visits, it was still a place I didn't know too well and I soon found myself lost among unfamiliar back streets.

At first I didn't hear him and walked straight ahead.

"Hey man!"

I turned and saw him walk towards me.

"Hey man. Where you going?"

"Just walking," I said.

"You need anything?" he said.

I looked at him, a man in a leather jacket who, unlike me, looked as though he knew his way around. I looked at the street I was in, at the signs in the windows, at the men and women standing on the corners and realized I had walked a little too far.

I wasn't sure that the term red light district was still used, but if Bristol had one I had definitely wandered into it.

The man was still following me.

"You look like a man who needs something," he said.

"I'm fine, honest."

I carried on walking, suddenly terrified that he was about to make some kind of Invitation. I felt my new resolve melting.

"Whatever you want I've got it."

"I said I'm OK."

But the man was persistent, keen to offer me his menu.

"You want a girl? I got it. You want anything I got it. Skunk? I got it. E? I got it. Speed? I got it—"

"No really," I said, cutting him off.

I needed to get away before he framed anything as an Invitation, so I turned around and started to walk in the direction I had come.

He followed.

"I got good skunk," he said. "Why don't you come and try some of it?"

"Sorry," I said, "I didn't catch that. What did you say again?" I wanted the words to be different.

"I said come and try some of my skunk."

I stopped and turned to him. "I thought so," I said.

"What about it then?"

"Try some of your skunk?" I said. "I'd love to."

It would have been safer and more sensible to have found a way of avoiding this, to have run away as soon as he started to speak, or to have pretended to be foreign and unable to speak English. This was exactly the kind of situation I needed rescuing from, not a peaceful game of pool with Wiggy.

As I followed the man down a side street I realised just how dangerous a situation I was getting myself into. Anything could happen. He could lead me anywhere and rob me or beat me up. And even if he didn't, the chances were he was going to show me some drugs and possibly get me to try them. It just wasn't my kind of thing. I may have been crap at pool but even that was more my kind of thing than drugs. Apart from the occasional casual joint back at college I had stayed well clear of the stuff, unlike Alex, of course. He had kept up all kinds of habits, and may well have been taking stuff just before he died, but I had always (as so often in my relationship with Alex) decided not to follow his wild ways.

And, from what I read in the papers, the whole thing had changed. The innocent stuff we had dabbled with back in the seventies was nothing, apparently, compared to this thing called skunk. Ten times as strong, and likely to lead to serious mental problems. We'd had a few kids at college who had got into real trouble with it.

These were some of the thoughts running through my head as we headed down a back street and through a door at the side of a Chinese takeaway. As he opened the door I followed him in and he gestured for me to head up the stairs. The place stank. Paint peeled off the walls and as I started to walk up it felt like mounting a scaffold.

This was it. I had no idea what lay up those stairs, no idea where this was likely to lead. Yet this was what the whole thing was about. You go where the Invitation leads.

The man was walking up behind me.

"It's good shit," he said. "You won't regret it."

I turned and saw him reach into his jacket pocket.

This is it, I thought, he's reaching for a knife. Or a gun.

He took his hand out of the pocket and brandished a key, holding it up towards me with raised eyebrows as if we were about to enter Aladdin's cave.

He turned the key and held the door open for me, standing aside and looking furtively down the stairs, as if we might have been followed.

"Go on in," he said.

I paused in the doorway. Anything or anyone could be in that room, and, once in there, who knew what might happen? My imagination raced, and so did my pulse.

"Go on," he said. "Don't be frightened."

Then I heard a voice from inside. "Yeah," it said, "come on in man, ain't nothing to be scared of."

The voice was deep and terrifying. I stepped forward nervously.

Then my mobile rang.

"Dad, is that you?"

"Ellie, what is it?"

"Wiggy rang me. He said you had to cut short the pool because something happened to Danny. He said he didn't know what, but it sounded urgent. Is he OK?"

"What? I don't believe it!"

"Dad? What don't you believe?"

"Really? Where?"

"Dad, what are you talking about?"

"The Police you say?"

"Dad? Are you all right?"

"The Police?" I repeated.

I turned to the man, who had stopped on the stairs at the mention of the word "police"

"Shit!"

I hung up and swivelled to the man behind me. "Let's go!" I said and I ran past him out on to the street.

I didn't stop running until I reached the theatre.

21

I took it easy in the stalls. In fact, I took it so easy that I fell asleep. At one moment Willy Loman was in a restaurant and the next moment Maggie was uttering the final words of the play.

It wasn't just that I had missed most of the emotional, climactic moments of the play, it was that I had missed Maggie's best lines and, as I walked out of the theatre and headed for the stage door, I began to rehearse what I would say about her performance, in particular the parts of her performance I had slept through.

I met her at the stage door where she greeted me with a huge embrace and an extravagant theatrical kiss.

"You were great," I said, "really great."

"Do you mean it?" she said. "Do you really mean it?"

"Fantastic," I said, "moving, powerful and above all intelligent."

"You're so sweet," she said, "I wasn't sure tonight went so well. Maybe it was because I knew you were coming."

"Don't be silly, you were brilliant," I said, "the best Linda Loman I've ever seen."

"Make sure you're around to write my obituary, won't you?"

"My pleasure," I said.

"And now," said Maggie, "I know a great little place where we could have a drink and a bite to eat. You up for that?"

"Of course I am," I said. But I knew it wasn't the truth.

It wasn't that I didn't like Maggie, and it wasn't that I hadn't enjoyed any of what we had got up to, or that I didn't ever want to do any of it again. It was just that it had been a tiring day in all kinds of ways and all I really wanted to do was drive home and get a good night's sleep. So, when we reached the French restaurant round the corner I was already thinking of how to avoid The Invitation.

Throughout the meal, Maggie seemed in good spirits. She spoke about her performance and I did my best to say the right things, treading particularly carefully when she referred, as she did quite frequently, to any of the long section I had slept through.

By the time of coffee, though, her mood had changed. My role up to this point had been very much a supporting one – the attentive and responsive listener. Maggie had spoken mostly about herself and I had been happy to let her deliver her high-spirited, post-show anecdotes, happy to let her take centre stage.

By coffee, though, she seemed to have worn herself out and was far less buoyant, a very different person from the bouncing runner who had charmed me at Harry's drinks on New Year's Day.

"Shall I tell you something, Rick?" she said, leaning close to me across the table. "You might think I'm a happy-go-lucky kind of woman, given what we've done and everything, but underneath it all, you know, I'm really very very sad."

It wasn't what I had expected and it wasn't what I wanted.

"You know what they say about actresses," she said, "how insecure they are, how vulnerable – every word of it is true. I say that because right now, at this very moment, that's exactly how I feel."

She reached across the table and put her hand on my wrist.

"The truth is Rick, I'm lonely. I'm very very lonely and I need some comfort."

Here it was. An Invitation loomed.

"But not that kind of comfort. I need something, I don't know, more permanent, more secure."

"We all do," I said inadequately.

"And the thing is, Rick, I like what we've had. It's been fun and everything, but I think I'm becoming more and more attracted to you and I think what I want is something more – I don't know – regular."

It wasn't what I expected. I had feared an Invitation to more fun and games in costumes and handcuffs, but this all seemed far more serious.

"I'm not sure what you mean," I said.

"Well, when I'm back in Richmond again, I was thinking, rather than have you pop over every now and then and rather than us have this very casual thing – and don't get me wrong it's been a very fun casual thing – maybe you could…"

Alarm bells rang in my head. If I was reading this correctly the invitation that was about to be offered was more serious than any I had been offered so far, far more binding than fluffy handcuffs. Maggie was about to ask me to move in with her.

This was where she was heading and the chances were that whatever words came out of her mouth, however she chose to phrase it, it was likely to sound like An Invitation.

"Maybe you could… I don't know, maybe it's a silly thing to ask and I really don't mind if you say no. I really don't mind at all."

I needed to move quickly.

I looked round the table. A half-full glass of wine, and two cups of coffee sat between us.

"Please," I said, leaning forward, and reaching my hand out as if about to touch her gently and reassuringly on the arm, "just ask."

Then, as my hand moved across, I slipped off my chair towards the floor. As I fell the hand hit my coffee cup, turning it over, and spilling its steaming contents all over the tablecloth.

Maggie shrieked as I crashed to the floor. Then she loomed above me, full of concern, and waiters rushed to join her.

"Rick," said Maggie, "are you OK?"

I hauled myself up quickly.

"I'm fine. I just caught my shoe on the table leg."

"Are you sure?" said Maggie. "You didn't black out at all?"

"No, I'm fine, honestly."

"How much have you had to drink?" asked Maggie.

"A couple of glasses of wine. It's not that."

Maggie shook her head in a mixture of disapproval and disbelief.

"You should get it checked out. You never know."

"I caught my shoe, that's all," I said. "Look." I stood up and pretended to catch my shoe in the carpet to show exactly how I had fallen, and then turned to the waiter. "I'm terribly sorry about the coffee."

"No problem, sir." He started to mop it up. "No problem at all."

I asked him to bring the bill and then looked at my watch.

“I think I’d better be heading back,” I said. “It’s getting late, and...”

“But you can’t drive back like this,” said Maggie.

“I just fell off my chair,” I said. “It was nothing more than a tumble.”

I knew I had to make my getaway quickly.

If I didn’t do something else she might remember what she was about to say or she might invite me to spend the night with her. And if she asked me back to her place she was bound, at some stage, to get back to the invitation that was forming on her lips before I took action to prevent it.

I needed something else

“Shit!” I said, checking my pockets dramatically. “Shit! Shit! Shit!”

“What is it?” said Maggie

“I’ve left something at Ellie’s. Something important.”

“Won’t it wait? You could pick it up tomorrow morning.”

“No, I need to get it back tonight – I have to get it to someone tomorrow morning.”

“Why’s it so important?”

“It’s something she wants me to give to Sarah,” I said, congratulating myself on such a smart move. Family stuff never needs elaboration.

“But couldn’t you stay with—”

“No, no, it has to be tonight.” I cut across her quickly, sensing what she was about to say.

I leaned towards Maggie and gave her a peck on the cheek.

“I really must go,” I said. “I really must. Let me know what the bill is. I’ll settle it when you’re back. And well done, by the way, you were great. I had no idea I’d left it at hers and I really do need it. It’s urgent.”

Maggie looked baffled as I turned away.

As I walked towards the door I heard her call behind me.

“What I was going to say before you fell over, Rick, was would you...”

Oh no. She had remembered. And she was about to utter The Invitation. Surely not. Not in a loud voice, shouting to me as I left a restaurant? Maybe I should run out before she could finish?

“Would you come running again?”

Had I misheard?

"Come running with me again. I really enjoyed it."

I turned and walked back to her.

"Did you say would I come running with you again?"

"Yes, when I'm back. Come down to the runners, I enjoyed it."

I smiled.

"Of course I will."

"That's great," she said, "and Rick? I'm sorry about tonight."

"What are you sorry about?"

"That you've had to go. I would have asked you back to my place, but—"

"That's fine."

"It's just that it's all a little tiring. But I'll be back soon, and then—"

"Great," I said, heading out of the restaurant again, "I'll see you then."

Never had I faced the prospect of a drive back up the M4 with a greater sense of relief.

22

It was a meeting and a conversation I had been meaning to have for some time. And it was one I had imagined turning out in different ways. The best possible version was the one in which Colin threw himself at my feet, asking forgiveness, begging mercy and apologizing for having so spectacularly fucked up my life. The worst version was the one in which I broke his nose as soon as I saw him, spitting on his face, and marching out of the pub, pointing my finger at the other customers saying "And the same happens for anyone else round here who fucks with my wife." Or maybe that was the best version.

"Cheers!" said Colin.

It seemed an inappropriate gesture, but I breathed in deeply and joined him in it.

"Yeah," I said, "cheers."

Then we both leaned back in our chairs, Colin raising his eyebrows as if waiting for me to start. It was like some kind of interview.

"Colin," I said, "I thought we should get together to have a talk about what's been going on."

"Sure," he said, "I know it must have been very difficult for you."

A punch seemed seconds away.

"Yeah, well maybe it has," I said, "but I just thought I'd ask you a few questions."

"Go ahead."

"OK," I said, "let's start with that trip to the theatre, shall we?"

"*Death of a Salesman* What did you make of it?"

"I'm not here to discuss what we thought of the play. I'm here to discuss what you were doing there. You were with some woman."

"Yeah, Kim, it was her idea. Theatre's not really my kind of thing, or at least not that kind of theatre, but Kim wanted to go, so..."

"So you weren't with Sarah."

"No"

"Did Sarah know?"

"I think so. I think I mentioned it."

He thought he *mentioned* it?

"It just seemed to me – and I may have got this wrong – but it seemed to me as if you and this Kim were on quite intimate terms that evening."

At least he now had the decency to blush.

"Oh dear," he said, "was it that obvious?"

I nodded. "I'm afraid it was, yes, and when I saw it I have to admit I was more than a little shocked."

"Shocked? Well, I can see how the theatre might not be the kind of place where you should do that kind of thing, but you know how it is."

I couldn't see a wink, but one was clearly implied.

"My question is – " I paused and steadied myself. "My question is did Sarah know, and if she did, what did she think of it?"

Colin shrugged as if he couldn't see what all the fuss was about.

"Oh Sarah doesn't mind, honestly – she doesn't mind at all. We have this understanding, you see."

"Understanding? What kind of understanding?"

"Well, when she moved in we said we didn't need to tell each other what we were up to. We should just get on with it. Come and go as we please."

I tried to take it in. My wife had left me to move into an open relationship with a man called Colin. She had been sleeping with him while we were still together, and she had made a decision to leave me and move in with him on the basis that he could carry on sleeping with whoever else he wanted to.

I looked closely at Colin. He may have been handsome, he may have been a little bit younger than me, and he may have been considerably more in shape, but surely there was more to sexual attraction than that?

"Anyway," he said, "it didn't work out with Kim. I'd hoped it would, but there you go."

There you go? Was there no shame, no shred of decency in the man?

"The thing is, Colin, I'm a little worried about Sarah."

The more I thought about it, the more I could see why Sarah had been so desperate to come back. How could anyone survive in such a set-up?

"I think," I said, "that she's not very happy."

"I know," said Colin, "it's not been easy for her, has it? When she asked to move in I knew things were pretty bad and I guess they haven't got much better since."

"Hang on – she asked to move in with you? It was her idea?"

"Initially, yes, but as soon as she said it, we knew that it made sense."

Maybe now was the moment to tell him that she had asked to come back, that she had admitted the error of her ways, that she thought the whole thing with Colin had been a miserable mistake.

That would sort him out, that would wipe the smug we-have-an-open-relationship grin off his handsome face.

Or maybe now was the time to hit him.

"So let's get this straight," I said, "Sarah knew about you and Kim?"

"I think so."

"And she knows about any other women you… see." I chose the word carefully.

Colin nodded.

"I tell her. Sometimes I ask her advice as well, she's very good at that."

"And Sarah's happy with that?"

"I think so."

"But overall you'd agree with me that she is not in a very good state, emotionally."

"It's been tough for her. Just like it must have been tough for you, I guess."

I felt my fist tighten.

"And have you ever thought that her unhappiness might in some way be linked to the fact that you are sloping off to the theatre with other women? More than that, that you are actually telling her and asking her advice?"

Colin looked bewildered, as if the thought had never come close to him.

"You mean," he said, "that she might be jealous?" He laughed. "You really think so?"

These open-relationship guys clearly lived on another planet.

"Look", I said, worried that a punch was imminent and standing up to go, "I've got to dash. And I'm glad we had this chat."

"Do you have to go so soon?" said Colin. "I was enjoying it. It's good to talk about these things."

For you it might be, pal.

"I must. But before I go, can I just say one thing."

I leaned down close to his face. Colin leaned back, alarmed by my proximity.

"Be careful, she's still my wife."

"I know that, Rick. I know that."

"And she may have walked out on me, but I still care for her. I care for her a lot."

"Sure."

"And if you do anything more to harm her or upset her..."

Colin held up his hand.

"Hang on," he said. "I haven't upset her, and I certainly haven't harmed her."

"Well keep it that way," I said, "or I might do something I'll regret."

I wasn't sure what the something might be, but I had no doubt about the regret part.

"Don't worry, Rick, I'll look after her and if there's anything I think you should know, I'll give you a call. How about that?"

He'll give me a call? What kind of call would that be?

"Look after her, OK?"

And with that I marched out of the pub.

***

As I strapped on the padding, stuck on the beard and moustache, checked that my glasses were straight, adjusted my cap and headed for the pub, I reassured myself that it was perfectly reasonable to test out my disguise on Jerry. If a job was worth doing, then it was worth doing well, and when the stakes were as high as these I needed to be sure that I wouldn't be discovered. After all, it wouldn't only be Danny on stage who could spot me in the audience. In all likelihood, his college friends Hayley and Caroline would be there as well. So would Ellie, if she kept her promise to come up from Bristol, and she might decide to bring Wiggy, who was exactly the kind of person I could imagine ruining everything by penetrating my disguise immediately.

Outside the doors of The Red Lion I took a deep breath before pushing them open. Scanning the pub quickly, I saw Jerry sitting by himself at a table between me and the entrance to the gents. His head wasn't buried in a newspaper or a book. He was just staring into space. In fact he was staring straight at me.

Perfect.

I started to walk past him towards the gents. My eyes were fixed on the toilet door as I moved forward but, as I went past Jerry's table, I couldn't resist shooting him a quick sideways glance

His eyes didn't shift.

When I came out of the gents, carrying my disguise in a big sports bag I had brought specifically for this purpose, I walked round the other side of the bar, and approached Jerry's table as if from the side door.

Jerry got up, asked what I was drinking and headed for the bar. He had noticed nothing, and I sat down, flushed with success, more than ever confident that I could make the trip to Oxford with a real chance of not being discovered.

"I'm glad you're here," said Jerry as he carried two pints towards the table, "because I've been longing to tell you what's been happening."

I took the pint, and raised it towards him.

"What do you mean?" I said.

"This invitation thing," he said, "it's amazing."

"So you're still doing it, then?"

He nodded enthusiastically.

"I sure am."

"But you're not doing it properly are you?"

"Well, that's the thing I need to talk about."

"Why? What's happened?"

Jerry took a few seconds, as if gathering himself. "Nothing's happened. Well, not yet at least, but ever since that phone call when you made those ridiculous invitations to prove some kind of point. You know, the invitation to suck your dick and all that—"

He said it loudly, and I turned round to check that no one was listening.

"Well, when I hung up I thought about what you'd said. And I knew it wasn't meant entirely seriously and I knew that you'd said it as some kind of device, some kind of strategy, so in a way I thought it was perfectly OK for me to ignore it. I thought I could treat it as something that wasn't a proper invitation. But then I thought about it, and I realised that you were right."

I gulped.

There was only one prospect more worrying that Jerry doing the thing half-heartedly and that was Jerry doing the thing properly.

"And I thought about all I'd said to you that New Year's Eve and I thought about my life and, yes, I know it all sounds very sad and mid-life crisis, but I thought what the hell."

"But Jerry, I've told you before. You don't need this. You didn't have a problem. You weren't in a fix like me."

"That's what you think. My fix might not have been as obvious as yours, but it was there all right. And then I started thinking about Alex and the way he lived his life and the way my life has been so safe, so predictable..."

"But Alex is dead. You're alive. Which would you prefer?"

"Alex is dead because he was knocked down by a car, not because of the way he lived his life. What I'm trying to say is that I thought about what you said and I thought – fuck it – let's do it properly and see where it leads. You know," he said, with the astonished tone of a man who had made a great discovery, "when

I made that suggestion to you on New Year's Eve, I didn't realize what a fantastic idea it was."

"You don't need to tell me this, Jerry. I know."

"OK, yes, and I know you couldn't see it through. I know you obviously found it all too difficult."

Was this some kind of accusation? Was he delivering some kind of challenge?

"I see," I said, resisting the temptation to tell him that I was still in the middle of it, that I had done this whole thing, from the beginning, with a lot more commitment than him, that I had lied when I told him I had given it up.

"But the reason I wanted to tell you, Rick, is that I'm on it now, and it's proving to be quite a ride."

"Really?" I said. "And where's this ride taken you?"

I listened as Jerry told me, but it all seemed very tame. At first it had been taking up the offer of drinks after work – something he had avoided for the majority of his working life, or at least ever since he married Caroline and the kids came along. And this, it seemed, had set off an invitation trail of the kind I now recognized. Someone in the pub asked him for a game of tennis, then someone had asked him to a concert and then he had been asked to join a local charity. I stopped listening after a while. The nature of the invitations you received was limited by the kind of circles you already moved in. Jerry led a boring life, so the invitations he received tended to be boring as well. Only Jerry could turn something so dangerous, so edgy, so liberating, into something so safe. It was like playing Russian roulette knowing all the barrels were empty.

"That might sound all fairly dull to you," said Jerry draining his pint, "but then something else happened. I'm still trying to find out about Alex, you know. I haven't forgotten."

He hadn't let me forget either. Our phone calls still always contained some reference to his theories.

"I rang up Freddie," said Jerry. "Remember him?"

I nodded.

"We had a good chat and then at the end he asked me if I wanted to come round to some drinks party he was having. So, of course,

I said yes. Anyway, I went to the drinks and there were quite a few Balham people there, including Helen Manson." Jerry winked. Helen Manson had been his first college crush. "And guess what? She asked me out for a drink."

"Helen Manson, eh?"

"Yeah," said Jerry, unable to prevent a sudden blush, "imagine!"

"She knows you're married, does she?"

Jerry shrugged.

"I don't know. That's not the point. The point is I did go out for a drink with her. And it was fantastic. You know when you started you had Maggie. Well, I started and I've got Helen."

"But Jerry," I said, "You can't do this! Is she married?"

"Yes, but she seemed to suggest that things aren't all they could be."

"And does she have kids?"

"Three."

"This is crazy," I said. "You can't do this."

"You did it."

"But it was different for me."

"How? How's it different for you?"

"Because I hadn't done anything wrong. I wasn't betraying anyone. I wasn't fucking up anyone else's marriage, anyone else's family. I was the one who'd been fucked up. Remember?"

Jerry gave a worldly-wise, cynical smile, as if I was a mere apprentice in a game he had been playing all his life.

"And have you," I said, "done anything yet?"

"No," said Jerry, "not yet."

"And did she give you any indication – any invitation?"

"Put it this way," said Jerry, "she'll be at the gaudy and she said that it would be good to be there together. It's money in the bank, Rick, I know it is."

"You can't do it, Jerry. You just can't. You've got a wife. You've got kids. Everything's fine. Don't do it."

"It could happen tomorrow."

"What could?"

"The car. The Skoda in Chiswick High Road that did for Alex, could do for us."

"But it's such a dangerous thing, Jerry, it really is. That's why I stopped."

"I can see why you did. Maybe you didn't have, I don't know, the guts or something, but I'm determined to see this one through. Just watch me."

"OK, then," I said. "How long?"

"What?"

"How long are you going to do it for? Mine was a year and I didn't make it. How long will you do it for?"

Jerry looked baffled and, for a moment, I could see the old lawyer-straightness grappling with a difficult question.

"I don't know," he said.

"But you can't do it forever, can you?"

"Why not?"

I shook my head. This thing had me firmly in its grip, but I liked to think I had, throughout it all, managed to keep my sanity. I wasn't so sure Jerry would be able to do the same.

"And, by the way," he said, "Helen saw Alex a couple of weeks before he died. He was in a restaurant with someone she thought she recognized. But she didn't say who."

"So where does that leave your ideas about Alex then?"

I wasn't particularly interested in his ideas about Alex, but it seemed preferable to his enthusiasm for Invitations and the prospect of adultery.

"I don't know," said Jerry. "But maybe the gaudy will throw something up. As well as Helen that is."

He couldn't keep away from it.

"Don't do it, Jerry," I said, trying one more time to get through to him. I wasn't being judgmental about this, I wasn't occupying any kind of moral high ground or anything, but it did seem as though what he was doing was fundamentally wrong.

"It's not a risk worth taking," I said, "it really isn't. Since Sarah walked out it's been shit – really shit. Living by yourself, working out new relationships with the kids, going through all the doubt, the blame, the anxiety. I just can't believe it's worth it."

"But Sarah obviously did."

"And she regrets it. She asked to come back, remember."

"So why didn't you take her?"

Again the truth crept towards my lips. Again I resisted.

"It's just not right, not yet."

Then I told Jerry what I'd discovered about Colin. He couldn't understand it either, but, newly liberated from his boring years, he gave a good impression of finding open relationships interesting and permissible.

It wasn't long before he was back to talking about Helen Manson and what he hoped would happen at the gaudy.

23

June

Oxford Comics Showcase
Waddell Theatre
Tonight. 8.00 p.m.

Larry Porter
Mary O'Connor
Jim Mundy
Danny Matthews

Come and see Oxford's rising stars
Admission: £4.00.

I stared at my son's name and wondered, not for the first time that evening, what the hell I was doing there.

This is silly. I should turn round, get in my car and drive home.

But then I heard a voice behind me.

"Can I help you sir?"

I turned round to see a porter emerging from the lodge.

"Are you looking for anything?" he said.

I looked at the few students gathered round the notice board and realised he could only be talking to me. So much for my not attracting any attention. And then I realised that there was something I had overlooked completely. In all my efforts to disguise myself visually – the padding, the beard, the moustache, the cap – I had forgotten one crucial factor, one thing that could give me away instantaneously and unintentionally – my voice.

This all ran through my mind in the few seconds it took for the porter to walk out from behind his sliding glass panel to stand by my side.

I looked around again. The chances were that Caroline or Hayley wouldn't recognize me from just my voice, but you couldn't be too sure about these things. I was, after all, a novice in the world of disguise.

"Sorry, sir. Are you all right?"

The porter seemed worried by my delayed response.

I had to say something. And for reasons I still can't quite understand I reached for the first accent that I found in my limited repertoire. Irish.

Begorrah, Bejaysus. Jesus Mary and Joseph.

"I'm just looking for the comedy," I said in my best brogue.

I may not have sounded like the real thing and my voice, even within that very short sentence, may have travelled through several different Irish regions, but what came out of my mouth sure as hell didn't sound like me and, in that respect, wasn't a bad result.

I would be Irish for the evening.

Emboldened by the prospect and keen to get away from the porter, I gave no more thought to the idea of going home, and, head down, followed his directions and walked through several arches to the ugly sixties construction that housed the college bar and theatre.

Keeping an eye out for Ellie, and for Caroline and Hayley, I bought my ticket and walked in. I was deliberately early, figuring that it would be easier to be sitting at the back of a theatre when others came in than it would be to walk in later to an already-full auditorium, when all eyes would be turned in my direction.

I headed up towards the back of the quarter-full theatre and chose a seat in the corner. It felt secure and, as I waited for the show to start, I opened the programme and, casting the occasional wary glance at new arrivals, I started to read:

Danny Matthews

First year English student, Danny, has been a regular at open mic sessions through the year and is beginning to build a reputation for himself. That such a reputation should have come from drunkenness and debauchery and throwing up at parties rather than the quality of his comedy act is not, he thinks, a problem. He cites as his influences Bob Dylan and Leonard Cohen ("both much funnier than they're ever given credit for"), Shakespeare ("my goldfish, not the playwright") and God ("now there's a guy with a real sense of humour"). His act "They fuck you up…" shares its title with the opening line of a Larkin poem, but, he claims, "I have no problem with stealing someone else's gags. As long as they're good."

I looked up from the programme as Caroline and Hayley came through the door. I hunched my shoulders and turned my head towards the wall, sneaking occasional glances out of the corner of my eye as I sensed them walking up the narrow aisle looking for a seat. At one stage they stopped and looked in my direction as Hayley pointed at the seats beside me, but they didn't seem to recognise me, and I turned back with relief to the programme notes as they headed for a pair of seats on the other side of the aisle.

With a minute to go before the show's start there was still no sign of Ellie and I started to relax a little, thinking that there would be one fewer person who could potentially see through my disguise. Just as I thought this, she rushed in, holding on to Wiggy's arm, and looked up towards the back of the theatre, searching for an empty seat.

With a shudder of horror I realised that one of the few places where there were still spare seats was in my row. Ellie noticed them, pointed in my direction and led Wiggy up the steps.

I put my bag on the chair beside me, and looked hard at the programme as they came into the row. I kept my head down, hoping that they would choose the two vacant seats close to the aisle, but I heard them moving along the row, Ellie offering her apologies to the two students who had to stand up to let her pass.

Then I heard her voice.

"Excuse me," she said, "is anyone sitting there?"

I froze.

She wanted me to move my bag.

If I were to behave normally, I would turn to her, smile, and say, "No that's fine", move my bag and turn back to my programme as they sat down beside me. What I actually did was turn to her without raising my face, grunt something in an Irish accent which I hoped sounded like "No that's fine", and went back to reading the programme, checking that my padding was in place, giving my beard a thoughtful reflective stroke just to check it wasn't about to fall off, making sure my glasses were firmly hooked behind my ears, and subtly adjusting my baseball cap.

I also shrank closer to the wall.

I didn't want to listen but, much as I tried to concentrate on something else or to block my ears, there was no way I could avoid hearing what was being said beside me. For the first time ever I wished I had an iPod.

"This better be good," said Ellie, "and I hope he appreciates it."

"It'll be fine," said Wiggy, "he sounds like he's a funny guy."

"Yeah," said Ellie, "but there's a difference between telling a few gags in the pub and doing it on stage."

And then they went silent for a while. I shot a quick look out of the corner of the glasses, and my fears were confirmed.

They were snogging.

No law against it of course. Anyone is allowed to kiss and canoodle in public, as Colin had proved so well at The Lyric, and they, of course, had no idea that they were sitting next to one of their parents. But, even so, it was unnerving. I was a tolerant, liberal parent, well aware that my children were leading active sexual lives, but there were limits, and, as Ellie and Wiggy continued their intimacy beside me, I buried my head in the programme, praying for the show to begin, almost willing Larry Porter onto the stage, and consoling myself with the thought that hearing the silence of their snogging might actually be better than hearing them talk.

When Larry came on I clapped with relief.

"Good evening," he said, strolling to the mike and lifting it off its stand, "and welcome. I was on my way here tonight, and I went past one of those charity muggers. 'Spare a minute for cancer research?' he said. 'Yeah,' I said, 'won't get much done in a minute though, will you?' Chuggers, that's what they're called, isn't it. It's a coinage, a new word, though I don't see myself why we need one. I can think of plenty of old words that describe them even better, like wankers."

And so it went on. Charity workers, teachers, football pundits – they all came under the comic scrutiny of Larry Porter. I even almost laughed a couple of times. Mary O'Connor bounced on with a question.

"Do you all want to hear the funniest joke in the world?" No response. "Come on, say yes if you do, or at least put your hand up. I know this is Oxford but there's no need to be so restrained." Some muted cries of "yes" and a few raised hands followed.

"OK," said Mary, "Here it is. Two New Jersey hunters are out in the woods when one of them collapses. He doesn't seem to be breathing and his eyes are glazed. The other guy whips out his phone and calls the emergency services. He gasps, 'My friend is dead. What can I do?' The operator says, 'Calm down. I can help. First let's make sure he's dead.' There is silence. Then a shot is heard. Back on the phone the guy says 'OK, now what?'"

Mary looked expectantly into the audience. There was some laughter. "So," she said, "funny, but not that funny, eh? But that, according to research, is the world's funniest joke, and here are the reasons why…"

Mary O'Connor then went on to explain the theories of comedy that made the New Jersey hunter joke such a winner. It was a brave act, a comedy act about comedy itself, with jokes about jokes and the kind of low-key self-referential irony that undergraduates might find funny. This group, though, didn't, and the audience greeted most of the act with a silence which, for the sake of Danny, I hoped was sympathetic but feared was coldly critical.

Jim Mundy was a different thing altogether.

"Funny things words, aren't they? What are they after all? Just breath? So if I tell you to fuck off and you get angry all I have to say is 'pardon me for breathing'. But if they're just breathing, why are they so offensive? See, when I was young I was taught this phrase 'Sticks and stones may break my bones but words will never hurt me'. But you never hear that any more do you. Of all the black people I've called nigger not one of them has ever come back at me with that one. Someone should teach it to them. But they're funny these little sayings aren't they? You know these little mottos we're taught. Here's a couple I like: 'Slow but steady wins the race' – didn't work for me. As advised, I took it slow, very slow. And I took it steady, very steady. And I came last every time. And here's another one: 'More haste, less speed'. I never got that one until I started drugs."

Jim was going down well, and I feared for Danny having to follow him, but I soon developed a different fear when I realised, halfway into his isn't-language-funny act that a girl in the front row kept looking at me.

She wasn't doing it in an obvious way, just the occasional turn of the head after a joke and when the audience was laughing. At first I thought she was looking elsewhere – maybe she knew Ellie or Wiggy or someone else who sitting close to me – but the more she did it the more I realised she was definitely looking in my direction. I shrank further into the wall.

Jim finished to great applause. Even Ellie and Wiggy had taken their hands off each other and were clapping loudly.

As we waited for Danny to take the stage I tried to tune in to Ellie's conversation, but I couldn't make much of it out, hearing nothing decipherable between the string of "yeahs" and "likes". Their intimacy and togetherness, though, was clear. Any futile hope I may have entertained that Wiggy was back with Ellie merely as a friend, or some kind of platonic, emotional support, had been firmly dashed.

I looked down towards the girl at the front, who looked back at me. This time she seemed to give me a smile and a half-wave.

I turned behind me, but there was only wall. Unless she was badly cross-eyed she was definitely waving at me. It unnerved me. Did she somehow know who I was? How could she, if I was in disguise? Or maybe she had rumbled my disguise? Or maybe she was singling me out for the special "oldest in the audience" award?

Whatever it was, there was nothing she could do until after Danny's act and there was always the chance that, as the theatre emptied, I could slip away unnoticed before she reached me.

"Good evening everyone, I'm Danny Matthews."

My stomach tightened with nerves, and I was sitting beside Sarah at his first Nativity play, watching him make a nervous entrance as one of the three shepherds. How things had changed. He had moved from supporting role to centre stage and I had moved from one of a loving couple to a single parent in disguise, sitting undetected beside his snogging daughter and her boyfriend. The circumstances may have been absurdly different, but that feeling of parental pride, that fearful nervousness, that sense of *responsibility* seemed just the same.

"Have you ever looked at your parents and said to yourself – 'so you're to blame?'"

Danny took the mic off the stand and walked round the stage with a confident swagger.

"Because when you think about it, they are to blame, aren't they? If it weren't for them you wouldn't be here. If it wasn't for them you wouldn't be pointing at them saying 'so you're to blame'. And the whole thing is so fucking random. I mean who could possibly devise a system where you decide to have a kid and you have no idea what you're going to have. It could be male or it could be female. It could be clever, could be thick. It could be pretty, could be ugly, and despite all the advances in technology, despite all this test-tube stuff, it's still pretty much the same. I mean we talk about designer babies, but who are we kidding? Forget designer babies, babies with a good label. We haven't even got as far as Tesco or Sainsbury babies, let alone Versace. Parents don't know what kids they're getting and kids certainly have no control over the parents they end up with. So what I propose is not designer babies, not even Primark Babies, but eBay babies. No hang on, let's make it eBay families. A huge cyberspace family swap. You put up your kids for auction, you put up your parents for auction. You put up their photos, and start an auction. A bit free market perhaps, and I've no doubt that the kid who's advertised as 'Slightly damaged, three ASBOs,' will probably not go for as much as others, but there you go, at least everyone will know what they're getting. You see, the government's missing a trick here. Not only would it make the world a happier place because everyone would end up with kids and parents they wanted – or at least if they didn't want them they'd have no one to blame but themselves if they made a bad choice, and then they could always trade them again later if they got fed up with them – but if you gave a bit of your profit to the government everyone would benefit. Better schools, better hospitals, better transport, and happy fucking families!"

I sat rigid in my seat. I couldn't hear whether or not the audience was laughing. I felt numb all over. Everything I saw was through tissue paper. Everything I heard was through cotton wool. All I could see was my son on stage and all I could hear were his words about children and parents.

There was no doubt about it – he was talking about me.

"Of course," said Danny, "it's not an entirely original idea of mine, this eBay family fortunes thing. Jonathan Swift had the idea of selling babies as food in his wonderful, fantastic, satirical work *A Modest Proposal*, but my idea is a little more environmentally friendly, a little less savage if you like. It's a kind of green idea, if you like. You don't eat them, you recycle them."

I snuck a look at Ellie. She was laughing, and so was Wiggy. I still felt numb, unable to decide whether or not anything my son was saying was funny.

"But they do fuck you up, don't they, your mum and dad? I don't mean to go too English Literature on you all here, but that line is Philip Larkin's. It goes 'They fuck you up, your mum and dad, they might not mean to but they do. They fill you with the faults they had and add some extra, just for you.' A wise man Larkin. A racist, sexist bigot it turns out but, when it came to parents, he got it spot on. Like, how many of you here have got parents who aren't together? I mean they may be together, in that you might have a mum and dad but it's not the mum and dad who conceived you or they might not be together in that one of them's dead or something. You know what I mean, don't you? Show of hands?"

It seemed that every stand-up comedian drew on the same repertoire of linguistic devices and tricks. One of them was the observational tic of "Have you ever noticed?" followed by some outstanding insight. Another was this "hands up" device. It felt like you were back in primary school.

About a third of the audience had put up their hands. I noticed that Ellie had kept hers down but that Danny, on stage, held his own hand up, while he pretended to count audience response.

"OK," he said, "so all of you will have noticed something else about parents – the way they come out with ridiculous clichés. They do it all the time, of course, but when they split up it's worse than usual. Like, for example, 'We're not going to be living together but we'll still be friends.' Oh yeah? How do they work that one out? We're such good friends, we like each other's company so much that we're going to spend as much time as we can out of each other's way. And these are the people who used to tell you that if you put your tooth under the pillow a tooth fairy would come and take it and leave money. Or 'we need space'. Oh yeah? And why's that? Have you got bigger? Or has the house got smaller? And best of all 'It won't make any difference to you. We both still love you.' Yeah, right. We love you so much that we are going to give you the choice of two places you can be with us! We love you so much that we're never going to be with you together, that's how much we love you. And if you're really lucky one of us might shack up with someone new and then there'll be so many people who love you!

"You see? That's the point. You should put them on eBay – see if anyone else fancies taking them over, starting again with them."

Beside me Ellie was not only laughing – she was nodding her head in agreement. It may have been funny, but it was also true.

I tried to smile but I couldn't. I tried to listen but I couldn't. And I tried to nod my head slowly in appreciation, but I couldn't do that either. I was paralysed with fear and shock. As Danny continued to explore the way I had managed to fuck him up so comprehensively since his birth, all I could think about was how I could get out of the place as quickly as possible.

An early departure was out of the question – it would involve getting up and being noticed not only by Danny (who would, in the tradition of stand-ups make some comment about me – probably, in this case, something like "What's the problem, daddy-o? Can't face a few home truths?") but also by Ellie as I asked her (in my Irish accent) to excuse me as I walked past her and Wiggy and the rest of my row. It would also attract the attention of the girl at the front who, in my numbed state, I hadn't noticed looking at me for some time, but who, I was sure, would say something to me on my way out.

I had to wait until Danny finished. When he did the applause was louder than it had been for Larry. Ellie even whistled, standing up as Danny bowed – not, I think, in an attempt to get the whole audience on their feet, but just to let her brother know she was there.

Then, as the audience started to leave, I stood up. Beside me Ellie and Wiggy were picking up their bags.

"That was, like, great," said Wiggy, "he was really funny, really cool."

"Yeah," said Ellie, "and so true. Just imagine if either of my parents had been here. No wonder he didn't want Dad to come."

"Oh I don't know," said Wiggy, "your Dad seems to have got a sense of humour from somewhere."

I stood beside them trying to exercise it.

"I mean, he came and played pool, didn't he? Maybe he's, like, chilled out a bit about things."

All I wanted to do was get out of the place as quickly as possible.

"Anyway," said Ellie, "let's go and say hello."

They moved towards the end of the row and started to walk down the steps to the exit. As the audience made its way out, I waited until everyone had passed and joined the back of the line, keeping my head down and remembering to stick to my altered walk.

Then, just as I saw the light of the world beyond the theatre, Danny walked in. Ellie threw her arms round him and gave him a big hug while Wiggy stood grinning beside her waiting to offer a congratulatory handshake.

I tried to move past them but they were blocking the way, so I hovered behind, trying to keep my head down as much as possible.

“Well done, Danny,” shrieked Ellie, “you were brilliant! I’d no idea you had it in you.”

“It went OK, then?”

“I was saying to Wiggy, just as well Dad wasn’t here.”

“I know,” laughed Danny, “maybe he can see me when I’ve got a different act.”

I moved forward, trying to squeeze past the three of them.

Then Caroline and Hayley bounced up and joined in the congratulations. There was now a large group between me and the door. I tried to squeeze past it unobtrusively but Wiggy saw me and started to move out of my way, gesturing with his hand to the others to let me pass.

They shifted to the side and I was just going past them, congratulating myself on having accomplished my mission and got through the evening undetected, when I heard a voice behind me.

“Excuse me!”

At first I ignored it and carried on walking towards the door.

“Sorry! Excuse me!”

The voice was louder.

Again I tried not to turn.

Then a hand rested on my shoulder. Not to turn now would only attract more attention.

“Yes?” I said, turning my head slowly and cautiously.

In front of me stood the girl from the front row who had been looking at me throughout the evening. Just behind her stood Ellie, Wiggy, Danny, Caroline and Hayley. They had turned in my direction and Danny, I thought, was looking straight at me.

“Sorry to grab you like this,” said the girl, “but I’m Sophie MacFarlane.”

I smiled. Was I supposed to know her? Was she expecting me to introduce myself?

“We were told you were coming, so I thought I’d just have a word before you went back to London.”

She knew where I lived.

I looked at her blankly. Over her shoulder I could see Danny looking at us, as if he was keen to hear what was being said.

"Why don't you come and have a quick drink in the bar before you go back?" said Sophie, flashing me a smile that in any other circumstances I would have found charming.

I looked at my watch, trying to deny the reality of what I had just heard.

An Invitation.

Sophie looked at me waiting for an answer.

Silence.

"I'd love to," I said, "But…"

But I had forgotten to speak in an Irish accent.

Begorrah. Bejaysus. Jesus, Mary and Joseph.

"I'd love to," I said, my brogue restored, "but I have to catch the next train."

That sounded better.

"That's OK," said Sophie, "It's just that it'd be great to know what you think. I mean, even if you don't want to take it any further I'm sure the acts would like some kind of feedback."

Who did she think I was?

I looked at my watch again. It was definitely An Invitation, but I couldn't accept it. If I had a drink with Sophie I would be hanging around, exposing myself even more to the risk of discovery.

I looked over her shoulder. Danny was still looking towards me.

Had he rumbled the disguise? Maybe my beard and moustache were hanging down. Maybe my padding was showing.

"Just a quick drink," said Sophie.

"OK," I said, "I'll have time for a very swift one."

There, I had done it. I had said yes.

I looked over Sophie's shoulder. Danny had left the group and was walking towards us. He came up to Sophie's side and looked at me with searching eyes.

I was rumbled. I knew it.

Sophie turned to Danny. "Danny," she said, "this is Freddy Price, the man from the BBC."

Was it?

Should I tell her?

Danny stretched a hand out towards me and looked in my eyes.

"Hi," he said.

"Hallo," I said. It was a hello with a limp and a moustache, the most Irish hello ever uttered.

"Hope you enjoyed the show," said Danny, "I'd love to know what you made of it."

"We're going to have a drink in the bar," said Sophie, "so we can get the official BBC Comedy Department view of things."

I was Freddy Price and I worked in the BBC Comedy Department.

"Not that we expect anyone to be snapped up and given their own show immediately," laughed Sophie, "but it's always good to know what the professionals think and it's so good of you to come. When I rang up and asked if you could send anyone I was so pleased when they said they would. I just hope you weren't sneaking out just now because you didn't like any of it."

Sophie laughed nervously and so did I, as I followed her out of the theatre and into the adjoining bar. Behind me followed Danny, Ellie, Wiggy, Caroline and Hayley.

There was no way I could sit down with them all for a drink and not go detected. Danny looked like he already had his suspicions.

I tapped Sophie on the shoulder.

"I just need the loo," I said, "then I'll join you."

"Great," said Sophie, "we'll be at that table."

She pointed to a corner of the bar and I headed off to the loo.

What I needed to do was escape. I had said yes. I had kept faith with my resolution. If I made a getaway now I might not be acting in the spirit of the scheme but I would be OK. I could hold my head up.

I needed time to think, so I sat in the cubicle trying to come up with a plan. I could hear the comings and goings outside, the opening and shutting of the doors, the tinkle of urine, the matey conversations, the running of taps. And all that time I sat on the loo, my head in my hands, wondering, not for the first time that evening, how I had managed to get myself in this mess.

One thing was for certain. If I went into the bar and sat down with Sophie I was more than likely to end up sitting down with my two children, and, good though my disguise was, I had no doubt that I would be recognized.

Although Danny's performance had smacked of absolute confidence and self-belief I knew that he was a troubled soul. His academic future – his whole life in effect – hung in the balance. He had specifically requested that I didn't come to see him perform. So what would he do if he discovered not only that I had, but that I had also gone to such preposterous lengths to deceive him? It didn't bear thinking about.

But what should I do?

The answer was so obvious it amazed me it had taken so long to think of it. Sophie was expecting Freddy Price, the man from the BBC, to come out of the loos and join her for a drink. She was expecting the bearded, moustached, bespectacled, paunchy, Irish man wearing a cap to come out and tell her what he thought of the comic potential of the Oxford University Stand-Up Society.

What she was not expecting to emerge from the loos was Rick Matthews carrying a bundle under his arm. Danny and Sophie weren't expecting it either.

That could be the only explanation for how I got away with it.

I took my cap off, walked out of the loos, kept my face turned away from their gaze, headed straight for the bar exit, ran through the front quad into the road, and sprinted as fast as I could towards Norham Gardens.

Even if they had spotted me, and even if they had taken off after me in pursuit, I doubt whether they would have come close.

All that running had served me well.

24

So that was what my son thought of me.

That was all I could think of as I drove back to London in a cold sweat, terrified that either Danny or Ellie had seen me slope out of the gents, creep along the side of the bar with my head turned to the wall, and sprint like hell towards the college exit. I expected my mobile to ring at any moment and for my whole sorry charade to be exploded by my children shrieking in outrage at my stupidity.

But no phone call came, and I was left for the next couple of weeks to ponder the significance of Danny's act, to come to terms with what he really thought of me and with the fact that he was prepared to share these thoughts with a paying audience in the cause of advancing his comedy career.

Ellie did casually mention her visit to Oxford in one of our phone conversations. I tried to respond in an equally casual manner.

"And what was he like?" I said.

"He was good," said Ellie.

"Lots of laughs?"

"Yeah," said Ellie, "he got quite a few."

"That's great," I said, "and when you say 'good' does that mean good enough to do it – you know – professionally?"

"You mean is it worth him jacking in Oxford to be a stand-up? You know what the answer to that is, Dad."

"Only asking," I said. What I really wanted to know was whether Ellie had noticed anything strange about the bulky, bespectacled, bearded man in the seat next to her. "And what was it about?" I asked

"What do you mean – what was it about? Have you been to any stand-up comedy?"

Well, yes, actually. As it happens I was sitting next to you.

"I just wondered whether there was a theme or anything."

"Look, Dad, all you need to know is that I went and he was good. Much better than the others who were doing it, and Wiggy thought so too."

"I see, so Wiggy went as well, did he?"

As the call descended into the frostiness that always came with a mention of that name, I decided that my presence at the Oxford Comics Showcase had definitely passed undetected.

***

I had no desire to return to Oxford for a very long time, but the gaudy loomed closer, and the closer it came the more Jerry's excitement intensified.

"Can't wait," he said on the phone one evening, "it'll be great."

"I'm not convinced."

"Come on, it'll be fantastic."

"You're only saying that because you think you're going to sleep with Helen Manson."

"Of course I'm not."

"I don't believe you."

"Well, it would be a nice extra, but that's not the only reason. I'm sure we'll find out more about Alex as well."

Whenever he spoke about his Alex theories he had a habit of saying "we", not realising that I had lost all interest in it long ago. Sure I missed him, sure it was sad and unexpected, and sure it had made us all reflect on our own mortality. But I just couldn't see the point in Jerry's obsessive interest. I was more concerned with my own predicament.

As the summer term unfolded, as my own sixth form students went on study leave (i.e. they were excused from lessons on the school's misguided assumption that they would cram in last-minute revision at home), as Ellie's finals loomed and as Danny came closer to his first year exams, I tried to get things back, if not to normal, then at least to a situation where I thought I still had some control of my own life.

I still, though, laid myself prostrate before the god of Invitations. Not one Invitation came my way that I didn't accept: cups of tea with old ladies, stepping into shops to view new ranges of furniture, meetings where I considered the benefits of joining both the Conservative and the Labour parties, evenings where I was sold the advantages of pyramid selling, or the benefits of investing in a time-share property. Quite what all this was doing for, or to, me I had no idea, but I did it anyway, occasionally thinking that I had the whole thing under control, only to be thrown off course by an unexpectedly tricky invitation that made me realise it was still a crazy, dangerous game.

***

When Maggie got back from tour she asked me in for a coffee, but that was all it was. I waited for the Invitation to go upstairs, but it didn't come. I should have been relieved, but there was definitely a part of me that was disappointed. Was I such a bad lover, so unexciting, so undramatic that she didn't want to repeat the experience? Had she gone off me so quickly? Had she met someone else?

Whatever the reason, the only Invitation that came my way was the one she had made in Bristol – the request that I should take up running again.

And so I did. I went down to Richmond Green for the next few Sundays and joined the Runners again. I knew there were risks involved, but I was prepared to meet each of them.

"Hallo," said Big Ron as I trotted up to the group, "fancy seeing you here!"

"Hi Ron," I said, moving away from him to limber up beside Maggie, and thereby avoiding any reference to the Running Mare quiz and The Fist fight.

"Rick!"

I turned and saw Veronica, trotting up towards me, her face twitching in time to her steps.

"I hope you got your medication OK," she said, "I've been worried."

"I have to watch it," I said, "I'm under doctor's orders. Running's OK, but I'm off certain games, if you know what I mean." I gave her a wink and, suddenly realising that she might think I was imitating her facial imbalance, I turned it into a laugh. “So Scrabble’s out, I’m afraid.” I tried as hard as I could to make Scrabble sound like a euphemism for sexual activity, but Veronica didn’t seem to respond, so I moved away, raising my hand in acknowledgement to Andy and Mark safe in the knowledge that their memory of my poor goalkeeping performance was likely to prevent them asking me back to Real Richmond.

I managed to avoid both Ron and Veronica on the run itself, pacing myself to keep far enough ahead of one and far enough behind the other to avoid any further conversation, and I also managed to avoid talking to anyone new. Given that my outings with the Richmond Runners had so far produced sexual invitations from both Maggie and Veronica, I was particularly keen to avoid bumping into any more Richmond Runner women, and it was with a sense of relief that I finished the run and caught up with Maggie.

“How about a coffee,” she said, “at my place?”

***

In Maggie’s kitchen I braced myself again for an Invitation; again it didn’t come.

“Is everything OK?” I asked.

“Fine,” she said. “Some good reviews, and, as tours go, it wasn’t a bad one. I haven’t been flooded with offers, but then I’m used to that.”

“I hope you don’t mind my asking,” I said, “it’s just that...”

I didn’t *want* her Invitation. That was the last thing I needed, and yet there was something worrying about the way the Invitations had just stopped. It wasn’t as though I felt rejected or anything like that, and it wasn’t as though I was being over-sensitive or vulnerable, it just seemed odd. I realised that, in a strange kind of way, I actually cared about her, and was worried that there might be some sort of problem.

“It’s just that,” I repeated, “we used to... you know... and now...”

“Is that what you’re after?” she said. “Like the rest of them?”

“No,” I said, “no, really, not at all. I was just wondering...”

And then she started crying.

At first I didn't notice, but then I saw a small tear creep out of the corner of each eye and, as she reached for a tissue, her shoulders started to shudder.

"Maggie, are you all right?" I said, moving towards her.

"I'm fine," she said, trying to gather herself. "I'm sorry."

"No. I'm sorry," I said. "That's not what I meant, not what I meant at all."

"Don't worry," she said, "I'm used to it. And, yes, you're right. I know I haven't been acting like I did before. I know..." She reached for a euphemism but couldn't find one. "I know we haven't done it recently. I know it's what you expected in Bristol."

"No," I said, "no, I didn't. That was the last thing..." I stopped myself before I made it any worse.

Maggie dabbed at her eyes, straightened up and looked at me. "The thing is, Rick, I want more." More? So I was definitely a disappointment then? "I don't mean more sex. I mean more – more love."

From who? From me?

"What do you mean?" I said.

"What I mean," she said, "is that when I was on tour I was thinking about a lot of things, as you do. I was thinking about you a lot, and how I really enjoyed our time together and how you made me laugh, and how it would be good to have something that was a little more – I don't know – permanent."

What was she about to suggest?

"That's why I wanted you to come running again, so that we could be doing something together. Not just all this wild sex. And so..." She looked up at me again. "I was thinking – you're by yourself, I'm by myself, why don't we...?"

An Invitation was on its way and it didn't look like a good one. She was about to say what I had thought was coming my way in Bristol.

"I mean," she said, "the thing is sometimes it gets a little lonely, and I'm sure it gets lonely for you too, so I was thinking why..."

Why don't I move in with you? Why don't you move in with me?

"I was thinking why don't you move in with me?"

Oh no.

"Are you inviting me to move in with you?"

"Yes."

I paused. It was only a matter of seconds but it seemed like forever.

"You don't want to, do you?" she said, and she started crying again.

"No, I do," I said. "I just need..."

"You need what? Time?"

"Yes. That's exactly what I do need."

"How much?"

"Well, there's no hurry is there?"

Maggie shrugged.

"Look if you don't want to, then just say it. At least we'll know where we stand."

"No," I said," it's not that. I just need to take it in."

She sobbed again. I moved towards her and put a hand on her shoulder.

She looked at me through pools of tears.

"You see, Rick," she said, "I think I've fallen in love with you."

Oh no.

"Take your time by all means, but please don't say no."

No pressure then.

"Yes," I said, "I'll think about it. Just give me time, that's all I ask."

Maggie dabbed at her eyes and smiled.

And then she asked me upstairs.

***

"It may be nothing to do with... with what's happened."

Sarah looked at me across the table.

"Why else, though?" I said, "why else would they get back together?"

"I don't know," said Sarah, "Maybe they..."

I thought for one horrible moment that she was going to say that they loved each other.

"Maybe," she continued, "it's just one of those things."

"One of those things? What the hell does that mean? The same as you walking out on me? Was that just one of those things as well?"

"Rick, I know neither of us was particularly fond of Wiggy."

"*Was*? It's is! That's the whole point. We were so relieved when we could put it in the past tense and now we can't. It's back."

The Return of The Wiggy. It sounded like a horror movie. It certainly felt like one.

"We can't choose her boyfriends, can we?" said Sarah, sighing deeply.

"I know that," I said, "but we can let her know what we think, can't we? Isn't that what parents are for? To give advice when they think their kids are screwing something up?"

"Maybe it's not what you think. Maybe she's just feeling low and wants him back for... I don't know... companionship."

My wife seemed to have lost her brains since moving in with a PE teacher.

"If there's one thing Wiggy is not back with Ellie for, it's companionship."

Sarah may not have seen them together at Danny's comedy night, Sarah may not have sat next to them while they snogged their way through half the evening, but surely she must be wise enough to know that Wiggy had come back into Ellie's life to carry on where he left off – to revive what had been an intense two-year relationship and one that had done absolutely nothing for our daughter.

"Well," she said, "there's not much we can do about it, is there? She's an adult after all."

"That's great," I said, "and I suppose there's nothing we can do about stopping Danny dropping out and becoming a fucking stand-up!"

"We don't know for sure though, do we?" said Sarah. "He hasn't decided definitely, has he?"

"That doesn't make it any less of a problem, though, does it?"

"I'm just saying we should wait," said Sarah, "take the pressure off, give him time."

"Maybe that's what he doesn't need. We should be putting the pressure on, not taking it off, and I'm not sure that time is going to make any difference, is it?"

"Has Ellie spoken to him about it, do you know? I know she went to see his act."

"Really?" I said. "And did she say anything about it?"

Did she, for example, say anything about a bearded figure running out of the college bar or a mysteriously disappearing man from the BBC?

"She didn't give any details, just said he went down well and was very funny."

"So funny that he could jack in university and make a living out of it?"

"Now you're being silly."

"Am I?"

I paused and looked away.

"And how are things with Colin?" I asked. If we were talking about being silly, why not get to a *really* silly situation?

"Fine."

"Is that it? Just fine?"

"Look," said Sarah, "I really didn't want to come out to talk about Colin, OK?"

I nodded and we sat in uneasy silence, avoiding each other's eyes.

Then Sarah turned to me.

"How's Jerry?" she asked.

"Are you trying to change the subject?"

"I'm just asking after Jerry."

"Well, he's fine," I said, "in fact he's more than fine. He's pretty excited. It's the gaudy, he can't wait for it. Funny, isn't it? Some people can't wait to leave all that stuff behind them and some people can't wait to get back. I think Jerry's quite looking forward to getting together with some of our old mates."

"Anyone in particular?"

"Remember Helen Manson?"

Sarah furrowed her brow.

"I think so, I didn't know her too well."

"Jerry had a big crush on her, but nothing came of it."

"Nothing came of any of his crushes if I remember."

"That's because he was too frightened to do anything about them. But apparently he bumped into her recently and she was giving him all kinds of signals… and now it seems Jerry's not too frightened any more."

"Not Jerry!"

"Why not?"

"Well, look at him – happily married, kids."

"Just like us," I said.

Silence.

Sarah looked up at me with imploring eyes and I thought she was about to repeat her plea for me to take her back.

"You can't take anything for granted can you?" I said. "I mean, look at poor old Alex. Maybe it's got to us all. It's certainly got to Jerry. He's still talking about him. He told me that Helen saw him with some woman in a restaurant just before he died. She thought she recognized her but couldn't place her."

"Could have been anyone," said Sarah dismissively.

"You're right," I said, "given Alex's track record with women, it could have been exactly that – anyone."

"Yeah," said Sarah, "we all know what Alex was like."

"Funny to think of going back to Balham after all these years, though, isn't it?" I said. "All those old faces, all those old memories. Are you looking forward to it?"

Sarah shook her head.

"Well actually I've changed my mind. I'm not going."

"Why not?"

"I've been thinking about it. It's not really my kind of thing."

"Your choice," I said, "but I hope it's nothing to do with – you know – with us."

"No, of course not."

"Are you sure? All those old friends asking about us and how we're getting on?"

"It's fine," she said, "you go by all means, but I've decided it's not for me. I mean, if I'd wanted to keep in touch with any of those people I would have, wouldn't I? In fact I still find it difficult to believe that *you're* going. You used to run a mile from this kind of thing. Still, I suppose we change our minds about these things as we get… older."

"Maybe that's it," I said, "maybe we've all reached that age where we don't feel we have to prove ourselves to each other all the time, where we don't feel we always have to compete."

She didn't seem convinced.

"I don't believe that for one minute. But if you want to go, I certainly can't stop you."

"You don't want me to go, do you?" I said.

"Don't be ridiculous!"

She said it with such venom that I still didn't believe her.

"I can understand why," I said, "and if you really don't want me to—"

"Go, for fuck's sake, will you? Just go! And come back and tell me just how terrible it was and how right I was to stay away."

"Don't you think you're overreacting a little about all this?" I said. "I know things haven't been easy…"

"I'm not overreacting!" she shrieked. "Just go, will you? Go, see if I care!"

"OK," I said, getting up to leave, "it's no big deal, is it? Just a bloody gaudy. It's just people going back to their college to get pissed, nothing to be frightened of."

But as I looked down at her, I felt that was exactly what she was – frightened. She looked as though she was about to cry.

"Look," she said, "I'm sorry. I'm so so sorry about everything."

"Please," I said, "not again. We've been through all this."

"I just want some kind of understanding, some forgiveness."

"Forgiveness? I'm not a priest."

I sat down again and reached out for her hand. Despite it all, there was still something that made me want to do it. I held it in mine and looked at her. She kept her eyes down. I squeezed her hand gently and then she looked up.

"Take me back, Rick. Please, I've made a terrible mistake. Take me back and I promise it will work."

How much longer could I resist? It would have been so easy just to say yes and put the whole sorry mess behind us.

Across my mind scrolled pictures of how it had been in the good times: the four of us together as a family, laughing and happy. Christmases, birthdays, holidays – all those captured moments neatly labelled in chronological photo albums and tucked away at the bottom of a bedroom cupboard, all those smiling images suddenly burst out of their pages and blurred my vision.

Perhaps now was the time to just say yes.

I squeezed her hand one more time, leaned over and pecked her on the cheek and got up from the table.

It would be so easy to give in.

"Just give me time. I said a year. Just give me to the end of the year."

"That's a long time when you're unhappy," said Sarah, her face and lips creased with nerves.

"I know it is," I said, turning to go, "but look after yourself won't you?"

I left the café without turning back.

***

Ellie was the first to return. Finals over, parties finally finished, tears finally shed and final handshakes delivered, she came back, removing all that amounted to her world from the back of the car and dumping it in her old bedroom. All, she said, had gone well. She was hoping for a 2.1 and she was happy to talk to me about jobs and her future once a week and no more. In the meantime she promised to find something temporary and to give me something for her keep once she had been on a holiday jaunt to Greece with Wiggy. Wiggy, it seemed, was destined to last beyond university.

Her return was followed, a couple of weeks later, by Danny's. His world occupied less car space than Ellie's and he made no mention at all of the future, refusing to talk about it in any shape or form. He too moved back into his bedroom, promising to find some holiday work, but giving no clue as to how his first year exams had gone or whether he intended to go back for his second year. He said nothing about his drop-out stand-up plans and spent most of his first few days back in stony, unsmiling sit-down silence. Having a full house again after so many weeks of being alone meant I had to tread more carefully in certain areas. I kept up the running and I kept up my half-hearted liaison with Maggie, giving no firm answer to her invitation to move in and pleading the return of the kids as some kind of mitigating circumstance. She seemed to understand, and we spent some enjoyable evenings doing the kind of things that dating couples do – a trip to the cinema, a walk along the river, and dinner in town. In fact, the more I got to know her, the more I grew to like her. All that sex stuff, I realised, was just insecurity, the kind of thing you did when you just weren't sure of yourself. And even that started to change. Maybe we were just getting used to each other or maybe she was beginning to realize how all this theatrical palaver just wasn't my thing – whatever the reason, it all seemed to calm down.

One evening the unusual happened; I found myself in the kitchen at the same time as both Danny and Ellie and neither showed signs of leaving in a hurry. It looked like some kind of conversation might develop.

"So how have things been, Dad?"

It was Ellie who kicked it off. Danny's head was buried in a newspaper.

"Things?" I said. "What kind of things?"

"I don't know, Dad. Global warming, strength of the Euro, Chelsea's home form, that kind of thing? The important stuff we need to talk about as opposed to all that domestic trivia, like how is it without Mum, and how is Mum, and what's going to happen to you, like is it going to be like this for ever?"

"Irony doesn't suit you," I said. "Leave that to the resident comic."

I nodded towards Danny who kept reading the paper.

"And talking of which, how is the comedy? How did the act go? You never told me."

"I saw it," said Ellie, "I went up for the night and it was great. You're too modest Danny. You should tell Dad how well it went."

"Really?" I said, addressing the top of Danny's head. "What was it about?"

Danny's head moved.

"What do you mean – what was it about? You can't summarise a comedy performance can you?"

I backed off, pleased that I had at least provoked some kind of response.

"Only asking," I said.

"You should have come," said Ellie.

"I would have," I said, "but Danny made it clear he didn't want me to. I'm still not sure why."

"The time will come," said Danny, sounding like the prophet of doom, "the time will come."

Ellie leaned forward. "Don't try to change the subject, Dad. I still want know how things are."

"What's Mum said?"

"Not much, but I don't get the impression she's particularly happy, do you Danny?"

Danny said nothing, but he shook his head.

"And I've always had this problem with Colin." She paused. "You are OK talking about this stuff, aren't you?"

"Fire away, tell me your problems with Colin."

"He's a tosser," said Danny.

"What kind of tosser?"

"I don't know," said Danny, "A boring kind of tosser, I suppose."

Boring! Music to my ears.

"I know what you mean," said Ellie, "there's something odd about him, something odd about the whole set up."

Was this the time to tell them about their Open Relationship, to let them know that, boring he may have been, but Colin was a babe magnet of unimaginable proportions?

"We all got a shock when you told us about Mum, but we got even more of a shock when we saw Colin, didn't we?"

Ellie looked at the top of Danny's head, which nodded its response.

"I don't know what to say," I said. "It's not what I wanted. It's not what anyone wanted."

"Apart from Mum," said Danny.

"Well, yes," I said, "I guess so."

A brief silence followed. We sipped our coffees. Danny turned a page of the newspaper.

"So Mum's got Colin. How about you, Dad?"

"No," I said. "I don't fancy Colin."

"That's not funny," said the bowed head.

"Sorry, forgot I was in the presence of a professional."

"And that's not funny either."

"OK then, I'll say something unambiguously serious, shall I? Like how did your exams go and are you going back next year or are you dropping out?"

It just slipped out. I knew a hands-off, softly softly policy was what was needed and as soon as I spoke I regretted it. It did, though, cause the head to lift.

"Do you know what?" said Danny, "I was wondering when you were going to ask."

"My fault then, is it? Perhaps I'm just a bad parent."

I was suddenly back in the theatre, listening to Danny's act. Ellie and Danny exchanged a quick glance. Perhaps they were back there as well.

"The exams were OK. I think I've passed and I don't know yet about next year. I'm still thinking about it. Is that OK?"

"That's fine," I said. "Sometimes it's good to know where you stand, isn't it. Sometimes things have to be said, questions have to be asked."

"So let's ask some," said Ellie. "In fact, let's get back to Danny's question. Have you got anyone?"

I felt cornered and, for some reason, guilty. It was the old story. I hadn't been the first to do anything wrong, but I felt as if I'd betrayed everyone.

"No," I said, "not really. Well, when I say not really, I mean…"

Danny looked up again.

"You mean not really that woman who lives opposite. Maybe she doesn't count because she's a neighbour?"

"What do you mean?"

"We're not stupid, Dad," said Ellie. "We've seen you."

Seen me? Seen me doing what? Surely none of the upstairs action?

"Going over there," said Danny, "and walking down the street together."

"Yeah," said Ellie, "you looked very much a couple."

"Though she does look a bit younger than you, Dad," said Danny. "Are you sure you're up to it?"

Up to it? What was he suggesting?

“Look Dad,” said Ellie, “in one sense, it’s nothing to do with us, but in another we do have a right to know.”

I sat there at the kitchen table, completely lost for words. Maggie’s Invitation still hovered over me. By the rules of the bet I had to say yes, I had to accept her invitation to move in. But saying yes to it had never seemed right, and it seemed even less right now, faced as I was by the enquiring faces of my two children.

What was going on inside their heads? How much had Sarah’s walk-out disturbed them, and how much had my behaviour since just added to their confusion?

They fuck you up, all right. Never had something comic been more serious or true.

“Look,” I said, still feeling cornered, “we’re just good friends.”

“I see,” said Danny, “so you’re just good friends in the way that you and Mum aren’t together but you’re still good friends too. Is it that kind of good friends or another type of good friends?”

“You know what I mean.”

“No, Dad,” said Danny, “I don’t think I do. Explain.”

“I’ve been seeing her, yes. I won’t say I haven’t.”

“Sounds like some kind of mid-life crisis to me,” said Danny. “She’s almost half your age, and you’ve taken up running. How crisis-like can you get?”

“OK,” said Ellie, sensing the conversation heating up and stepping in as peacemaker, “we were only asking, that’s all. The reason why is that we’ve been talking, and we’ve been talking to Mum and we wanted to say something.” She looked at Danny as if for support and he nodded his approval. “What we want to say is that we would very much like you two to get back together. Everything just doesn’t – doesn’t seem right somehow and the longer it goes on the less right it seems. I know that things have happened and there may be things we don’t know about but we reckon it’s what Mum wants as well. We don’t expect you to turn around and say yes straight away, but we would like you to think about it.”

I nodded slowly, trying to take it all in. Was this An Invitation? No. As much as I would have liked it to be I couldn’t kid myself like that. It was my children saying what they felt, and I knew that deep down I felt it too. I knew that Danny's intention to drop out was far more likely to be rooted in what had happened to his parents than any conviction about his own comic destiny, and maybe Ellie's lack of clarity about the future came from the same cause.

What was stopping me? What was stopping me picking up the phone and asking Sarah back, rescuing her from Colin and getting our lives and our kids' lives back on track? Some silly New Year's resolution. Some stupid scheme that I could break tomorrow. Some strange feeling that breaking the rule would amount to a betrayal, not of anyone else, but of myself.

"I'll think about it," I said. "I promise."

25

July

Balham College Gaudy

July 7th 2007

For those who matriculated 1977-80

Programme

6.00 p.m. Arrive. Drinks in Buttery Bar
7.30 p.m. Formal dinner in Hall
10.30 p.m. Drinks in JCR
"The What We Danced to Disco"

I looked at the sheet of paper as the M40 unfolded in front of us.

"I'm not too sure about the disco," I said turning to Jerry. "What about those who didn't dance?"

"And who were they?"

"You know – all those weirdoes who preferred Beethoven to The Buzzcocks."

Jerry kept his eyes on the road ahead, drumming his fingers excitedly against the wheel. His smile had grown broader and broader ever since we had left London.

"Sounds great," he said, "just like the old days."

"It won't be though, will it? That's the whole point. It'll be some perverse, distorted version of the old days. We're all grey, bald, fat, divorced. We're all old. And getting pissed and dancing round to Ian Dury and Blondie isn't going to make us feel any younger."

"Well if you go into it with that kind of attitude you're not going to have any fun are you?"

"Unlike you, of course. You'll be having fun with Helen Manson as soon as we get there, I suppose. Straight upstairs for a long overdue shag."

Jerry shook his head, as if I was a little schoolboy who just didn't understand these adult things.

"It may happen. It may not. Now if she invites me of course I'll just have no choice."

"Yes you do," I said. "You chose not to suck my dick or lick my arse and I bet there are a whole load of other invitations you've 'chosen' not to accept."

If only he knew. If only he knew the proper way to do it. The way I was doing it.

"You'd be making a terrible mistake," I said. "Think about it before you do anything rash."

"Don't worry," he said, "I will."

To me he was still Captain Sensible, the Boring One, and he always would be. In my eyes he was forever fixed in his college image – perhaps we all were. As others gathered from distant corners of countries and continents to attend the Balham gaudy, I realised that I too would be fixed in others' eyes and memories as I was all those years ago. Just as I would meet them and immediately place how they seemed now against my image of them as they once were, so would they do the same to me.

It was a terrifying prospect.

"So why's Sarah not coming then?" asked Jerry.

"She just said she couldn't face it."

"Maybe she'd feel a little awkward with both of you there – you know, under the circumstances. I can see her point I suppose. After all, it's where you met. Maybe she'd find it painful."

"I think anyone in their right mind would find it painful, don't you?"

Jerry drummed his fingers gleefully.

"Not me, I can't wait, and just think, if you hadn't been keeping my bet when the Invitation arrived you might not have been coming either."

"Don't rub it in."

"Although, technically, given that you've stopped the whole scheme you could, I suppose, turn it down. Some kind of retrospective deal. You're no longer honouring the contract so all previous obligations are annulled. Did you ever think of that?"

"Of course I did, but..."

"But a little part of you still wanted to come, didn't it? That's why you're here. You see, for all you say about this, you really are curious to see the place again, to see what's become of everybody."

It was easier to agree. "OK," I said, "maybe I am, but only a very tiny teeny bit, you understand."

"Good, nothing like a bit of honesty, is there?" Jerry laughed. "So," he said, momentarily taking his hands off the wheel to rub them together in delight, "what's happened to them all then?"

Jerry had been a regular reader of the *Balham College Gazette* over the years, the yearly publication that kept all college members up to date not only with what was happening at Balham but also with news of Old Members. It never told you about everyone, only those who were self-important enough to feel they merited inclusion or thought they had achieved something worth boasting about. I remember reading it a few times and wincing at the smug announcements of promotions, publications, marriages and births. There was never anything about those you wanted to hear about – the failures, the cock-ups, the things that weren't going right. What you really wanted were true-life confessions and gossip. What you got were miniature CVs. Occasionally there would be an entry that caught the eye – someone might have dropped out of a high-flying career to live on the West Coast of Ireland, another might own up to having been out of work for several years, and another might even admit euphemistically to "hard times", but these were rare.

From his annual reading of the *Balham College Gazette*, Jerry was already familiar with what many of our contemporaries were up to and, as the outskirts of Oxford loomed, he took me through all that he knew – the MPs, the multi-millionaires, the high-flying lawyers (amongst which he didn't include himself – he was merely a lawyer), the writers, the actors, the ones who read the news on TV.

"Of course," he said, "there'll be a lot of people asking about Alex."

"I know," I said, "and it's frightening to think he might not be the only one who's not made it this far."

"So, carpe diem, and all that."

"Well I don't think Alex made that mistake, did he?" I said. "If ever anyone carped his diem, it was him."

"And yet," said Jerry, "for all that he was never quite happy, was he?"

I shrugged, and as the M40 rolled past I listened to Jerry hold forth on various matters: about Alex; about Helen Manson; why they never got it together all those years ago and why they might now; his sense that, after so many years of being the boring one, he was beginning to change; and his conviction that his idea for a New Year's Eve bet had turned out to be more of a life-changing idea than he had thought it at the time.

The centre of Oxford couldn't arrive too soon.

The low sun behind the Hall threw its light across the mellow Oxford stone, and, as I walked through the front quad, I was overcome by that easy nostalgia I had been so determined to resist – all those faces and names, all those places, all those events. The bops, the parties, the pubs, the essay crises. The long summer evenings, the walks across the parks, the punting, croquet.

I let it flood over me as I walked, still looking round to see faces I recognized. I was suddenly overwhelmed, not by that generalized nostalgia which the low-lying sun had ignited, but by a very specific thought and a very specific face.

Sarah.

She should have been here with me, walking this walk, in the place where we met and fell in love, the place that launched us into so many years of happiness together. When I reached the bar I was brought out of my reverie by the chatter, laughter and the clink of glasses. I grabbed a drink and moved into the group that had spilled out onto the lawn, sticking by Jerry as if for security, smiling and nodding at those who were doing the same to me, but not really recognizing anybody or seeing anyone I felt like rushing up to and greeting like a long lost friend. Soon Jerry left my side, and moved towards a woman who I recognized as a late forties version of the Helen Manson I half-remembered.

"Rick! Rick Matthews!"

I turned to see a man with a smiling tanned face walking towards me with outstretched hand.

"Remember me?"

I shook his hand and grinned.

"Bill Grainger, we shared a tutorial."

It came back to me. The English Civil War in the third year.

"And we played football together. Not very well, and not very together, but we definitely shared a pitch."

Of course, Balham 3rd XI. How could I forget?

"So how are you, Rick? Tell me what you've been up to for the past thirty years."

And so I told him – seriously at first, but speeding up and embellishing it a little when I realised he wasn't really that interested and I was in danger of appearing boring.

Then I reciprocated, and he gave me his story.

"Went into the City," he said. "Stayed there, made a bit of money, made a bad marriage, made a bit more money and then last year I decided I had enough so I stopped."

"What?" I said, "so you've retired?"

"Yeah," he said, "I suppose so. I don't really think of it like that, but I figured I had more than enough so why carry on making any more? I divide my time between London and a little place in the South of France."

"Very nice," I said.

And I was much better than him on Cavaliers and Roundheads, much better at football too.

"It is. You should come down and see me in the summer. You must have loads of time in those long holidays you get. Come down."

"Is that an invitation?"

"Of course it is. I mean it. I'm not just saying it. Come down, I'd love to see you. Bring your wife."

"Ah, we're not, technically, together."

"Sorry. Put my foot in it, have I? Fucked it up like me, did you? Oh well, I don't think we're alone in that this evening."

"Yeah," I said, "We married straight after Balham. You might remember her, Sarah Griffiths."

"Sarah? Of course I remember her. Now you mention it, I remember you two being a couple as well. Oh well, these things happen."

It was a pattern repeated many times throughout the evening – through drinks, through dinner and even through the "What We Danced To Disco". Everyone varied the phrasing of the question, and everyone gave their response a different kind of spin, but the principles remained the same. As the evening progressed, though, and as the level of drunkenness increased, people went for jokes rather than seriousness when describing what they had been up to – any early signs of competitiveness disappeared as we all regressed to a state of youthful parity.

The more I drank, the more the Invitations seemed to arrive with increasing speed and generosity. By the time we all headed for the JCR (and with countless glasses of champagne and wine inside me, the idea of dancing to what we had danced to now seemed irresistibly attractive) I had received the following:

1. Stay with Bill Grainger in his South of France house (just across from St Tropez) in the summer.

2. Join Colin Foulkes (another old 3rd XI player) for a very relaxed informal game of 5-a-side football with other Balhamites in North London once a week.

3. Go along to Mary Salmon's book launch.

4. Have dinner with Tim Berensfield at his club.

5. Go sailing with Steve Hawk on the Isle of Wight.

6. Go on a pub crawl with Harry, John, Bill and Fred next Boat Race Day.

That, I think, was the extent of the list by the time we reached the JCR. I hadn't written any of them down, but I had, in the true spirit of the scheme, accepted each and every one of them. They may have been offered half-heartedly (and very drunkenly) and the likelihood of those who offered them actually remembering them, let alone, reinforcing them was very remote. But I was more than prepared to act on each and every one of them.

At least I was still doing this thing properly.

Half an hour into some undignified and unrestrained dancing to Eddie and the Hot Rods, Talking Heads, The Police, Joe Jackson and Elvis Costello, I was approached by a woman I didn't recognize.

"Come and have a dance," she said, pulling me away from a group of fist-pumping men singing along to the chorus of *Sex, Drugs and Rock and Roll.*

"Is that an Invitation?" I said, conscious that I was slurring my speech, but beginning to place her.

"Of course it is," she said, slurring hers.

"You don't remember me, do you?" she said.

"I think I do," I said.

"Who am I then?"

Ian Dury had stopped and *Oliver's Army* had started. One of my all-time favourites, and one of Sarah's.

"Hang on," I said, "Angie?"

"Very good."

"You did History."

"Even better."

"And I'm not going to ask you what you've been up to for the last thirty years."

"That's good, because I'm not going to tell you, but I am going to tell you a secret."

"What's that?"

She leaned towards me and I bent my head to hear.

"I always fancied you and I still do."

She pulled her head back and swivelled her hips to Elvis.

"That's nice," I said.

She leaned in again. "The problem was you hitched up with Sarah very early on and stayed together, so all I could do was admire you from afar. I was so sorry to hear that you split up."

"Well, "I said, "these things happen."

"They do bring their opportunities, though, don't they?"

Then she smiled the kind of glazed-eyed, out-of-control smile that leaves you in no doubt about its intention.

"So how about it? You and me – tonight. It would make me very happy…"

I added it to the list.

7. Sex with Angie (I couldn't remember her surname).

I had to say yes. It was just one of those things. We were both drunk, there was no doubt about that, but I wouldn't want to produce that as any kind of excuse. And it seemed to be going on everywhere we looked, though I wouldn't want to use that as an excuse either. Did this happen at every college gaudy or was it just unusual that both Jerry and I spent the early hours of the morning copulating with women either we had fancied or who had fancied us in those long-off years?

Afterwards I lay there, wondering whether what I had just done was a good idea. I didn't want to talk, but Angie, unfortunately, did.

"We probably shouldn't have done that," she said.

"Thanks," I said, "that makes me feel a whole lot better."

"But I enjoyed it," she said.

"Yeah," I said, "and so did I."

"And don't worry," she said.

What was she about to talk about? There couldn't have been any risk could there? Disease of some kind? Pregnancy? It couldn't be that – I had been responsible enough to buy some condoms from the JCR vending machine before heading off to my old college room.

"Don't worry about what?" I said.

"I'm not doing the dirty on anyone. I'm not married, never have been. And I'm not in any relationship."

"Oh," I said, "good."

"Hardly the word I'd use to describe it."

"I mean—"

"Yeah, I know what you mean. And given that I knew you and Sarah weren't together, I thought…."

"I'm glad you did."

"Yes," she said, leaning in and talking loudly in my ear, "when someone told me about you and Sarah I was surprised. It was a bit of a shock really. You were like some kind of institution. I never thought you wouldn't last. I didn't believe it at first, just like I couldn't believe Alex died. I just couldn't believe it. First of all I saw them together. And then it must have been only days later I heard he'd died."

"What? You saw them together? Who?"

"Alex and Sarah."

"Where was this?"

"In London, I didn't speak to them. I don't think they saw me. I didn't think it was them at first. It took a while to recognize them, but I when I looked at them closely it was clear who they were. But I didn't know about you and Sarah then, so I didn't really expect to see them together, not like that."

"What do you mean? Like what?"

"You know, holding hands, arms round each other."

I suddenly felt very sober.

"Hang on. You saw Sarah and Alex holding hands only a matter of days before Alex died?"

"Yes, I'm sorry. Should I not have mentioned it? I thought—"

"Hang on," I said again. My head was feeling very muddled. "Where was this?"

"Well that's the thing. It wasn't as if they were walking down the street or anything. It wasn't anywhere public. It wasn't as though they didn't care if anyone was looking. I was on Hampstead Heath walking and there was this area, a quite secluded area and there was a bench that I sat on, and—"

"So where were they?"

"They were on another bench."

"Holding hands?"

"Well, yes. And kissing."

"Oh my God."

"I assumed that was why you split. I assumed you had already broken up. I mean…"

Oh my God.

As I lay in my old college bed, beside a woman from my student years who I could barely remember and with whom I had just made drunken, middle-aged love, I saw my world turning faster and faster until it was just a blur.

Then I leaned over the side of the bed and vomited.

Just as I had done so many times, thirty or so years ago.

***

Next morning I said an awkward goodbye to Angie, uncertain whether the etiquette of late seventies one-night stands was at all appropriate so many years on, uncertain whether I really meant it when I said it would be good to see her again, and sensing that she felt the same when she reciprocated and headed off for breakfast.

My head was throbbing with hangover and guilt, spinning from the revelation about Sarah and Alex. All I wanted to do was get back to London as fast as possible. I ate breakfast quickly, keeping an eye out for Jerry, who I expected to walk in at any moment with Helen Manson, and left before anyone could engage me in more conversation or, even worse, extend an Invitation.

Jerry didn't make breakfast. The next thing I saw of him was when he was walking towards the Lodge, bag in hand, ready to depart.

For the first five or ten minutes of the journey back we said very little beyond the obvious platitudes about time flying, people going bald and getting fat, how with some people you would never have guessed how they had turned out and how with others it was all very much as you would expect.

"Lots of people asking about Alex," said Jerry, "everyone was… you know… shocked, but no one I spoke to had anything new to say about him. How about you?"

"No," I lied, last night's words coming back loudly, "nothing new."

If I ever were to tell Jerry, now was definitely not the right time.

We drove back down the M40 in silence, both of us thinking of, but neither of us mentioning, what had happened the previous night when the dancing had stopped.

I was the first to break.

"And how was it for you?" I said.

"How was what?"

"You know what I mean."

"Fine," said Jerry, "it was fine."

"Is that all you have to say?" I said.

Jerry shrugged.

"Come on Jerry let's not fuck about. How was it with you and Helen?"

I expected a smug smile to creep across his lips, a blokish did-it-last-night grin to light up his face. Instead he frowned.

"Nothing happened," he said.

"And what does that mean?"

"It means nothing happened."

"Why not? I thought she was, what is the phrase, money in the bank?"

"It wasn't her," he said, "it was me."

"What? Too much to drink?"

"No it wasn't that. I just couldn't bring myself to do it. It just felt wrong, somehow."

"So you could have if you'd wanted to? I mean, she asked you to?"

"Oh she asked all right."

"So it was an Invitation then? A proper Invitation."

Jerry turned and gave me a regretful, tight-lipped nod. "It was a proper Invitation all right, but as I sat there, all that drink running round my head, all those songs from our youth ringing in my ears and all those complicated thoughts about the past and the present and all that lies ahead – what's left of it, that is – I thought, what the fuck am I doing? Why the hell am I thinking of sleeping with this woman who, let's face it, means very little to me? Why am I jeopardizing everything I've got, everything I've achieved because of some stupid fucking game?

So do you know what I did? I pecked her on the cheek, said goodnight and went to sleep. And do you know what? I think I feel a hell of a lot better than I would have if I'd done anything last night."

"So what about the whole Invitation thing, then?"

"I'm stopping, Rick. It's led me too far. That time when you tested me, when you asked me over to suck your dick and lick your arse – you were right. That's when I should have realised. That's when I should have stopped. I'm Captain Sensible, Rick. Always have been and always will be. Going to something like last night just drives it home. Some things run through us. Some things you can't change."

I looked towards Jerry, wondering whether I should tell him about my night – what I had done and what I had discovered.

"Now I can understand why you stopped," he said, "I really can. I didn't at the time. I thought you were chicken. But now I see it. It's time just to get on with things. You were right all along – it was different for you. You were by yourself. You'd done nothing wrong and I think we were both thrown by Alex's death more than we might have realised."

Alex who had always been the wild one, Alex who Angie saw with Sarah on a park bench a matter of days before he died, Alex who had been sleeping with my wife.

I said nothing for a while, taking in what Jerry had said, mulling it over, letting it sink in.

"You know what, Jerry?" I said. "You're probably right to stop it. I mean, I'm certainly glad I did."

It was a lie, and for the first time I felt uncomfortable delivering it. At that moment I wished that I, too, was in Jerry's position, that I, too, had stopped this thing for real. I had just spent a night in bed with a woman I had barely known and who I probably would not want to see again. I was heading home to give an answer to an Invitation to move in with the woman across the road. My son was thinking of dropping out of university to become a comedian, my daughter had taken up again with a tosser called Wiggy, and I had just discovered that my wife had been sleeping with one of my oldest friends just before he had died.

I didn't need any Invitation game to make my life interesting.

26

"I've got a few questions for you, Colin."

"Fire away," he said, raising his beer.

He had been reluctant to come out at first, but I knew I had to see him and I had insisted.

"First of all," I said, "how's Sarah?"

"She seems fine," he said, "from what I see of her."

I had spent a lot of time thinking about it, framing my questions, my line of enquiry. I felt like a policeman.

"You have a bit of a strange relationship, don't you, you and Sarah?"

"Do we? What do you mean?"

"Well, you don't seem to spend an awful lot of time together and you go out with other women…"

"It's not a problem."

"When she moved in with you last year," I said, "I was a little surprised."

"Yeah. So was I."

"You were surprised? Why?"

"Well, when I put the notice up on the common room board it was mainly in case any other teachers knew of anyone who'd be interested in sharing. I didn't expect another teacher to be interested themselves, and I certainly didn't expect Sarah."

"Hang on," I said, "you put up a notice advertising a house-share?"

"Yes." Colin gave me a puzzled look. "I'm surprised Sarah hasn't told you any of this."

"Go on."

"You see I had been sharing before – well in fact I had been in a relationship before and it folded – and I needed some extra money and I was feeling a bit lonely so I thought rather than rattle around all on my own why not rent it out. If I could find someone nice it would mean company and a bit more cash. So I put up the notice and I was staggered when Sarah came up and said she knew someone who would like to look at the house, and that someone was her."

"When was this?"

"Just into September."

Just before Alex had died.

"I didn't ask too much about why, or about what had happened between you two – because I'd always thought her marriage was very happy – and that's how it happened. She moved in and she's been there ever since. And it all seems to work out fine."

"So," I said, "Let's get this clear. You have never slept with Sarah?"

"What? Slept with Sarah? Of course not!"

Colin shook his head, amused and alarmed.

"So Sarah moved in as a tenant, not as a lover?"

"She moved in very gradually. In fact when she took it she said she wouldn't be around all that much but she needed the base, needed the address and the room. Again, I didn't ask much. I was just pleased to let the room and pleased to help her. I'm very fond of her, you know."

"I'm sure you are," I said. "And tell me, how was she in those first few weeks?"

"Well, as I say, at first I hardly saw her and there wasn't even a lot of stuff in her room. She popped in occasionally but not very often. And then after three or four weeks she moved in properly."

Just after Alex died.

"And when she moved in," said Colin, "she seemed very quiet, very low. Not herself at all."

"Was she upset at all?"

"Difficult to tell. Didn't one of your friends die round about that time?"

"Yes," I nodded, "he did. Knocked down by a car."

"Goes to show," said Colin, "you can't take anything for granted, can you?"

"No," I said, "you can't"

***

For someone who had spent three years at the place, Sarah showed little interest in the Balham College gaudy. It had taken some persuasion to get her to come out for a drink, and now it was taking some effort to move the conversation in the direction I needed it to go.

"How's Colin?" I said, casually.

"Fine," she said, "we get on with things."

"Is he seeing anyone at the moment? Apart from you that is?"

She shrugged weakly. "I don't know," she said. "I really don't want to talk about it."

I knew she could explain it, and I was determined to make her do just that before I got up from the table.

"I know you might not want to talk about it," I said, "but I think it's important that we do, because I think I've found something out that might have some bearing on everything – on us, on the kids, on everything."

She looked up and a flash of real fear and terror contorted her face.

"What?" she said. "What have you found out?"

Her eyes darted with nervous anticipation.

"When you walked out on me to move in with Colin," I continued calmly, "did you know that Colin was the type of guy who would want to carry on with other women, the type of guy who would indulge in an "open" relationship?"

Another weak shrug.

"I guess so. I wasn't really sure..."

"Because what I don't get is that you walked out on me, a faithful, loving husband and you walked out on our kids when they still needed you very much, to move in with a bloke called Colin who didn't seem to love you at all. Or at least not love you in the way I understand the term. Not love you in the way that I did, that I do."

Tears welled up in her eyes. She reached for a tissue.

"And I've been thinking a lot about this. You moved out to live with Colin and then a couple of weeks later Alex died. I've never thought of the two as being connected at all. Until now, that is. Because, you see, Sarah I know."

"How much do you know?" she said. "How much?"

"That's what I'm here to find out," I said. "I know for a start that you haven't been sleeping with Colin and I know that you moved in to share his house not as a lover but as a rent-paying housemate."

Sarah nodded, as if some kind of game were heading towards its inevitable end.

"For some reason," I said, "when you walked out on me, I got the impression that it was to 'live with' Colin in the generally accepted sense of the term. That's why when I saw him on intimate terms with another woman I was a little surprised."

Sarah nodded again, not even trying to find any words.

"And I now know why you didn't want to come to the gaudy. You were worried that something might come out, weren't you? That something might be revealed? Shall I have a guess at what that was? I think you were worried that there would be a lot of questions about us, and about Alex. Poor Alex. And I think you were worried that someone, somehow, might have picked up on something you were desperate to keep hidden from me."

She sobbed gently and wiped away a tear

"I won't tell you how I discovered it," I said, images of Angie flashing through my mind, "but I think I found out what it was you were trying to hide from me."

Sarah looked up at me.

"Don't torture me like this, "she said, "just get on with it."

"You were sleeping with Alex before he died."

She nodded slowly and sadly.

"I don't know how long you'd been doing it, but when you moved in with Colin you weren't sleeping with him, you were sleeping with Alex. Am I right?"

"Yes."

"And when you first moved out you weren't at Colin's house at all. You were using it as some kind of cover. Am I right?"

"Yes."

"And then, when Alex died, you moved into Colin's properly. Shortly after that you told me you'd made a terrible mistake and you wanted to be forgiven, you wanted to come back. Am I right?"

"Yes."

I took no pleasure in being right, and I felt uncomfortable in the role of prosecutor, but Sarah's sequence of simple, unadorned yeses amounted to some huge personal breakthrough.

I sat back, sighed, and looked at Sarah, saying nothing and waiting for her to speak.

When Sarah had gathered herself, wiped away her tears, had taken deep breaths and composed herself, she delivered her story. It was the story I had been expecting.

"I can only say again that I'm sorry," she said. "I'm sorry it's all happened this way, and I can quite understand everything you mighty be feeling – anger, hurt, bitterness. I understand it, and I'll say it again, all of this has been entirely my fault. It has nothing to do with you. It's not going to be easy to tell you all this but I'm going to do it as clearly as I can. When we were at college and when we started going out together I had a fling. I had a fling with Alex. It was a one-night stand, a drunken student thing. We both did it and I suppose we both regretted it and promised never to say anything about it. I'm not proud of it but these things happen."

Like they happened to me, with Angie.

Like they didn't happen to Jerry, with Helen

"And then we got married. And it was fine, but then—"

"Oh, no, Sarah, no, please tell me you didn't!"

"Again it was only a fling, it was a couple of times—"

"Only a couple of times! Well, that's OK then isn't it?"

"Look, Rick. This isn't easy for me. I've been living with this for some time, and I'm trying to tell you it all clearly. Please, just listen."

I backed off, putting my hands up, inviting her to continue.

"Nothing else happened for a while, but in the year before he died we started seeing each other a little more and we started to go out together. Something brought us back together– I don't know what it was."

You didn't love me. Or maybe I'd become boring.

"I just felt something had gone out of our marriage—"

Yes, you.

"I'm not trying to justify it, but the kids were getting older, one was at university, the other about to go, and we'd stopped doing a lot of the things we used to."

So, boring then?

"And Alex was by himself..."

Between relationships? Resting?

"And we started to see more and more of each other, and eventually he asked me to move in with him. He knew it was difficult, being a friend of yours for so long. He knew it was going to be a difficult thing to handle, but he really wanted to do it."

I couldn't contain myself.

"And you wanted to do it too? Despite our years of stable marriage, despite the fact that Alex had shagged his way through half the world and his relationships had never lasted longer than about half an hour? Despite all this you were happy to walk out on me and Ellie and Danny? To throw all that away?"

Sarah shook her head, as if only now was she realizing quite how stupid the whole thing had been.

"It's because it was so difficult that I couldn't at first bring myself to tell you. That's why I moved in with Colin, it was so that you wouldn't know."

"But I'd have found out, wouldn't I? You couldn't have kept it secret for ever?"

"We would have told you. Once we had got used to the idea, once we were ready..."

"So I thought you were sleeping with Colin and all the time you were sleeping with Alex? I don't believe it."

"But then Alex died, and..."

She started to cry again. I looked around, as if trying to find something to anchor my racing thoughts.

"So," I said, "why didn't you tell me then? Surely that was the perfect time?"

"I moved into Colin's house and that's when I told you I'd made a terrible mistake. That's when I asked to come back. I was going to tell you everything then. I was ready to come clean and try to patch it up. I was ready to say sorry. And then you said no."

That's when I asked for a year. A year to follow the god of Invitations, a year to keep faith with a ridiculous bet.

"And since then," said Sarah, "I've been miserable beyond thought."

"It hasn't been too great for me," I said.

"Not only leaving you and leaving the kids, but losing Alex. It was all too much. If you'd agreed to take me back, I would have told you everything there and then. I would have come clean. I would have tried to sort it out, but I can understand why you didn't. Believe me, I can understand."

It was pretty much what I had expected. After Angie's revelation and after my chat with Colin I had been working ferociously at trying to create some coherent picture of it all. I could now see that picture a little more clearly.

"So," I said, hoping I didn't sound too much like a teacher concluding a lesson, "What do we do now?"

"I don't know," she said.

"No," I said, "Nor do I."

27

The following days and nights blurred into one. I didn't sleep, I didn't eat, I didn't function. I just couldn't take it in. How could I have been so wrong? How could I have been so stupid? Of course Sarah wouldn't have left me for Colin. I may have become boring, but not so boring that an unremarkable PE teacher – handsome though he was – could seem a better option, an option worth breaking up your family for.

Leaving me for Alex, though, was something else entirely, and I wasn't sure whether it hurt more or less. When it hurt more Alex was the object of all my blame, the man who had destroyed my family, the man who had seduced my wife and betrayed me. When it hurt less, Alex was the old friend who just couldn't stop himself behaving like that, the wild-living man who nobody, Sarah included, could quite resist, and the one who had met with a tragically early death.

My sympathies shifted, almost by the minute. At times I felt most sorry for Ellie and Danny – both innocent victims of their parents' foolishness. At others I felt sorry for Sarah who had found the guts to walk out on me and then had lost her reason for leaving, trapping herself in the charade that was her life with Colin. Then I would feel sorry for Jerry, drawn into a game of his own devising that he had no need to play, before moving on to Colin, who had done nothing other than rent out a room in his house and be younger and more handsome than me. And then I would feel sorry for Maggie, central to so much of what had been happening in my recent life, still looking for something that kept eluding her, and still waiting for my answer to her Invitation.

Lying on the sofa one evening, I was brought out of such whirling thoughts by a call from Jerry.

"How are you?" he said. "Recovered from the gaudy?"

"I don't know that I ever will," I said. "And you?"

"Just about. You know, Rick, I'm glad I did what I did. Or rather that I didn't do what I thought I might. I don't know what got into me. That Invitation thing, dangerous isn't it?"

"Yeah," I said, "very dangerous." I paused, and then remembered that I still had a lie to maintain, "That's why I stopped it," I added.

"Do you know," said Jerry, "when I got back, when I walked in and there was Caroline and there were the kids I just thought to myself – what the hell was I thinking of? What was I trying to prove? Still, I'm glad I went. In a strange kind of way it makes me feel better about Alex. It's almost made me come to terms with it all. How about you?"

I had drifted off into thoughts about Alex and Sarah.

"Rick, are you still there?"

I came to.

"Yes, I'm here."

"I was saying that the gaudy made me feel differently about Alex. Made it all easier in a way. A bit like visiting the scene of an accident, I suppose. Did it make it easier for you?"

"About Alex?" I said, "not really, no."

"It takes time, I guess. But anyway, give me a ring. Let's go out for a drink some time? Or even better why don't you come over for dinner one evening. Caroline hasn't seen you for some time. It would be good."

An Invitation.

An Invitation to go over to Jerry and Caroline's, to see them happily married and together, to hear them talk about their kids and their lives, to look at Jerry and think how close he was to fucking it all up and how he pulled himself back. To sit there and listen to Captain fucking Sensible being smug. There were better and more important ways to spend an evening.

Then I thought again of Maggie's Invitation and, as if from nowhere, there came an overwhelming feeling.

I tried to resist, but couldn't. I tried to fight it off with the dogged resolve that had got me this far, but failed. I tried to reason it away, but its own logic seemed invincible.

***

"Rick, good to see you. Come in."

I walked into Maggie's house, following her into the kitchen and sitting down at the table. So much had happened since I first came in all those months ago.

"I won't stay long, Maggie, but I just want to say something, something very important."

"What's happened?"

"Nothing's happened. Or rather, yes, I suppose something has happened. I've been thinking about things, thinking about us, and Maggie, I don't know if you realise this, but you've helped me over the last few months one hell of a lot. I've been through quite a few changes and I think I've become someone different. I don't know if I'm better or worse – that's not for me to judge – but I think I'm a different man from the one who met you at Harry's drinks and who came down with you to go for that first run. And all I want to say is thank you for helping."

"Helping? What do you mean? You make me sound like some kind of nurse."

It struck me that a nurse's uniform was one of the few Maggie didn't seem to own, but now wasn't the time to point that out.

"I don't see how I've helped," she said, "apart from teaching you the art of disguise."

"Well, maybe that's it," I said. "Maybe that's exactly what you've done."

Maggie laughed.

"You're sweet, you know that?"

I wondered whether an Invitation was about to follow. I may have made my decision, but the instinct was still there, the Invitation antennae were still tuned.

"And so are you," I said, "but the thing is..."

I could see from her face that she had guessed what was coming.

"You're going to call it off, aren't you?"

"Yes," I said, "I am. It's not that I don't like you, or that I don't want to be with you—"

"I'm too old for that bullshit, Rick. Just give me the truth, will you?"

"There's no truth to give," I said. "It's just that I've thought things over and I'm not ready to commit."

"Not ready to commit! You're nearly fifty, for fuck's sake! When will you be ready? When you're eighty?"

"It's not just that," I said, "it's Sarah."

Her face fell.

"She's coming back. We're getting back together."

It just came out. I had no intention of saying it, but as soon as I had I realised that it was exactly what I did want to happen. It was what I had wanted from the moment she had walked out, and the revelation about Alex, rather than making me more reluctant, had, in some strange way, made me want her more.

"So is that it?" said Maggie.

"I guess so," I said. "I hope we'll still be friends."

Maggie forced a smile.

"Well, we'll certainly still be neighbours."

"And," I said, "I hope…" Maggie was looking at me with sad resignation. "I hope I haven't hurt you, because I've enjoyed our time together and… I like you a lot. I really do."

"It's fine," said Maggie, with an eloquent shrug of her shoulders, "I'll get over it, I guess. I always have done."

"And if you're performing in anything," I said, "let me know, won't you?"

Maggie nodded, got up, and showed me to the door. I leaned to give her a kiss on the cheek, but she pulled out of it, forcing another smile and holding up a half-hearted farewell hand.

"Don't worry about it, Rick," she said, "I understand."

The door shut behind me and as I walked back across the road I felt an enormous weight lifting.

I might never need to go running again.

***

One evening when Ellie was out I found myself watching TV with Danny. It was a comedy show, and so it seemed only natural to use this as a starting point.

"Not very funny, is it?" I said, casually from behind the *Independent*.

Danny shrugged.

"I should think you're probably far more funny," I said.

Another shrug.

"How's it going, the comedy?"

"Ask Ellie, she came to see me."

"I have asked her and she said you were really good, the best of the bunch." I paused. "I'd have liked to come along."

"Oh well," he said, "next time maybe."

"I'd like to. All you have to do is... invite me." I hesitated before I said the word.

"OK," he said, "I will next time."

"Next time? Same place?"

"That is – if I'm still there."

"Sorry, I wasn't trying to probe, I was just asking."

"No it's OK. I still haven't decided yet. I'm still thinking about it."

"And what about Caroline and Hayley? How are they? Have you spoken to them about it."

"Yeah, I have, and they both say exactly the same thing."

"What's that?"

"That I'd be stupid to chuck it all in now. They say I should just get on with it. Everyone has doubts, everyone goes through rough patches, and everyone has problems. They say I should just get on with it – even if I scrape through academically, I'll be in the best place to do stuff."

"Stuff like your comedy?"

"Yeah, like my comedy."

And that was it. Suddenly Danny was talking to me in a way he hadn't for a long long time. It all came out, not in a rush, but over the next hour or so as we sat there flicking channels.

"Yeah," he said, "the comedy's going quite well. In fact some bloke from the BBC came to see it last time, just to check us out."

I tensed.

"Really? What did he make of it?"

"Well it's all very odd. He sort of – disappeared."

"Disappeared?"

"Yeah, went to the loo and we didn't see him again. He was probably drunk or drugged, but we never got to find out what he thought."

"Any reviews?"

"Yeah, we got a couple. In fact, I've got a copy upstairs if you want to see it?"

"I'd love to," I said.

When he brought it back I scanned it quickly and read out the relevant section, "'Rick Matthews's act 'They Fuck You Up' was full of wit and insight. He is definitely one to watch, a star of the future.' Very good. So that's the Larkin poem is it, *This be the Verse*?"

He nodded.

"I see," I said.

"But the next one will be different, come to that one."

***

Two weeks after the revelation Sarah asked me round to Colin's for dinner, pointing out that Colin wouldn't be there. It would be just the two of us.

No longer bound by the rules, I knew I could refuse, but I didn't want to. We needed to talk. Every time I had spoken to Sarah in those two weeks I had felt a strange mixture of emotions – blame, anger, accusation, doubt. Sometimes I just couldn't forgive her, but at others I found it easier. Sometimes it seemed that her act of betrayal was so huge that nothing, not even the passage of time, could make it easier to bear. Sometimes the deceit, sustained over so many years, seemed to have destroyed any possibility of my ever recovering my feelings for her.

And yet there were also times when I was able to see things from her point of view. How much courage must it have taken to walk out when she did, to turn her back on her kids and the home she had built for so long to start something new with an old friend? How much must it have taken to face up to the truth about herself and her past, and to prepare to tell me?

And as I thought that, I went back to my New Year's Eve discussion with Jerry and that ridiculous bet, undertaken in the wake of grief at Alex's death and in response to the accusation that I might have been boring. Maybe I had been, but if the bet had shown me anything it was that I didn't need to be. I had it in me to do things – look at what I had done with Maggie, look at what I had done on that revelatory night with Angie. Of course the truth was I hadn't enjoyed either, and it had all felt wrong. Maybe, in time, Sarah would have reached the same conclusion herself.

"What should we do, then?" Sarah reached for the second bottle of wine.

"About what?" I said.

"About everything."

We spoke sensibly and unemotionally. First about the kids.

"He still hasn't made a decision," I said, "or if he has, he's kept it quiet."

"Don't put any pressure on," said Sarah, "you know how Danny's never liked pressure."

I smiled at the thought of all the times we had spoken about the best way to deal with our son. I wondered whether Sarah was thinking the same.

"The funny thing is," said Sarah, "I don't even know if he's any good. Is this all just a reaction to what's been going on, or does he have a chance of making it?"

"No one has a chance of making it as a comedian. You might as well drop out of college and say you're banking on winning the lottery."

"I suppose what I mean is," said Sarah, "I've never seen him, so I've no idea what he's like."

"No," I said, thinking of my evening at the Comics Showcase, "nor do I, but he's always had a good sense of humour."

"And I guess he's needed it recently."

"But they're quite understanding about these things," I said.

"Quite a few take a year out and then come back when they feel better about things."

"Sounds a bit like Ellie and Wiggy then, doesn't it?"

"Ah," I said, "Ellie and Wiggy, well I think we probably have to do the same thing there as well. No pressure and see what happens."

"And you think that was another reaction as well?" said Sarah. "Another way of coping?"

I shrugged.

"Who knows what will happen? These university romances don't always last when they reach the real world."

"I know," said Sarah, "I mean look at us."

I reached out across the table for her hand and squeezed it gently. She squeezed it back and we looked into each other's eyes in a way we hadn't done for years.

"You know," I said, "the funny thing is I still love you."

"Do you? Do you really?"

I nodded.

"I always have," I said.

"Even after I walked out? Even after I told you the truth about Alex?"

I nodded again.

"Look," she said, "I've made a terrible mistake and I don't know how I can ever make it up to you, but what I'd like to say is – and it's as simple as this and there's no other way to say it – I'm sorry. I know you're not going to believe this either, but I still love you, and I always have. Even..."

"If I asked you," I said, "would you still come back?"

A smile lit up her face.

"I'd come back with you tonight."

"How about it then?" I said. "I think it's the only way we can make anything work out."

Then we went upstairs and made love.

After Maggie, and after Angie, it felt like coming home.

28

December

"Whose idea was this, then?"

Ellie stood on a chair in the kitchen, sticking decorations to the wall.

"Blame me," I said.

"And how many are coming again?"

"About fifty," I said.

"Don't tell me," she said, "fifty of your closest friends."

"Well, when I say fifty I mean I sent out fifty invitations. Not everyone will come, and some have already said no. These things aren't everyone's cup of tea, you know."

Danny came in and headed for the fridge.

"And if I remember," Danny said, "it wasn't your cup of tea for quite some time. You never used to do anything on New Year's Eve. Now you're throwing a party. It's the first one I can remember in this house."

"It is the first one," I said.

"And why fancy dress?" said Ellie, climbing down from the chair.

"I don't know," I said. "It's just something we used to do."

"And who are you going as then?"

I laughed.

"A well-kept secret," I said, "and if you want to find out you're going to have to come along."

"All under control?" said Sarah, coming in with shopping bags brimming with party food.

"Yeah," I said, "all under control."

I had never thought I would be looking forward to a party, let alone one I was throwing myself. When I sat down to write the invitations, it felt a little odd to be involved in a process I had avoided for so long and to be creating the very things that had made my life so complicated for much of the year. But as the day grew closer, I grew more and more used to the idea, and as the acceptances came in, from old friends and new acquaintances, I even began to feel a little excited.

As I looked at the four of us together in the kitchen it seemed entirely appropriate that the end of the year should be marked in some way.

Ellie had graduated with a 2.1 and was, as anticipated, looking for work in a half-hearted way that suggested a couple of Gap years might lie ahead. She seemed happy, considerably happier since Sarah's return, and although she was still with Wiggy, I found myself increasingly relaxed about their relationship. In fact, I was, at times, even beginning to like Wiggy, or, at least, not finding him as unambiguously awful as I had done. It was no major shift in attitude, but I could definitely feel a slight move, and I sensed that Sarah might feel it too.

Sarah herself had moved back in with noticeable relief and happiness, and set about making the place much more attractive and comfortable than it had been during her absence. Everything she did seemed to have a new enthusiasm about it, as if, for all those years, she had been taking it all for granted and was determined not to do the same this time. And that was certainly how I felt about things – glad to have it back, even if it was all in a slightly different form.

Danny had decided to go back to Oxford, figuring that it would be the best way to keep him close to Hayley, who was now his girlfriend, and that continuing with his degree wouldn't necessarily prevent him developing his comedy ambitions. The place, as he put it, was full of comedians anyway. He even extended a formal invitation (I pressed him on this and he did actually use the word 'invite') to Sarah and me to come along to his next performance.

The Invitation game was behind me. I had ditched it in the summer, turning my back on some of my already accepted invitations with a twinge of regret (the South of France with Jimmy Grainger, for instance) but wanting to start again with a clean sheet and an open mind. I would, I knew, be different from now on, more open, more likely to think carefully before refusing to go anywhere or do anything. I would certainly be more fit, given my decision to keep on running, and, who knows, I might even be less boring…

I looked at the crowd of New Year's revellers, drinking, chatting and dancing. I waved at Mary Poppins (Maggie) dancing happily opposite The Pope (her partner of several months). I raised a glass to Captain Sensible (Jerry). I smiled at Tarzan, Mickey Mouse, and assorted cowboys, punks, nuns and prostitutes, and, when I walked with Sarah past a mirror, I glanced at our reflection and blew a kiss at Boy George and Siouxsie Sioux.

I knew there was still a good deal of unfinished business and that things could never be the same again but, as I danced with Sarah and held her tight, I also knew that I loved her. And as New Year approached, I held her even tighter, knowing that we had something worth keeping, and feeling, despite all the difficulties, despite all the hurt and betrayal, and despite the fact that I had only managed it for six months, this year of no regrets had been worth it after all.

Big Ben chimed, and we linked arms and sang *Auld Lang Syne*, and with every sound of the bell I heard a new year inviting me.

New Year. New Me. RSVP.

I scrawled the answer across my mind in big neon letters.

Yes, it said, and "Yes" was the word that echoed through my head in response to the sound of each chime.